Dixie Siegel

DARK RIDDLE

Dixie,

It was a pleasure to meet you. Best wishes for your new book club.

Deborah Madar

by Deborah Madar

NFB Publishing
Buffalo, New York

Copyright © 2020 Deborah Madar

Printed in the United States of America

Dark Riddle/ Madar- 1st Edition

ISBN: 978-0-9978317-9-5

1. Fiction. 2. Drama. 3. Family. 4. Current Issues (Mass Shooting/School).
5. Madar

NFB
<<<>>>
NFB Publishing/Amelia Press
119 Dorchester Road
Buffalo, New York 14213

For more information visit Nfbpublishing.com

Dedicated to the parents and teachers who care enough to ask the important questions and are brave enough to heed the answers

"For love's sake, we must never stop trying to know the unknowable."

-Susan Klebold, 2016

Prologue

NOVENA A SAN JUDAS

When Gina Clayton was four years old, she and her mother would board a metro bus once a month to go to the "funny farm." That's what her father had called the place. But those Saturday morning visits had been disappointingly unfunny to the little girl. The one clear memory from those trips to the Buffalo State Hospital was of trailing close behind her great-aunt Concetta up and down a long hallway while the old lady, holding a beautiful blue rosary in her wrinkled hands, muttered to herself in Italian.

"What's she saying, Mommy?" Gina had asked in a whisper.

"She's praying. She's making a novena to Saint Jude. She's asking him for his help," her mother had said.

"His help? Why does she need help?"

Her mother listened intently to the old woman's murmuring before she answered. "For us. For you and me. She's asking Saint Jude to protect us."

Decades later on a stormy November morning, Gina repeated that same prayer she heard all those years ago in the halls of the mental institution.

Just moments before, she was sound asleep, but a blast of shrieking static jolted her head off the pillow. She turned and squinted in the direction of the sound, listening for several seconds before she could discern its source. The police scanner in the twins' bedroom across the hall, a relic of her former life with her felon of a husband, had rarely been turned on since his arrest. One of the boys must have been listening to it while she had been at work. She sat up and strained to make out the dispatcher's hiccupping transmission. **"Lake Hinon School ....shooter....all responders....."**

Before she realized it, Gina was praying.

"Saint Jude, protect Luke, John, Tom, and Lisa."

Frantically pulling on her jeans, she begged the saint to safeguard her four children who were at the school. She collapsed to the floor and tugged on her boots. The phone in the upstairs hallway was ringing, but she ignored it; instead she worked at tightening the rawhide laces, fighting her crazily trembling hands.

The answering machine blared as she stumbled out of her bedroom and into the hallway. **"This is the Emergency Notification System from the Lake Hinon School District. We are in lockdown due to a crisis situation. Parents and family members are NOT to go to the school. The authorities will decide when it is safe to end the lock-down. When we are advised to do so, we will transport our students to the Langston Fire Hall on Oak Street. Households will be informed when this happens. Again..."**

She recognized the robotic voice. It was Wendy, the school secretary, the first person she had met when she had registered the kids. As Gina flew down the stairs, she heard the woman's mechanical tone repeating the words that would change everything. **"This is the Emergency Notification System from the Lake Hinon School..."**

"Saint Jude, protect Luke, John, Tom, and Lisa."

She knew as she prayed that she would not follow Wendy's dictum. She *would* go to the school. She had to see her children—to make sure that they were safe.

Where had she put her purse? She looked for it on the entryway bench where she thought she remembered dropping it, but it wasn't there. She couldn't recall going into the kitchen when she got home from work earlier this morning, but she had been so tired, maybe she had.

Then she saw it on the table and grabbed it, intent on retrieving her car keys. She fished for them in every compartment of the bag. "God damn it!" she said, clenching her fists in an attempt to halt the bizarre shaking. With a clatter that echoed throughout the empty house, she dumped the contents of her purse onto the table. Her keys were not there. Did Luke leave them in the car this morning after their driving lesson?

She tripped over a kitchen chair as she bolted back to the foyer. Grabbing her red parka from the hook, she opened the front door to the sound of wailing sirens. At first a duet, and then a trio, the alarms beckoned all emergency volunteers from everywhere along the twenty mile shoreline.

"Saint Jude, protect Luke, John, Tom, and Lisa."

A mini blizzard had been well underway as she slept. Gina fought the wind as it snatched the knob from her hand. She grabbed at it and managed to slam the door closed. Blowing snow blinded her as she pulled on her parka and fled down the porch steps. Halting as she reached the bottom stair, she put her hand over her eyes, attempting to shelter them from the blustering flakes as she made her way to the car.

But there was nothing to see. The Pontiac was gone. In its place was a foot of snow. As she stood in the white drifts staring at her carless driveway, Gina frantically continued to mumble her novena to the patron saint of lost causes.

"Saint Jude, protect Luke, John, Tom, and Lisa."

She was renacting the old lady's slow march down the halls of Buffalo State Hospital, pacing up and down the length of the driveway, from the street to the small shed in the backyard, desperate to put her thoughts into some kind of order. She *had* to get to the school. She closed her eyes and fought the panic that threatened to engulf her. Opening them, she glanced up and down her street. Which neighbor's door should she pound on to beg for a ride? It would have to be Mr. Simpson's, although the old man had never been neighborly in any sense of the word. With her head down in order to brace herself against the strong gusts of wind, and still praying out loud, she turned toward the old man's house.

"Saint Jude, protect…"

When she heard tires crunching snow behind her she turned and saw the flashing lights. The state trooper got out of his car and walked toward her. Gina's knees buckled.

"Mrs. Clayton?" he asked. "Is Luke Clayton your son?"

Gina, kneeling in the snow, nodded, closed her eyes and continued to pray.

PART I

CHAPTER ONE

PROBLEM ONE

Gina stifled a yawn and hurried back to the largest table in the dning room. Thank God the ten rowdy hunters were her final customers of the overnight shift at the Linwood Street Diner. The men took their time with the menu and then dawdled over huge breakfasts and multiple cups of coffee.

"Hey, sweetheart, how about a warm-up?" one of them asked. As she carried the carafe to the table, several more beckoned her.

"Can I get a little more syrup, honey?"

"I'd like Tabasco if you have it. Can't stand the taste of that Red Hot."

"Of course," she replied. The men watched appreciatively as she moved from one to the other of them. Today, like most work days, her thick mane of dark brown waves was banded in a ponytail and pinned into a tame bun. Throughout her life, she had often been mistaken for Irish because of the green eyes she had inherited from her Sicilian grandfather. Petite and trim, mainly due to waitressing and worry, she buzzed around their table like a perpetual motion machine.

She knew these guys were definitely from the city. The locals who had grown up hunting would order without looking at the menu and efficiently swallow their eggs and coffee and head to their tree stands with no unnecessary banter. Gina put on her game face for the out-of-towners. She smiled down at them and tried to imagine how a woman who *didn't* have teenagers at home on this Monday morning might respond to their small talk. All during the meal they shouted over one another, arguing about who would be the first to bag a deer on opening day, but their good-natured repartee caused Gina to punch out twenty minutes late. Oh well, she thought as she headed into the cold morning, she could use the overtime pay.

She traipsed through the foot of overnight snow that had fallen in the parking lot, her headache bouncing from one temple to the other. Listening to the hunters' raucous laughter for the past hour had caused it. On this morning Gina felt eons older than her forty years. Her back hurt, and her feet throbbed inside her boots. Thank God the city guys had tipped well.

As she drew closer to the car, she was relieved to see her son sitting in the driver's seat. Now she wouldn't have to worry about nodding off at the wheel during the drive back to Langston. Gina yawned loudly as she opened the car door and slid onto the cold vinyl seat. Concentrating what little strength she had after working two shifts, she slammed the stubborn door closed.

"Morning, Mom," Luke greeted her quietly and turned the key in the ignition. As soon as the engine turned over, she was reminded that a new exhaust system was the next item on her constantly growing list of unaffordable necessities. Before the dome light dimmed, it cast its glow on her son's handsome face. Gina was startled by what she saw in those few seconds. The years had flown since Luke's birth; in her mind's eye, his infancy and childhood were limited to a few shadowy scenes. The birth of the twins eleven months after Luke's had usurped his place in the family photo albums and in Gina's memory bank. As she glanced at him, her tired brain woke up to an epiphany: my boy is a man.

She recognized, too, the confidence in his posture as he sat in the driver's seat. Was it possible that he had grown taller over the past sixteen hours? He was wearing his new varsity jacket. Maybe that was it. "Hi, honey," she said as she placed her purse in the space between them and pulled on her seat belt. Gina turned away from her son and watched for cars in her side view mirror as he backed the old Pontiac out of the parking spot. When he pulled onto Lake Drive she asked, "Everything okay at home?"

"Pretty much. I shoveled the driveway, so I should be able to pull the car in, and I woke Lisa up so that she could get into the shower before the twins," he explained.

"Thanks," she said, too tired to add how grateful she was for his taking responsibility for his younger siblings. "It was nice of Travis' grandpa to drop you off here on his way to work."

"Yeah."

"Any trouble finding the keys?" she asked.

"No. They were under the mat, like you said they'd be."

She raised her hand to shield her eyes. They were headed into the rising November sun, brighter than usual for this time of year in the Northeast. It was supposed to snow again later, but you could not tell from this early morning sky. She leaned her head back against the seat and closed her eyes.

Before she had left for work yesterday, her son asked if she would take him out for some driving practice before school. Luke's desire for a license so soon after his sixteenth birthday was a reasonable one. Gina worked so many hours at the restaurant—her own shifts and those of the "slackers," as Linda, her boss, dubbed them, those who called in sick "whenever they had a fart caught crossways"—she couldn't be counted on to take her son to his job at Sumner's Groceries in Lincoln. The city was ten miles away, too far from home for him to bike. After football practice throughout the fall, Luke relied on his friend Travis' grandfather, who worked the third shift every other week. When that didn't work out, and when Gina's schedule prevented her from taking him, he had admitted to his mother that he had actually resorted to hitchhiking. The last time he had stuck his thumb out on Route 44, he told her, a middle-aged man had pulled over, and within five minutes, Luke had felt a hand on his knee. Gina had forbidden him to do that again. She was looking forward to him passing his driver's test, possibly more than Luke himself was.

Now he sat beside his mother, tracing the curvy lake road with the ancient Pontiac. He reached for the dial and turned the radio down. The rotten egg smell of the paper mill invaded the car's interior. Even though the plant was down to a one shift operation, the odor was noxious and ubiquitous on this part of the lake when the wind blew from the south. But Gina, like all residents of the area, was used to it, and so she kept her eyes closed. In spite of the fact that he had just recently gotten his permit, she trusted Luke's driving, as she trusted everything about her son.

Luke was an anomaly in the Clayton family. Her other kids brought her constant worry; her two younger boys, fifteen-year-old twins, were already known in the county's juvenile court system, mostly for chronic truancy, although recently Johnny had been caught shoplifting. The two girls, her oldest and youngest children, had problems too. Luke was different. Mature beyond his years from early childhood, he seemed to understand how difficult his mother's life was, and he did not want to burden her further. His quiet reserve bothered her sometimes. But he was a good student, an athlete, who had a part-time job. Luke asked for nothing, and because she had nothing, that's what he usually got. His sobriquet, given to him by his four siblings, was "Problem One" because Gina often proclaimed while scolding or lecturing the others that that was what Luke had *never* given her.

Last night Gina worked her three-to-eleven shift and when another waitress had called in sick, she took the overnight too. Three years into it, the job was becoming more and more physically taxing and less and less mentally stimulating. Gina was too tired most days to realize the extent of her boredom, but on her rare time off, she daydreamed about going back to college to finish her bachelor's degree. When she mentioned it to Linda one day, her boss agreed to hire her part time if she decided to enroll. The schedule would be exhausting, Gina knew, but then again, she probably hadn't slept more than four hours a night since she had left her parents' house decades ago. And she knew she could count on Luke to pick up the slack at home.

Her inhalations deepened as her son guided the car along the winding road. Gina dreamed she was climbing a lakeside cliff, not an actual precipice, but one conjured by her tired imagination. In her dream she grabbed onto rocks and underbrush in a long, slow-motion ascent toward the apex of the steep hill. Suddenly, the earth gave way beneath her feet. She gasped and startled awake just before her dream-self plummeted into the water.

Shaking her head to clear it, she turned toward her son. His window was opened an inch or two in spite of the frigid morning, and he clutched the steering wheel so tightly, his knuckles were white. "Everything okay?" she asked him.

"Yeah," he answered, staring straight ahead. "There was a deer on the shoulder back there." Something unfamiliar in his tone, a cold detachment, startled her. For a fleeting moment, she felt like she was sitting next to a stranger. She shook her head again, attempting to remove the cobwebs that still clung to her from the dream.

She looked at the dashboard clock, trying to focus. The kids had to catch the school bus in the next half hour. "Head home, honey," she said, and Luke turned left at the next intersection.

A few minutes later, he pulled slowly into their narrow driveway, the

Pontiac mere inches from the rail of their next door neighbor's porch. Gina could see the disgust on old man Simpson's face as he lumbered down his front steps, snow shovel in hand. He shot a disapproving glance toward the Claytons' bungalow, obviously for Gina's benefit. Her too-small rental was filled to overflowing this morning with the sounds of music blasting from someone's speakers and Luke's sisters and brothers bickering loudly. She and Luke were going to put the storm windows in this weekend, so in spite of their being closed, their mother could hear the commotion as soon as she opened the screechy car door.

Gina shook her head and grabbed her purse. She climbed the porch steps, her head bent, her bed on the second floor her goal. Behind her, Luke had already picked up the shovel that had been left at the bottom of the stairs by one of his brothers and was pushing snow off of the steps.

"Hey, Mom, I need some money," Johnny said, as she walked through the front door, his hand held out in the universal salute of the teenager.

"I'm not paying for your cigarettes, John…" She took off her jacket and hung it up. The morning aroma of burnt toast combined with the odor of the several pairs of not-quite-dry sneakers on the rack in the tiny foyer assaulted her.

"It's for a lab fee! Jesus!" Johnny shouted. These days he and his twin seemed to have little control over the register of their changing voices, and John's curse had come out as a high-pitched squawk.

"Or your pot," she answered skeptically. This kid of hers, the most charming, the best looking of the lot had been in trouble both in school and with the law, taking after his father in this and so many other ways. "Turn the volume down!" she shouted up to the second floor.

Her oldest son closed the door and stomped his feet on the mat. "Luke," she said, turning her back on her pissed-off fifteen-year-old. She started to climb up the creaking wooden staircase. "There's a grocery list on the refrigerator. Get them before you leave work tonight, okay?" She dug into her purse for her wallet and handed him several wadded up bills over the railing, tip money from her shifts. "And don't hitch—call me when you're ready to come home."

"Sure, Mom," he said, picking up her parka that had fallen on the floor. He carefully hung it back up on the crowded hook. Their eyes locked for a second as he handed her the car keys. "Get some sleep, Mom," he said. Her son's smile assured her that everything – their nasty neighbor, her smart-ass twins, her own physical exhaustion – would all pass and they would be fine. He took the cash from her hand and headed for the kitchen to retrieve the list. "And thanks for the driving lesson," she heard him say. Too tired to respond, she tossed her keys into her purse and shoved her wallet into her back pocket so that John wouldn't be tempted by the few remaining bills. She dropped the bag over the railing to its usual place on the bench below.

As she reached the landing, Gina wished for the thousandth time during the past four years that she'd not had to depend on her oldest son as much as she had, that he hadn't had to grow up so fast. But what choice did she have? After her husband Pete was arrested, she had to increase her hours at her Kodak lab job, often taking overnight shifts. The position paid just a little more than minimum wage, so her then tweens, Shelley and Luke, had had to take care of the three younger kids in their parents' absence.

John's twin Tom passed her on the stairs. "Hurry up, assholes! We're late!" he noisily alerted Lisa and his brothers. She was too tired to deal with his foul language. They had missed the bus yesterday, and Gina had had to take them. It would be a relief when Luke got his license. She would let him keep the car some days so that he could drive his siblings to school.

Reaching the second floor, she turned in time to see Shelley beat her to the only bathroom in the house. "Hey, Mom," she greeted Gina, closing the door behind her. She looked at her watch. Her daughter's ride would be there in just a few minutes. She was going to be late to her job as a bank teller in Lincoln if she did not get a move on. Gina tried to swallow the disappointment she felt every time she looked at her oldest child these days. Just one year out of high school, Shelley would become a mother before she was twenty, just as Gina had.

Although she often felt guilty about her failures as a mother, she knew that she was doing the best she could and she was doing it without Pete. And in spite of the fact that her mother and father had offered many times, she was raising her kids without their help, too. Taking money from them would be admitting that their disappointment in her was warranted. The shame of it would weaken her, and for her children's sake, she had to be strong.

Gina closed her bedroom door and drew the shades. A hot shower would be nice, she thought, but she could barely keep her eyes open as she crossed her small bedroom. She peeled off her jeans and unbuttoned her Linwood Street Diner smock, tossing them onto the floor. Falling into her bed, exhaustion immediately trumped the commotion of the exiting teenagers a floor below, and Gina crashed into a dreamless sleep until the screech of the police scanner woke her.

CHAPTER TWO

OPENING DAY

With her arms folded across her chest, Janet Shelkowski stood in the back of her classroom surveying her first period seniors. Each head was bent steadfastly over the final test on *Hamlet*. Pens scrawling furiously across paper was the only sound competing with the buzz of fluorescent lights this morning. Remarkably, ten out of the sixteen students enrolled in her general English 12 class had shown up on this of all Mondays—the opening day of deer season.

In this part of the state, hunting was much more than a sport. It was an integral part of family and community life, perhaps more so than any organized religion. So the veteran teacher had been surprised as the majority of her kids had strolled in one by one before the first bell, greeting her in croaky, sleep-deprived adolescent voices. "Hey, Mrs. S., happy to see me?" "How you doing, Mrs. S.?" some of them affably nodding at her, a few yawning as they passed by on the way to their desks.

When the last straggler entered just as the bell rang, Janet turned the dead bolt on the classroom door. Any camouflage-clad latecomers would not be allowed in without a pass from the office. The absent hunters would have to stay with her tomorrow after school and write their essays, a warning she had issued at the end of last Friday's class. She was a hard-ass, she knew, but twelfth graders would be faced with the demands of the real world soon and so they must be held accountable for the choices they made.

Now she turned away from her focused seniors and looked out the window. The English suite was on the second floor of this state-of-the-art complex. Janet's eyes moved beyond the flat roof to the woods a few hundred yards behind the building. It was an almost daily occurrence this November with its early lake-effect snow that a small herd of deer would emerge from the thick shelter of the trees. The animals would graze on whatever provision was under the snow and eventually follow their leader toward the football stadium. The grounds crew had kept the stands and the field clear of snow throughout that late fall. The Lake Hinon Thunders had gone as far as they could in the post-season. As division champs they would be competing at St. John Fisher Stadium next month for the state title. Thanks to the winning football team, the deer could forage in this part of the campus with ease.

From somewhere in the distance, five blasts of gunfire shattered the bucolic scene and the teacher's reverie. The kids raised their heads and some turned around to look at her. "Just the soundtrack of Opening Day," she joked. They had no sooner turned back to their work when four more booms discharged. Half of the kids kept writing, but the rest were looking at Janet again.

"Those sounded close," one of the boys said.

"Stay focused," she cautioned. As she looked back to the window, she watched in dismay as the startled herd made their way back into the woods. Their exodus was a leaping dance, and Janet watched as the wind picked up and the snow blew sideways off the pines.

Two miles beyond these woods, the yet unfrozen waters of Lake Hinon were roiling with whitecaps. Every fourth grader in this region learned the origin of the lake's name in their social studies class. Hinon was a magical being, winged, powerful and benevolent. According to Seneca mythos, he was the grandfather of the race of gods called Thunders. Colorful construction paper mobiles suspended from the ceiling and fluttering in the grade school lobby depicted the sacred images of the Great Nation of the Iroquois who lived and reigned in this part of the country for eons before a white person had landed on the continent.

A century after the white settlers had come, steamboats churned and brought the wealthy city-dwellers to the natural wonder of the place. Ambitious entrepreneurs made a lot of money from the hotels, restaurants, and marinas that were essential to the resort economy. Many who had inherited this wealth now lived in these mansions. A number of the estates were occupied by seasonal residents, but the year-round inhabitants of these vast properties, those who eschewed boarding schools, sent their children to the Lake Hinon School District.

Up until two years ago, two schools had proudly stood on opposite banks of the lake. On the north shore was Jamesburg Central and at the southern end, Langston School. As enrollment declined in both institutions, costs and taxes soared. The citizens of each district had stubbornly held onto their autonomy until New York State's "bribe" of millions in building funds and tax rebates persuaded them to give up ownership of their local schools.

It had been a bitter, closely contested decision to merge. The two schools had been academic and athletic rivals for three generations. At raucous meetings held the year before the merger, people stood and shouted angrily about beloved mascots and the injustices that would be done to one or the other former school when the valedictorian was chosen or the new basketball team's starting roster was announced. In spite of these hot debates among the populous, the merger had passed by a few dozen votes, and Lake Hinon School District, a name students had chosen in a close vote, had opened its doors in September of last year. The twenty-first century progeny of these two communities were now joined under one impressive roof of the new school built on a beautiful woodland site.

In spite of the improvement to the physical campus, in the faculty room Janet's colleagues, old and new, continued to share in angry sibilance both the petty and the pedagogical reasons for the merger's inevitable failure. The differences in their teaching philosophies and practices made this experiment a sham, the naysayers insisted. Janet hurried away from these emotional "discussions," but she silently agreed with many of their points. From department meetings to casual conversations in the parking lot, most teachers referred to the halcyon days, the "pre-merger" era, with hushed reverence and longing. Janet had chuckled when she overheard one astute colleague refer to the merger as a shotgun wedding.

The particular bane of Janet's existence this second year of their union was Tony Brown. Because of the staff reorganization, the veteran high school English teacher from the Jamesburg district was now reluctantly teaching in the middle school. His classroom was directly below her own. The finicky pain-in-the-ass had complained on several occasions via one of his twelve-year-old student messengers that the constant scraping of chairs and desks on her classroom floor was noisily competing with his grammar lesson. Last week, she had brought him a morning peace offering—a blueberry muffin and a cup of coffee from the Yellow Goose, but he had been unyielding. His bristly attitude had put her off once again, and she had ended up giving him a mini-lecture on the history and effectiveness of student-centered learning.

From Janet's perspective, the kids seemed to have worked it out. It had happened somehow, somewhere, outside of the adult realm. When the high school students could be encouraged to discuss how they felt about the merger, the one constant their teachers heard was that it was okay;

maybe they wouldn't have to marry someone they had known since kindergarten. The expansion of the dating pool seemed to have excited them much more than the expanded building size and the additional AP courses being offered in the new district. After only a few months, they appeared to have settled into their new identity as Lake Hinon High School students.

Janet turned away from the deserted woods and looked at her seniors. All but one of them was still on task and writing frantically to beat the impending bell. Rob Turner always sat in the back seat of the row farthest away from Janet. The boy was in his favorite pose - his bare arms cradling his head as he lay slumped across his desk. The kid was always exhausted and usually dirty. His shirt, at least one size too small for his six foot frame, stretched across his wide back with every one of his deep inhalations. Janet stared at his arms. They looked like he had been lifting concrete blocks his whole life. He was one of those kids who more resembled a thirty-year-old man than an adolescent boy. Rob's peers gave him a wide berth. They knew he was quick to anger and that he wouldn't hesitate to punish any fool who tried to cross him. Janet thought about waking him, but decided against it. Her gut told her that the kid needed the sleep more than he needed to pass the *Hamlet* unit. She had had Rob's troubled older siblings as students, too, and she suspected that something was very wrong in the Turner household.

She continued the inventory of her seniors. A warm wave of affection washed over her as she looked at the young people in her charge. Most of them, whether they were from Langston or Jamesburg, had managed to do what their parents and teachers apparently could not. They had accepted the merger and each other. Janet had not been surprised by their level of tolerance. The one unwavering belief that she had held throughout her teaching career was, that although they could be annoying and sarcastic, teenagers brought from their recent childhoods an innocence and an optimism—a quality she called *heart*. And that's what she had felt connected to in this job that had been her calling. Throughout the decades she believed that she knew the *heart* of the teen, and she knew that it was *good*. Even Rob Turner's.

A knock at her classroom door preceded the inevitable cacophony that marked the end of the period and interrupted her thoughts. "I'll get it, Mrs. S," Megan Parkhurst, sitting in the first desk offered. Her classmates began shuffling papers and picking their bags up from the floor or from the backs of chairs as the tall senior walked toward the door. In the back of the room, Janet unfolded her arms and leaned to her left so that she could see who was there. A frowning seventh-grader peered in through the window. Obviously, she had been chosen as today's hapless messenger from Tony's classroom. Her mission would be to report that Janet's seniors were in some way disturbing the middle schoolers' concentration on the declension of verbs. Janet caught a glimpse of a camouflage pattern behind the child. One of her recalcitrant hunters, no doubt. She would make sure he had a pass and that she knew he would be joining her after school tomorrow.

Before she could take a step toward the door, Janet saw the black sneaker kick it open with a violence that knocked Megan to the floor. The little girl who had stood forlornly looking into the classroom seconds before was roughly shoved from behind. The teacher watched as she fell, landing on her hands and knees, her scream blending in sickening unison with Megan's. The hunter rushed in, closing the door with a backward kick.

He was wearing a black ski mask. A cold, numbing paralysis worked its way from Janet's feet to the top of her scalp. She was frozen in place, watching as he made a sweeping motion, tracing the room and all of its occupants with the pistol.

"Everybody. Stay where you are," he said.

CHAPTER THREE

ON YOUR BELLIES

Janet watched in horror as the intruder pointed the pistol at Megan. "Lock it," he said, gesturing with the weapon toward the door. Megan scrambled to her feet. Janet heard the click as the girl rotated the lever to the locked position.

"Stay calm and everything will be alright," he said to all of them. Now both of his hands clutched the gun, and he used it to direct Megan back toward the first row of desks. Before she could sit down, he spoke again. "Slide your phones to the front of the room." Janet, her seniors, and the little girl retrieved their devices from desks, pockets, and backpacks and slid them along the polished tile.

"You." He was looking at Megan. "What's your name?"

"Megan," she said, and Janet was afraid the girl might start crying.

"Count them, fast," he said. "Out loud," he added.

"One, two, three…" Megan obeyed.

When she stopped at twelve he spoke again to the group. "Now, all of you. Get down on the floor. On your bellies." His voice remained calm, as if this and everything else he might ask of them would be a reasonable request. These particular eleven members of the post-Columbine generation, all but one of whom had started high school the year that Adam Lanza committed the massacre at Sandy Hook, complied immediately.

"You too, Mrs. S." Janet was surprised by his conciliatory tone. It was not an order, but a request. She remained on her feet for a few seconds and then joined her students and the quietly weeping seventh grader on the floor.

"Put your hands behind your backs. Now, clasp them together," he said. Janet concentrated on listening for something familiar in his voice. From its pitch and register, she was pretty certain this was not an adult, but a high school boy. Was he one of her seniors? She didn't think so. Since she'd been teaching for years, many of the kids she saw in the halls and outside of school used the shortened version of her name in greeting her, so his addressing her this way did not necessarily mean he was one of hers. As she followed his instruction, Janet had an absurd flashback to last night's yoga class. She willed herself to breath deeper. She needed clarity. She needed to make a plan.

From her bizarre position on her classroom floor, Janet had a clear view of the gunman's shoes. The black Nikes turned left. They rushed past Kathy Harrington and Leah Meadows who had been taking the test in the first and second desk, and now Janet could once again see all of the intruder. She watched as he stood still, and with his free hand, folded the black ski mask up. Janet saw that his nose and bottom lip were bleeding. He dabbed at the blood with the left sleeve of his faded camo jacket.

The black sneakers were on the move again, this time toward the back of the room. Janet watched as the interloper stopped and pointed the gun at a student in the last row. It was Scott Wallace. Although her heart was pounding loudly in her ears, she heard the calm instruction the gunman gave him.

"You, Wallace. Get up." Suddenly, in an absurd counterpoint, she heard another voice amplified by the PA system.

"Students and staff. This is Mr. Walker. It is necessary at this time to

begin a school-wide lockdown. This is not a drill. I repeat, this is not a drill."

Janet felt nauseous as she watched Scott Wallace stand up. The boy had taken off his varsity jacket before he had started the test, and she stared at it now from her place on the floor. "Put your hands on your head," the gunman said, and Janet heard a new tone of urgency in his voice. He was standing behind Scott, who was inches taller than him. "Now, walk slowly toward the computer lab."

"I don't understand. Money? Do you want money?" Scott reached for the wallet in his back pocket.

For the first time, the gunman raised his voice."Put your hands back on your head!"

"Okay! Just take it easy, please," Scott begged.

"Keep moving." In spite of the order, Janet could tell that Scott was stalling, walking so slowly it seemed to her that time stood still. Scott was smart, she tried to assure herself. Not an outstanding English student, but wise in so many other ways. He was doing everything he could to avoid ending up alone with the assailant in the small technology space that adjoined the English classroom.

Scott stopped walking and turned toward the gunman. "You don't want to hurt anybody, right?" he asked.

"Turn around. Keep moving," The voice was calm and confident again.

Scott Wallace was one of Lake Hinon's most popular seniors. He had a charm and charisma that put him in a rare class of adolescents; he seemed to Janet to be everybody's friend. His father and uncles owned a successful corporate farm on the Jamesburg line, and Scott had attended that district until the merger. He was a Boy Scout working on his Eagle Badge and a 4-H member, but he wasn't considered geeky in spite of these uncool affiliations. Confident, at times even cocky, he had a warmth that seemed a part of his nature and a generosity that appealed to male and female classmates. A three-sport athlete, this year and last he had been chosen captain of the varsity football team.

At the pep assembly held last week to honor the team, Janet's colleague, Coach Rod Harrison, had told the group gathered in the gym that it was Scott's leadership that led Lake Hinon High School to the upcoming state title game. Janet had witnessed Scott's magnetism in her classroom, too. In the first week of Senior English she had introduced a public speaking unit. The first assignment was to explain a personal experience that led to something unexpected. Scott had thrilled all of them, including his teacher, when he had spoken about an encounter he had had that past summer with a black bear and her two cubs.

"One warm September morning, my mom asked me to go get my dad who was cutting wood about a quarter mile from the house. I was walking along the path at the edge of our woods when I saw her with her two cubs. They were about fifty yards ahead. I could see them through the underbrush and the trees. They were definitely moving toward me." He looked around the room then, like a pro, to make sure they were all with him. They were.

"The mother stopped and looked at me. She started swinging her head from side to side." He demonstrated the bear's movements. His audience was spellbound. "I knew that meant she really didn't want to charge me," he assured them. "I looked away from her and stood perfectly still. I didn't want her to think that I was challenging her." He froze, motionless for a few seconds, his speech transformed into a performance.

"I was a statue for what seemed like hours, but it was really only minutes. The babies were rolling around, playing, but the mama was still moving her head from side to side, glancing my way when she stopped. I started backing away from them. You never want to run away from a bear. They can book at thirty miles an hour if they want to. I'm fast, as most of you know, but not that fast." Scott flashed a wide grin at his classmates. They smiled back in unison.

"I was talking in a monotone the whole time, saying things like, 'Okay, bear. You're a nice bear. I don't want to hurt your babies.' Stuff like that." There was an appreciative group chuckle. Janet read the body language of the attentive audience. They were leaning in, engaged and in awe of Scott's ease and confidence in front of them. His pacing had signaled that his closure was coming, and he didn't disappoint them.

"And that's how I happened to walk a quarter of a mile uphill backwards on the first day of my senior year in high school," he concluded as spontaneous applause erupted. When the laughter subsided, hands were thrust in the air before Scott could ask if there were any questions.

"Why didn't you run?"

"How could you just stand there?"

"Scott The Brave." Janet thought of the compliment Mark Burt, who was lying on the floor one row over from him now, had paid his friend that day in September.

"Not really," Scott said. "I was shaking in my boots, but I was trying to determine what kind of personality she had. Bears are like humans—they're all different. Most won't charge at you, but if you move into their personal space, they just might."

"All students are to remain in class. All students in the hall are to report immediately to the nearest available classroom."

The principal's voice startled Janet back to the horror of the present. She could tell that Walker was reading from the school's emergency manual. The rustling of paper accompanied his announcements.

"I said keep moving, Wallace," Janet heard the gunman say to Scott, so quietly, the kids closest to the classroom door probably had not heard it.

But she knew that everyone in the room heard Scott's urgent attempt at persuasion as the gunman directed him to the front of the room and toward the threshold of the computer lab. From every corner came the sound of muffled weeping as his classmates listened to Scott beg. "No, please! Don't hurt me! Don't ruin your life. It's not too late. You don't have to do this!"

Janet watched helplessly as the gunman shoved the weapon into Scott's back. As the two disappeared into the small room, she heard Scott say, "Mrs. S?" He was calling to her the same way her boys had when they were little and a bad dream had frightened one or the other of them awake. "Mom?" It was a name and a question all in the same breath. It meant: Are you still there? Am I still here? Am I safe?

"*Teachers lock your classroom doors,*" Mr. Walker instructed. "*No one is to leave until an 'all clear' announcement is made by an adminis-trator.*"

Suddenly Janet heard Scott shouting, "Clayton! Why? What did I ever do to you?" His voice sounded strained as if he were choking. He might have been crying too. It was more than she could bear.

Janet pushed up on her hands and knees and began to crawl toward the computer pod. "Stay down," she whispered repeatedly to the kids as she crept along the wall. "Everything is going to be fine," she told them.

As she crawled toward the far corner of the room, she saw Rob Turner stand. From her position on the floor, he looked massive. Janet was their teacher, the adult in charge, but at that moment she stopped moving and silently prayed that Rob would save them. That he would grab the masked intruder by the throat, snap his neck, and end this nightmare. This kid who had slept through most of her lectures on Hamlet seemed to have a visceral connection to the most recognized soliloquy in the entire English language. He had decided. He was going to take action. But Janet could not let him do it.

"Rob!" she gasped. He turned and looked down at her. "Get down! Now!" she hissed. Something in her whispered command forced the hefty kid back to his knees and then all the way down to the floor. Janet clambered past him. She felt the eyes of every kid in the room on her as she stood and disappeared into the small computer lab.

———

"I KNOW YOU," Megan Parkhurst heard her teacher say. Mrs. Shelkowski was speaking softly, carefully, like she sometimes did when she was making an important point during a lecture. "You're Clayton, right? Johnny, right?"

Megan strained her ears listening for his reply, but the wild pounding of her heart was deafening. She held her breath to stop it, but she heard no response from the boy.

"Put the gun down, John. You're bleeding. Let me help you. *Please.* Let's figure this out together." The pleading tone in her teacher's voice was nightmarish. Megan's world had turned upside down from the moment she had unlocked the door to this horror. She felt like she was on the verge of hyperventilating, and she had to force herself to slow her breathing. Their teacher was in charge. Everything would be alright, she told herself.

"Go back into your room, Mrs. S," the imperturbable voice say. "I'm sorry I disturbed your class. I don't want to hurt you." Megan realized in that moment that it was not Johnny Clayton in that room with Mrs. S. and Scott. She had a study hall with that crazy freshman and he was constantly trying to get her attention by over-the-top flirting with her, telling her that fifteen-year-olds made the best lovers. He was annoying and funny at the same time, and Megan knew that his voice had not yet changed to the deep register of the gunman's.

Still on their bellies, everyone in the classroom flinched as the sounds of a scuffle broke out in the small room—chairs and desks scraping on tile, followed by a computer or printer crashing to the floor. As if they were playing some crazy version of Simon Says, Megan and the other kids simultaneously took their hands off their heads.

From the lab, Megan again heard Mrs. S's voice, strangely high-pitched, hardly recognizable. "NO!! GIVE IT..." The teacher's scream was followed by the explosive echo of gunfire, one shot immediately followed by a second. Megan and most of the kids around her covered their ears as the gun's discharge bounced off the walls of the small lab, but she was still able to hear the sickening sound of a body hitting the floor. Some of her classmates screamed or swore and their shrieks and expletives blended in a counterpoint with the principal's command as it came over the PA.

"Ignore any fire alarm."

Megan began to pray as Mark Burt and Rob Turner, two boys she had gone to school with since kindergarten, combat crawled toward the front of the room. Without thinking, she too began to slide forward on her stomach. She and the seventh grader who had come to the classroom moments before were moving together to the pile of cell phones.

As she inched closer, Megan could clearly hear Scott Wallace's pleading voice. "Don't! I'm sorry, Clayton...Wait!" Glass shattered and rained down inches from her as a bullet hit the small window that separated the lab from the classroom. She put her head down and continued her prayer as she slid closer to her goal.

Megan grabbed for her phone, and as she pressed the 911 icon, she heard Scott scream and cry out again, "DON'T..." A gunshot exploded, and seconds later, it was followed by two more. Still on her stomach, Megan felt the vibrations from the next room as computer equipment fell and crashed. She was aware of a loud ringing in her ears, but in spite of it, she heard the thud of a second body hitting the floor

"What's your emergency, please?" the dispatcher was asking her.

Every person but Megan began propelling him or herself to the door, sliding on their bellies. Kathy Harrington reached it first, and Megan watched as her classmate struggled to get to her feet. Wobbly and off balance, Kathy grabbed the lever, unlocked the door, and within seconds, was running down the hall.

As each of her classmates stood and followed Kathy's lead, Megan continued to talk rapid-fire to a 911 operator. "Yes, people have been hurt. Our teacher, a student...."

Next to her, the seventh grader was holding her phone and pleading, "Mom, come and get me, please!"

Megan screamed into her phone as the gun discharged one last time. "There's shooting!" she heard the little girl say.

The crashing sound of glass on tile as the small window blew out obscured the principal's final futile instruction.

"If we need to evacuate the building, an announcement will be made."

CHAPTER FOUR

TIME STAMP

Two hours after she had arrived at work, Wendy Levy sat trembling at the massive conference table in Superintendent Graves' office. The school secretary stared straight ahead at the large blank screen, awaiting the viewing of this morning's surveillance video. Dr. Graves was rushing back from a conference in Albany and would be there in a few hours. Principal Bob Walker, cadaver-pale, sat to her right. The laptop with the evidence the group needed to review was on the table in front of her boss. A wave of dizziness threatened to overtake her as she thought about the real possibility that in the next few minutes, she would have to witness the slaughter of Lake Hinon students and teachers. Wendy gasped softly and gripped the edge of the table in an attempt to steady herself.

Her sudden movement caused the man to her left, Iroquois County Sheriff Jeffery Greene, to turn toward her. Each time she had seen the sheriff on television she had found him intimidating, even though those criminal investigations had had nothing to do with her. Now that she was in his presence and under his scrutiny, she felt a menacing dread. "Are you okay, Wendy?" he asked, real concern in his tone.

"Yes," she lied, as she held her breath and willed her heartbeat to slow down.

Two of the sheriff's deputies and the Lake Hinon School District Re-source Officer, Joe Gloss, sat to his right. Joe had been a part-time cop for the Jamesburg force when he was hired by the new school, and he held both positions now. Wendy had known him for decades. He had been a year ahead of her at Jamesburg High, where he and her husband Rob had been on the football team. As Sheriff Greene began introductions around the table, Joe leaned forward and gave her a formal nod. As the video began to roll, she felt reassured by his presence.

The group stared at the screen for several minutes as teachers and students came streaming through the wide-opened metal doors. "Can you fast-forward to the time when the doors are first locked, Mr. Walker?" Greene asked. The principal complied. For several minutes, no one came to the door.

Suddenly, one smiling teen grinned directly into the camera. As he did, several other kids entered the "fishbowl" behind him. "Stop it there, Mr. Walker. Who are we looking at here, Wendy?" the county's leading crime scene investigator asked her. One of his deputies switched on a small digital recorder, while the other bent over a notebook and began writing furiously.

Wendy's stomach did another flip-flop as she stared at the frozen image. "Brett Lucas is the first kid. He pushed the buzzer for the whole group," she said. The time stamp at the bottom of the screen read 8:45.

"Okay, Mr. Walker. Let's continue, but slow it down, please," Greene said.

As the video began to play in slow motion, Wendy narrated. "That's Lisa Meeder, George Markham, Mark Pucci, Nick Alimo, Graham Reese," she said as they watched the motley parade of colorful camo-clad teens jostling each other through the door.

"Let's follow them, please," the sheriff said.

Bob Walker switched over to the view captured by the main office camera. The group of men at the table stared now at the back of Wendy's head as she bent over the written excuses each kid had presented. They watched as she took a pad of passes from a drawer and wrote with the speed and efficiency that came with years of experience. In the midst of the noisy chatter of the kids, Wendy heard herself good-naturedly chiding them as she continued to write each a pass. "Go straight to your lockers, and don't be making noise. It's still first block for those people who chose school over the woods this morning." As she sat there listening to her own voice, it struck her that she would never again be the woman the camera had captured that morning—casual, friendly, confident because everything in her domain was under control.

The electronic buzzer sounded in the background and Bob switched back to the front door surveillance tape, this time without the sheriff's prodding. A pretty blond woman shook the snow from her hair and smiled into the camera. "Hey, Wendy," she said, speaking into the microphone at the door. At the same time, she juggled a huge bag over her left shoulder and clutched the handle of a rolling suitcase with her right hand.

"Who's that?" Greene asked.

"Sydney Peck, a long-term substitute of ours," Wendy said. "She's taking over for our biology teacher who will be out on maternity leave after Thanksgiving. Sydney was coming in this morning to bring some of her stuff to the room and to go over Mrs. Lincoln's plans for the next three months. She didn't have a key card yet, so I had to buzz her in."

A figure in a faded camo jacket suddenly appeared behind the substitute teacher. They watched as he held the door open for her, his head bent and his eyes lowered as if he were examining something that had fallen to the floor. Sydney smiled over her shoulder at him. It wasn't audible, but they could read her lips. "Thank you," she said. The time stamp read 8:47.

Wendy's hands tingled and she felt a tidal wave of nausea sweep over her. Joe Gloss stared at her. She had to take a breath before she could speak. "That's Luke Clayton." She was repeating the words she had said when she and Bob Walker had been shown the picture of the dead boy, horrifically mangled yet somehow recognizable, on the floor of the computer lab. "I saw him when I buzzed Sydney in, but I had all of those kids at the front counter. He never checked in with me. I forgot all about him." Wendy shook her head. "Oh, God," she said.

Bob Walker switched to the main lobby video as Sheriff Greene instructed. They watched as Luke Clayton turned down the small corridor leading to the principal's door, the one typically used by teachers and staff when they met with him, not the door that students used through the main office. The camera in that hallway captured the boy's purposeful stride as he approached the door and grabbed the handle. Seconds passed as he attempted to open it, lifting up and then pulling down on it to no avail. Wendy glanced at her boss. Bob Walker flinched as the boy began pounding loudly on the principal's office door. When it remained locked, he kicked it savagely once and then again. The calm expression on his face as he turned back toward the lobby was weirdly out of sync with his angry body language of moments before.

"I had a Rotary Club meeting this morning," the principal told the group, although no one had asked. "They invited me to an executive committee breakfast to talk about the merger and how the kids were handling it this second school year. I got here just a couple of minutes after he came to the door. Jesus," he added in a loud whisper.

The sheriff instructed Walker to switch back to the lobby camera, and the group followed the dated military surplus pattern of camo worn by Luke Clayton as he descended the stairway leading to the school's lower level. "Can you change to the stairwell camera?" the sheriff asked.

Clayton had shot and critically wounded his first victim on the stairs. Sixteen-year-old Eddie Gatto was in the ICU at Rochester Memorial. He was in a coma and chances were that he wasn't going to survive.

The group looked at the black frame. "That camera must have malfunctioned. There's no footage," Walker said.

"How about the one on the lower level?" Joe Gloss asked.

"Yes, it's here," Walker said as he switched to the view of the long corridor. The new building had a state-of-the-art activity area on this level that included three sizable suites accommodating the physical education and music departments and the high school cafeteria. They watched as the shooter emerged from the stairwell with a black ski masked pulled over his face.

"Oh, God," Wendy said again. She caught Joe's eye as he leaned forward. She asked quietly, "Am I in trouble?" There was no response. Joe and everyone else turned their attention back to the screen.

"Pause it here, please, Mr. Walker," Sheriff Greene said. The frozen frame captured the clearest picture of Luke. The media would use this photo over and over again in the months to come, almost always with a caption that described the killer as "stalking" the halls of Lake Hinon School. "What can you tell us about this kid?" the sheriff asked the principal.

Bob Walker opened the manila folder in front of him, and as his eyes scanned the details from the permanent record, he read aloud. "Luke Anthony Clayton....birth date, October 20th, 1999. Parents, Peter and Gina Clayton. Transferred to Langston School from Rochester in September of 2011. Member of the Class of 2018, so he was a...." He hesitated, calculating.

"Sophomore," Wendy said.

He shuffled through the thin stack of papers in front of him. "Good attendance, a few tardies this year. Decent grades. Member of the track and football teams. Art Club..." The principal looked up.

"What kind of kid was he, would you say, Mr. Walker?" the sheriff asked.

"The kind I rarely get to know," the principal said, looking away from the sheriff. "I'm pretty sure he was never in my office for any disciplinary reasons." She should have spoken up then, but technically, everything Bob Hall had stated was true,

"How about you, Mrs. Levy? What was your experience with Luke Clayton?" Wendy's anxiety heightened. This was the first time the sheriff had not called her by her first name.

"He seemed like a very nice kid." She turned to her right and then her left and saw their skeptical expressions. "Mature. Polite. He never shared much in the office like a lot of the kids do, but I suspected home was not an easy place to be. Mom's a waitress, works a lot of hours. Dad's incarcerated. Pregnant older sister, twin brothers who are always in trouble. And the youngest sister in middle school – she's picked on a lot." Sheriff Greene nodded while his deputy flipped a page in the notebook and continued writing.

"And did you know he was a hunter?" She turned toward Joe Gloss who had asked the question. His typically ruddy complexion looked washed out.

"I'm not sure, Joe. Most of the boys and a lot of the girls in this student body hunt for one thing or another, as you know," she said.

"The jacket doesn't look right," Joe said.

The general consensus of the kids who talked to Wendy was that Joe Gloss was a bastard. He had his favorites, they said, but if you weren't one of them, you could be a target of his angry outbursts. Wendy stared at the man's right eye, which was twitching erratically. She wondered if she was the only one who noticed it.

"Okay, Mr. Walker. Let's keep going," the sheriff said, and Bob Walker played the video again. Everyone at the table jumped as the loud blare of a brass section echoed through the conference room. Now they watched the boy's back as he continued on his path along the corridor, moving faster than the tempo of the music.

This morning the Lake Hinon High School Marching Band had been in rare form as they practiced the national anthem with the high school chorale. Of the dozens of schools throughout the state that had auditioned, their band and chorus were among the five that had been chosen to play in the Macy's Thanksgiving Day Parade later this week in New York City. The thought suddenly occurred to the secretary—if Luke Clayton had wanted to commit a massacre with an even higher body count, he could have walked into that room where at least one hundred students and six teachers were. But he hadn't.

Wendy looked away from the monitor and down at her trembling hands. She drew them into her lap and under the table so that the men would not see them. When she looked up again at the screen, she saw Luke Clayton's back as he rushed past the band room toward the coaches' offices and the training center. The facility was the envy of sports teams all over this part of New York State. Wendy held her breath again as she watched Luke Clayton, polite, respectful Luke Clayton, open the door to the training room with his left hand. The right one was inside his pocket.

"Time?" the deputy who was scrawling notes asked no one in particular.

"8:52," Sheriff Greene and the high school principal answered together.

They stared at the camera's view of the empty corridor. The band surged triumphantly and Wendy found herself concentrating on the familiar lyrics the chorale was singing so that she could breathe. "*Whose broad stripes and bright stars, thro' the perilous fight, O'er the ramparts we watch'd, were so gallantly streaming. And the rockets' red glare...*"

45

Bob Walker had to turn up the volume to its maximum in order for them to distinguish the gunshots from the cymbal crashes and the booming bass drum. "8:53," the other deputy said to the note taker.

The principal rewound the tape several times to that spot and Wendy listened to Bob Walker and the sheriff, in unison and counterpoint with the band. "One...two... three... four... five."

"Coach Harrison, Brian Davis, Ryan Johnston," her boss said as he looked to Wendy for confirmation. The secretary nodded.

"Ryan must have called the office shortly after that," Wendy said, as they listened to that section of the tape for the fourth time.

"Pause it there, Mr. Walker. What did Ryan say, Mrs. Levy?" Sheriff Greene asked her.

Wendy would never forget that call. The horde of hunters had left her office moments before the inter-school phone rang.

"Call 911! I'm shot!" the young voice had said.

"Who is this? Where are you?" Wendy asked.

"Ryan. Johnston. In the training room. Coach Harrison and Mr. Davis too. They're not moving. Tried to stop him...hit him...in the face... with a weight." Ryan sounded very far away. Wendy wondered for a second if this was a sick senior prank, but then she heard a choking sound.

"Stay on the line with me, Ryan! Help's on the way." She could not reach the phone on Pam's desk, and it seemed crucial that she not put the receiver down. She reached for her purse inside her desk drawer with her left hand and frantically felt for her cell phone. She hit the 911 icon on the screen.

"Ryan! Ryan!" she called over and over again after the 911 dispatcher assured her that help was on the way. But the boy did not respond. Wendy bit her lip to keep from crying as she finished her account.

Sheriff Greene asked the principal to resume the video. The band had begun to play the school's fight song - the one all Lake Hinon students had planned on singing at the top of their lungs at the state football championship. The group around the table watched as Luke Clayton, wearing the black ski mask, burst out of the training room. His right hand was in his pocket. As he hurried in the direction of the cafeteria, two boys dressed in Mossy green camo emerged from the dining room and appeared to be rushing toward him.

Wendy watched as Luke Clayton froze. The first boy lunged at him, and Wendy prayed that Luke would not pull the weapon out, even though she already knew how this would end. His momentary second thoughts were over and Wendy saw the Smith and Wesson in his hand. She closed her eyes as tightly as she could. The men at the table watched as Luke Clayton fired once at each kid and then once again as the two boys fell to the floor.

"Rick Varos and Tad Burke, both seniors," Joe Gloss said. "I walk through the cafeteria every morning and today I noticed those two messing around and dawdling over their food. Told them they were going to be late to class and to get going."

"Time, please?" the writing deputy asked.

"8:55" Gloss answered. Both boys were pronounced dead just an hour later.

Wendy opened her eyes. The sprawled bodies of the two boys lay on the floor outside of the cafeteria. A sob broke loose from deep inside of her. The sheriff plucked some tissue from the box on the table and handed it to her. "Just a few minutes more, Mrs. Levy," he said.

Rick and Tad were two of her favorite seniors. They would stop in her office almost every morning on their way to catch the bus to the BOCES vocational center they attended for half the day. Rick was in auto mechanics and Tad took welding at the center, and they had shared with her how excited they were about the internships they would be doing with local businesses in the spring. "Bye, Wendy. Try not to miss me too much," she remembered Tad saying last Friday, waving to her on his way out of the building.

The tape began again and Wendy stared at Luke Clayton's back as he ran toward the elevator at the end of the long hallway. Except for disabled students or teachers, no one but the maintenance staff was allowed to use it. As the elevator door closed on him, Wendy stopped thinking of the masked figure as a real person, a student that she knew and liked. He was no longer Luke Clayton, but an evil force set loose in their school—and she had let him in.

"We found the empty clip in the elevator," Joe Gloss said. "He must have reloaded in there."

"Let's see the second floor footage, Mr. Walker. Go to 8:56," Sheriff Greene said.

Bob forwarded the videotape to a long view of the second level English suite. Because of the missing hunters and the many musicians attending the morning rehearsal, the hallway seemed eerily vacant. To Wendy, it looked the way school felt during the summer, silent and empty, wrong somehow. The group stared at the uninhabited corridor until 8:58, when a young girl emerged from the stairway that led to the middle school. She walked slowly toward the camera. From the far end of the hall, the elevator door opened. Wendy jumped as she saw the masked Luke Clayton noise-lessly overtake the child and grab her from behind. The group listened as she let out, not a scream, but a squeak.

They watched as Luke bent down and seemed to whisper something in her ear. From this angle, they could see the gun in his hand. He steered the girl toward Janet Shelkowski's English 12 class. They watched as the child tapped on the classroom window. The time stamp remained at 8:58 as the door swung open and middle schooler and Luke Clayton flew inside. The door closed behind them. Everyone around the conference table stared now at the hollow high school corridor.

"Turn the volume all the way up again, please," Sheriff Greene said. As the time stamp advanced to 8:59, they heard Bob Walker's first announcement echoing through the deserted hallway. And at 9:03, they heard the gunshots coming from inside the computer lab.

Again, Wendy listened as the men counted together, pausing intermittently as the shooter hesitated between shots. "One...two." Janet Shelkowski was the first to die in that small space.

Wendy and the men leaned toward the screen as the students' muffled screams began. The rumble of Mr. Walker's amplified voice bounced off the bare corridor walls as the terrified kids cried out from inside the classroom.

"Three...four...five...six" the men, except for Joe and the note-taking deputy, chanted as more shots were fired.

They listened as Bob Walker gave his final instructions over the PA. On the monitor, the Iroquois County Swat Team appeared from each of the stairways and ran toward the classroom. "Seven."

"That was it—the last shot he fired," Sheriff Greene said. They all looked at the time stamp. It read 9:05. Bob Walker rewound the video and played it again, as Sheriff Greene had requested.

As she watched, this time with her eyes wide opened, Wendy felt a final break with the woman she had been mere hours before.

Chapter Five

I'M DEPENDING ON YOU

It was one-thirty when the secretary walked out of her office, two hours earlier than her usual departure time. Moments before, her boss had pulled her to the back of the room, close to his office door. "Ed Gatto's father just called me. The doctors have advised the parents that Eddie is brain dead. They're waiting for his sister to get here from her college in Washington. Then they'll take him off life support," the principal said. Wendy's knees buckled, but Bob grabbed her by the sleeve of her blazer before she went down. Taking her by her shoulders, he guided her to the chair behind her desk. "Stay there," he said, and disappeared inside his office.

Seconds later he handed her a bottle of water and stood over her as she drank. "How could this have happened?" she asked, and the sob that came from deep inside her filled the room.

"Who knows?" Bob Walker shrugged his shoulders.

"But Luke Clayton? He was a good kid…"

"Look. There's no logic that can be applied here. The kid snapped. We're just lucky he ended it when he did."

Wendy didn't have the energy to say what she was thinking. *You're the luckiest one. You were at a meeting, and he was definitely looking for you.*

"We're going to have to pull ourselves together and carry on for the sake of the school, Wendy." He pulled a tissue out of the box on her desk and handed it to her. As he stood over her, the small-framed man looked like his body was lost inside a suit two sizes too large. To his secretary, he appeared to have somehow become more diminutive over the course of this horrendous day.

Throughout the first two years of the new district, she had witnessed her boss' silent anguish and desperation on a weekly basis when he met privately with Dr. Graves. She was not sure of the reasons for these frequent meetings, but Bob appeared to be shaken to his core when he came back from these consultations with the superintendent. Wendy left him alone in his office as long as was possible afterward so that he could regain his composure.

When Wendy joined Bob in a scheduled monthly summit with their superintendent so that he could "touch base" with his "PR" team, as he called them, he reminded Bob and Wendy that they were on the front lines. Everything they did in the high school office would be instrumental in convincing the public that the merger was the best thing that had ever happened to the two communities. Their boss' expectation was that Wendy and Bob Walker would handle any complaints about the merger from the kids, the faculty, and the parents so that he could tackle the "larger responsibilities" of running the new district. The secretary thought of these sessions with Dr. Graves as pep talks more than anything. But she noticed that Bob Walker often looked shell-shocked during and after these meetings with the "big guy."

At times, the principal reminded her of a humorless Don Knotts. In the high school office, Wendy observed how the man, whether he was dealing with students or staff, avoided conflict like the plague; yes, he was a shirker, she recognized that from the beginning of their association. But she took every aspect of her role as his secretary seriously, and the unwritten part of her job description was that she must do everything in her power to protect her boss, in spite of her personal feelings about him.

"Wendy," Bob Walker said, "I'm depending on you to help me bring Lake Hinon School back to the way it was last Friday. Before all this…" He stopped short of completing his thought and watched as she drank the rest of the water.

Once she composed herself and could stand again, he told her to go home. "But stay close to your phone in case I need you. The police may have more questions before the day is out, too. Dr. Graves and the board have decided to close until after Thanksgiving, but I want you here when the Crisis Team meets tomorrow morning at 7."

She walked out into the wide lobby, where on a normal day at two o'clock in the afternoon there would be a few stray teens, sitting on the floor, leaning against the walls and quietly chatting with one another. They might be waiting for parents to pick them up, to end their school day early for dentist appointments or other outside of school commitments. On this Monday as she turned toward the door, Wendy saw instead the county coroner flanked by three of his staff, two EMT's, and several sheriffs and state cops. She looked for Sheriff Greene, but he was not there. The men circled eight gurneys that bore eight occupied body bags.

Wendy stopped at the foot of one of the carts. For a moment she was stuck, grounded in a quicksand of motionlessness as she stared at the lifeless shapes. Three of those bags contained the bodies of people she had worked with. Janet Shelkowski had been a respected and revered teacher in Langston; she knew her least. Many people would be shocked and distraught by her violent murder, she was sure. But the two phys ed teachers, Brian Davis and Rod Harrison, she had known since her years at Jamesburg. Wendy's husband would be especially devastated by the death of Rod, his own high school football coach, and the man responsible for leading the Lake Hinon Thunders to play in their first state championship.

The other bags contained the corpses of young men. Four of them Wendy had known for nearly all of their lives. The fifth she had only met since the merger, and she had liked him very much. But as she stood frozen in that spot, she realized she had not known Luke Clayton at all. She watched as two of the deputies rolled one of the carts away from the lobby and into the main office.

"Thanks for your help today, Mrs. Levy," Joe Gloss said, taking her by the arm. "I'll walk you to your car." His guiding touch became a tight grasp as the two walked out of the school into pandemonium. The spaces in the visitor and handicapped parking lots would normally be vacant at this time of day, Wendy noted as she passed the police cars, fire trucks, and ambulances that took up every one of these spots. A barrier had been set up several yards beyond the emergency vehicles, separating them from the rest of the lined spaces.

Hours before, the students had been bussed to the Langston Fire Hall where they were released one by one into the arms of terror-stricken parents. The local media had captured those reunions for their Breaking News alerts, which had taken over their broadcasts for several hours now. In the main parking lot were vans advertising news logos from local and national media outlets, some already parked, more pulling into the lot in a steady stream. As she and Joe walked, Wendy saw at least a dozen technicians setting up sound equipment and cameras. A helicopter from a Rochester news station flew overhead.

Joe kept a firm grip on her arm as they headed toward her car. She would need to brush off the five inches of snow that had fallen since this morning before she could drive. She unlocked the door and reached into her backseat. From behind the barrier she heard the reporters shouting at her.

"Ma'am, what's your name?"

"How many are dead?"

"Are you a teacher?"

"Did you see the gunman? Who is he?"

"Is he a student?"

"A parent?"

"Get in and start the car, Wendy. I'll do that for you," Joe said as he took the brush from her hand. She climbed in and put the key in the ignition. Immediately the defroster blower blasted cold air.

As Joe pushed the heavy slush off her windshield, Wendy noticed a New York State Trooper vehicle pulling up to the curb at the main entrance. She glanced down at the clock on her dashboard: 2:06. Joe shook the snow from the brush and slid onto the passenger seat. He slammed the door and turned to face her. "Wendy, I'm telling you this off the record. For yours and Rob's sake." Joe looked unhinged. His usual semi-arrogant demeanor, the one that Wendy knew caused many students to give him a wide berth in the halls at school, had been supplanted by a nervous anxiety.

"Your life is about to change, Wendy. You are going to be hounded by people in the community and by the media. They're going to ask you for details about what happened today. They're going to ask you how well you knew Luke Clayton. Why you think he did what he did. They're going to ask you if you think that the merger had anything to do with it." She watched, fascinated, as his face flushed crimson. "And they're going to ask you how a murderer managed to get by you in the main office." She turned away from Joe and watched as a uniformed trooper stepped out of his car.

"They'll wonder how he was able to enter the building without your buzzing him in—how a psycho broke through the expensive security system to go hunting inside the school. How he was able to massacre eight people!" He was shouting over the noisy defroster. Wendy sat silently staring at the man's twitching eye.

Joe turned away from her. He seemed to be concentrating on calming his breathing. His voice was lower and quieter now. "You need to say nothing. You need to get a lawyer just in case, Wendy. Before the day is over. Get one."

He opened the door, and Wendy, stunned, watched him hurry back to the building. A few steps in front of Joe walked the state trooper. Wendy stared as the officer guided Gina Clayton through the front door of the school.

Chapter Six

CAMOFLAUGE

The state cop knelt down in front of her and clasped Gina's praying hands in his own gloved ones. As he stood, he lifted her off her knees and guided her down the driveway to the police cruiser. She had not zipped her parka and her shirt was soaked through from the melting snow. The battering wind lifted her hair, causing most of it to stand on end. An image of Concetta and the mental institution returned for a second time this morning. The desperate shouts and wails that echoed throughout the corridors came back to her and she wanted to scream at this stranger, *Where is my son? Is he hurt? Are you taking me to the hospital to see him?* but because she was terrified of the answers, she asked him nothing.

"Mrs. Clayton, my sergeant would like to talk with you. Please put on your seat belt," he said and closed the cruiser door. She was shivering so uncontrollably her teeth chattered, the clicking sound overriding the static of the police radio. Turning and concentrating with all her might on extracting the belt, she caught a glimpse of old man Simpson standing on his front porch. There was an expression of astonished concern on his face. As the police car pulled away, he held up his hand in a wave, but to Gina the gesture looked more like a signal to stop.

She remembered nothing from the thirty-minute drive to Lincoln except her wild shivering and the terrifying images that came into her head, unbeckoned. Luke, in a coma, unable to hear her calling to him. Luke in a hospital bed, hooked up to a ventilator like the one she had seen at her grandmother's deathbed. Luke in a wheelchair, his head resting on his shoulder, his eyes closed. And then she was walking into the New York State Troopers barracks. The officer took her arm and led her through a maze of beige walls to a small office at the back of the building. He pulled out a chair for her, and somehow a Styrofoam cup of hot coffee appeared on the table in front of her. "Take a sip," he said, the way one encouraged a child. "The sergeant will be in shortly."

Gina closed her eyes tightly, willing time to stand still, but too soon she heard heavy footsteps approaching. When she opened her eyes, a tall man in a white shirt and tie was reaching across the table to shake her hand. "Mrs. Clayton, I'm Detective Clairbourne." She let him take her hand in his. She could not speak. "I'm so sorry to have to give you some very bad news," he said as he sat down across from her. Gina focused on the movement of the man's bushy eyebrows and then at his closely trimmed mustache, avoiding his direct gaze. He spoke again, and now Gina watched his lips as they emitted meaningless sounds. "Your son, Luke, went to school this morning with a firearm and killed three teachers and four students. A fifth boy is in critical condition. I'm sorry to have to tell you that your son turned the gun on himself. He's deceased, Mrs. Clayton."

A numbness seemed to envelop Gina. It overrode the trembling, and like a thick fog, it wrapped itself around her, constricting and choking her as the sergeant began to ask her questions. "Mrs. Clayton? Do you understand what I just said?"

"Yes," she lied. She had heard, but she hadn't understood.

"Mrs. Clayton, I can't imagine how hard this is for you," the sergeant said. "At a later time, we'll sit down with you and have a more detailed discussion. But do you think you could answer just a few questions for me now?"

She nodded and he continued to talk. "Did you see Luke before he left for school this morning?"

"Yes." *A vivid image of Luke, his back to her, walking into their kitchen flashed through her mind. She wanted to call out to him, to stop him from disappearing from her sight. But this stranger had just told her that her son was gone. Forever..*

"Did he seem agitated or anxious to you?"

"No." *Thanks for the driving lesson, Mom, he had said.*

"Do you own a gun, Mrs. Clayton?"

"No."

"Would there have been a gun in your house for any other reason?"

"No."

"Do you know where Luke might have obtained a handgun and ammunition?"

"No." *Luke with a gun. A gun he used to kill kids and teachers and himself. This all had to be some horrible mistake.*

"Was Luke depressed, Mrs. Clayton?"

"No." *She saw her son again, hanging her parka on the hook, smiling at her. Get some rest, Mom, he had said.*

"Was he taking any medication for depression or anxiety or for any other reason?"

"No."

"Did he talk to you lately about being angry with anyone?"

"No." *If only she could form the words, she would tell this stranger about her boy's nickname. Luke was not depressed or anxious or angry. He was none of those things. He was Problem One. Oh my God, how could she tell his brothers and sisters that their brother had murdered people? That he was dead?*

Gina stared at the top of the sergeant's balding head bent over a piece of paper as he scribbled. "Alright, thank you, Mrs. Clayton. We'll be in touch again soon," he said. Detective Clairbourne came around to her side of the table and held out his hand. The tall man guided her to her feet. He took her gently by the elbow and walked her to the door where the first trooper stood waiting. "I'm sorry for your loss, ma'am," he added, as Gina left the room.

Inside the cruiser the trooper told her that they were going to the school. He explained as he drove that the county's medical examiner facility was too small to accommodate so many corpses. "As Luke's closest kin, we need you to give us a positive ID," she heard him say, but she didn't respond. "Mrs. Clayton, do you understand?"

"Yes." Another lie. *Corpses, Luke, positive ID.* She heard the words, but they made no sense at all.

As they pulled into the school parking lot filled with emergency vehicles and media trucks, Gina was still lost inside the numbing haze. They pulled up to the curb at the main entrance and she allowed the trooper to carefully steer her through the nightmare scene in the lobby. He rushed her past several policemen and women, emergency responders, medical personnel, all of them staring at her as she walked toward them. The trooper made a quick right turn down a corridor, but Gina was still able to glimpse several hospital carts beyond a crime scene barricade. It was true. Her kids' school had been transformed into a morgue.

He opened a door, and she was inside another small office. A policeman, not a trooper, she could tell by his uniform, seemed to be standing guard over a gurney in the center of the room. She could see the outline of a body under a sheet that covered it entirely. She was struck with an absurd thought. The sheet looked scratchy and gray, probably from too much washing. The shivering and shaking began again and she averted her eyes from the gurney to a table in the corner. She didn't want to look at or think about the sheet, the body beneath it, so she stared at the objects on the table. An oversized pair of scissors and a small tool box were there and folded up next to these things were some sort of camouflage fatigues. She thought of the hunters she had waited on at the diner early this morning. This morning when she had ridden in the car with Luke.

Gina jumped when the door opened behind her and she turned and saw an emaciated looking man. "Hello, Robert," the trooper said and then introduced her to the coroner. Without any words of warning, the man walked to the gurney and removed the dingy sheet. She closed her eyes tightly, challenging the dizziness that was trying to take her down. The trooper put his arm around her and steadied her.

"Is this your son, Mrs. Clayton?" the coroner asked her.

When she opened her eyes, she wasn't certain what she was seeing. It looked like some sort of bizarre mask that one of her twins would wear to scare her. She narrowed her focus and then she understood. It was Luke's face, a ghastly split version of it. One side belonged to the son she knew and loved, still young and beautiful. The other side was burned and mutilated almost beyond recognition. She felt the trooper clasp her tighter as she slowly reached out, and with her finger she outlined the small birthmark on her boy's left shoulder. "Yes," she whispered at last. "This is my son."

She couldn't remember how she got from the room where Luke lay to the trooper's car, but somehow she had, and the man with whom she had spent this horrendous day was suddenly driving down her street. The same man whose name would not stay in her head as many times as he told it to her was saying that an investigative team from the Lincoln barracks would be there soon with a search warrant. More than likely, because of the enormity of the crime, he told her, the FBI would be joining them. "Would you like me to call someone to come and stay with you, Mrs. Clayton? A friend or family member, a minister or priest?" He had asked her that same question about every ten minutes since he had guided her into the front seat of his vehicle this morning.

"No. Thank you," she said again, as the trooper walked her to her front door. She knew there was no one home. Earlier in the day, the school had contacted the emergency number she had written on the form in September for each of her kids, and at the moment they were with their grandparents and Shelley on their way to Buffalo. They would stay there until the Lombardos were sure that the police and the media would not be invading their grandchildren's home.

At some point during this endless day, the trooper told her that the police had contacted Auburn State Prison. The warden had informed Pete Clayton that his oldest son was dead. There really was no one else for her to call. Since their move to Langston, Gina spent most of her time working. There was no room in her life for friendships. And except for her run-ins with old man Simpson, she didn't really have anything to do with any of her neighbors.

"Okay. Just be aware that more than likely reporters will be showing up here shortly," he warned. "Call me directly if you need anything," he added, handing her his card.

"Thank you," Gina said. She bent down to retrieve the spare key from under the mat. The police had confiscated the Pontiac and with it her key ring that Luke had left inside the car. As she unbolted the door, she hoped the man couldn't tell how anxious she was for him to leave. The criminologist's team would show up with a warrant very soon, she knew. They would tear the place apart, just as the Rochester cops had done when Pete had been arrested.

"Take care, Mrs. Clayton," the trooper said.

The phone began to ring the minute she stepped inside. She turned on the light in the foyer as the answering machine picked up. "You have a collect call from an inmate at the Auburn State Prison. Will you accept the charges?" the anonymous voice asked, and then repeated the question. Pete. She couldn't face him or the conversation they would have to have. Not yet.

She took off her jacket and without warning, the memory of that warm June evening when she had first laid eyes on Pete Clayton, the night that had changed her life forever, returned. She had been a biology major at SUNY Geneseo on a full scholarship and was working as a lab assistant that summer. After her professor had left her in the lab to file the articles and slides they had been studying, Gina heard a noise from outside the propped-open classroom door. The biology building had been all but abandoned since early May when the semester ended, so the swooshing sound startled her. As she glanced up from the lab table, she watched as a tall young man walked down the corridor. Gina's eyes took in the long legs in tight, worn denim, the trim waist and wide shoulders, the blond hair, too long for a college boy in 1990. He seemed oblivious to her presence, but for some reason, her heart started to race when the push broom signaled that he was heading back her way. She looked up nervously from the pile of slides. Leaning on the broom he held in both hands, the stranger paused. From the empty hallway, he smiled in at her.

Although she couldn't have predicted it, that moment marked the beginning of the end of Gina's academic life and the termination of her newly budding independence. The magnetic storm that was Pete Clayton drew Gina in and away from her pre-ordained path, the path her parents had so fervently laid out for her. For the first time in her life, she understood the figure of speech "bowled over"—that's what Pete's smile, his charm, his body, did to her. He sated a hunger she had not acknowledged before that June night. The power he wielded knocked her down and when she got back up, she hardly recognized the woman she had become.

Dark Riddle

Gina was pregnant with Shelley by the beginning of her sophomore year. By the second semester, she was a married, part-time student and the mother of an infant. She was just barely keeping up in her classes and labs, and when Luke was born not quite two years later, she withdrew from school.

During these years, whenever she entered a room, her mother and father looked past her, as if they were expecting their real daughter to rescue them from this imposter. When her mother came to help out for a week after each of the children's births, Gina knew it wasn't post-partum hormones that caused the heavy curtain of sadness that weighed her down. Rather, it was her mother's unguarded glances of disappointment that set Gina down a black path. Her father, who said he was too busy with the stores to visit more than a couple of times a year, didn't meet the twins until they were a year old. Up until the time she had moved the kids to Langston, he had seen Lisa only once.

When Shelley was born, Pete was hired by the college in a full-time maintenance position. They were managing to get by, in spite of the increasing number of mouths that had to be fed. The VW bug that had been her parents' high school graduation gift could not contain the two of them plus two car seats, so she had reluctantly agreed to accept the offer of her parents' "old boat" of a Pontiac. As her father handed her the title to the car, he didn't try to hide his bitterness. "You know that husband of yours will never be able to afford a road-worthy vehicle." He practically spat the words at her.

She should have known, Gina chastised herself. Taking on a high-interest loan would have been better than accepting her father's "generosity." Her parents had given her a life full of opportunities, but she had been reckless with this gift, and she had squandered it. She could eventually pay a loan off, but she could never repay her parents, of that, she felt certain.

Five years later, when Gina was due with Lisa, the governor slashed the staff funding budget for state colleges. Pete was cut to half-time and the six, soon to be seven, Claytons could barely subsist on his reduced salary. Her father urged her to make her "janitor" husband get a vasectomy. He begged her to take "or borrow, if that's what your pride dictates" some money from him until things got better. Gina couldn't bear to accept his offer, and she never told Pete about it. She knew how angry that would make her husband. He recognized early on that his father-in-law couldn't stand the sight of him. So because she hadn't taken her father's money or told Pete about his offer, she wondered if she might bear some responsibility for her husband's arrest.

When Pete's buddy from high school whom Gina had never been able to tolerate got him a job "off the books" working several hours a week at a local assisted-living facility, she'd agreed that he must take it. Often during that year when Lisa woke Gina up in the middle of the night wailing to be nursed, Pete was gone. It wasn't until the sheriffs showed up with a warrant for his arrest that she discovered what Pete's second job entailed. He and his friend had been stealing prescription drugs from the facility's pharmacy and selling them.

Gina would never forgive herself for letting Pete Clayton control her destiny and that of her children. He was serving twelve to twenty years in Auburn and she was a waitress with five, soon to be six, kids under her rented roof. The magic between them had ended years before, and the only reason they were not divorced yet was because they couldn't afford to hire a lawyer. Resisting her parents' pleas to come to Buffalo and live with them "until she got on her feet," she had moved her children across the state to the small town of Langston shortly after Pete was incarcerated.

As she climbed the stairs to the second floor, in some part of her brain she understood that she was in a second phase of shock. The sight of her house from the trooper's car had seemed to snap her out of the paralysis that had kept the devastating truth of this day blunted. A keen sense of mission had suddenly taken the place of the numbness.

She had not cried yet, but she knew that once the sobs started, she might never be able to stop. Before she could allow herself to face the terrible new reality of her life, she told herself that she had to focus. She must search for the clues that would help her understand how her first-born son had become a mass murderer.

Logic overrode muscle memory and Gina unclenched her hand before it became a fist. It was typical for his door to be closed, but the civil gesture of a knock was unnecessary now. Gina had respected his privacy because he had proven his trustworthiness. Until today, Luke had never caused her to have even one moment of doubt or concern about him. He was the good child. The easy one.

She turned the knob and the door swung open.

Still, she felt like an interloper as she stood on the threshold of Luke's bedroom and tentatively peered into the darkness of the late November afternoon. Gina bit her lower lip as a groundswell of grief at last threatened to overpower her. She took a couple of deep breaths to fortify herself so that she could do what she had to do before the police arrived. Her hand searched for the light switch and as the overhead fixture lit the room, her eyes took an initial inventory of the small space.

Her first reckoning was that it was orderly and tidy, unlike any other room in the chaotic household. She stared at the neatly made bed in front of the curtained window. It struck her that on the day he planned to die, her son had efficiently folded the patchwork quilt her grandmother had sewn decades before and laid it across the bottom of his bed.

When they had first moved into the place, each of the five kids had picked out the paint color for their rooms. Her rowdy twin boys had chosen the deepest black for their walls *and* the ceiling. The two girls had rolled on a startling pattern of green and mauve stripes. Gina looked for an answer now from the non-color, a milky shade of beige that Luke had chosen. The younger boys had duct taped glow-in-the dark concert posters and sports franchise advertising onto their walls. In his room, Luke had hung only one thing.

Gina stood now in front of the poster-sized pen-and-ink drawing of an eagle-like bird, wings spread to their full span, prominent beak in profile. One staring eye gazed back at her. This was Luke's rendition of the Thunderbird, a version of the god Hinon, an important deity in the Iroquois culture for whom the first settlers had named the lake. Her son had used the red and black of the new school colors to outline the bird and mark its feathers. Below the creature, Luke's bold, black calligraphy spelled out the words - ***Power, Transformation, Unquestioned Authority.***

When Jamesburg and Langston had merged their districts, the newly formed school held a contest for the design of a new mascot. The art teachers and some community members had judged the dozens of drawings that were entered. Six were chosen and then voted on by the student body. Luke's design had won. A thirty-foot replica had been painted on the wall of the beautiful gymnasium and another in the main lobby of the new building. The school used the logo on its stationary, the school calendar, every uniform for every sport. The t-shirts, bumper stickers, notebooks, pens, and pencils sold in the school store carried Luke's design. True to his nature, her son had been modest about the fact that his drawing had been selected. Lisa and the twins had been the ones to tell Gina the good news. The fact that his original Thunderbird was framed and displayed on his otherwise barren walls showed the pride he took in his creation.

She turned away from it and her eyes took in the rest of the room. The furniture Gina had bought at the Salvation Army store and refinished in the back yard lined one wall of the small space. She crossed the room and began opening each drawer of her son's tall dresser. From the time he had been in middle school, Luke had insisted upon washing and folding his own clean clothes and putting them away. Underwear, socks, flannel pajama pants in the top drawer, t-shirts and a few sweaters in the next, jeans, and sweatshirts in the bottom two. She hurriedly searched the orderly stacks, but could not find what she was desperate to discover.

Gina slid open the pocket door of her son's small closet. One sports coat that he had outgrown and a couple of pairs of khakis hung neatly on hangers. Three tailored shirts, a denim jacket, and a couple of hoodies hung next to them, and the black varsity jacket with the words LAKE HI-NON FOOTBALL embroidered in bold red letters on the back was there too. Gina had planned on buying it for Luke's birthday, but he had paid for it himself that September. He had worn that jacket every day for the months he owned it, including this morning, the last time she had seen her son alive. But Gina saw now that he must have taken it off before he left for school today.

His mother was not looking for drugs or weapons hidden in his dresser or closet; instead, she searched frantically for any article of clothing with a camouflage design. Luke, unlike many of his peers in this rural part of New York State, had never hunted. As far as she knew, until today, he had never shot a gun. To his stricken mother, the waves of green and khaki on the jacket and pants the coroner told her he had cut off her boy had looked like a costume, a disguise. In those horrible moments in that tiny room, she had turned away from her child's maimed face and fixated on the unfamiliar camouflage. Focusing on it had kept her on her feet these last few hours, saved her from falling, held the truth at bay. But she could find no more evidence of this secret part of Luke's life here in his bedroom. With her failure to do so, the coldness that had sheltered her began to thaw.

She turned away from the closet, her movements more frantic. She stood in front of a stack of novels and textbooks on her son's desk, the one her parents had brought from Gina's childhood bedroom. Next to the large pile, a volume of short stories lay open and face down, as if Luke had been trying to keep his place. She picked the book up and looked at the cover. *Easy Listening, Short Stories by Adam Stoller,* Gina read, but the words meant nothing. She shuffled through the pages looking for what? She didn't know. Near the back of the book she noticed that several pages had been torn out. The coroner had told her that a story had been found inside the strange jacket that Luke had worn to school today—had it come from this book? She glanced at the small digital clock on the desk as she closed the volume and placed it on top of the pile. The search team would be arriving any minute.

The refurbished laptop she had bought Luke for his last birthday sat next to the printer. Gina trembled as she opened it and prayed aloud that the password would work. She had required that he give it to her as a term of his keeping the computer in his room away from his boisterous brothers. Gina held her breath to stop the shaking as she typed **Lukelhh.** When the home screen picture of the Lake Hinon High School football team appeared, she let out a sigh of relief. No matter how heinous Luke might become to the rest of the world, his mother could still count on his honesty. Clicking on **Search History**, she printed a list of all the sites he had visited in the past three months, folded the sheets of paper, and shoved them into the pocket of her parka.

Gina stood in the middle of the small room and suddenly a cinderblock seemed to have landed on her chest. She stumbled to her son's bed and sat down on it, completely exhausted. This was the worst day of her life and as it was unfolding, she was devastated by a variety of emotions - shock, disbelief, denial, horror, grief.

Now shame swept over her - not just because of the unfathomable acts that Luke had committed. Not only because her son had taken lives and destroyed families. Not just because the kids who had survived would never feel safe in their school the again. The burden of ignominy would weigh her down soon enough. But as she lay her head on the pillow, it was hot guilt that burned away every other feeling.

Luke's mother broke at last when she realized that before this day, she could not recall the last time she had been in her good son's room.

Chapter Seven

WAKING

Gina dreams of riding in the car with Luke. He is driving the Pontiac alongside a large body of water. The sun is shining on her face. She is smiling. Suddenly, Luke, staring straight ahead, wildly cranks the steering wheel. The car careens crazily from the guard rail at the water's edge to the shoulder on the opposite side of the road. Gina tries to grab the wheel, but the seat is so impossibly long. Each time she manages to slide within reach of it, Luke rotates it in the opposite direction and she is thrown up against the door. Finally, she manages to take hold of the wheel and turn it. Her heart stops in a frozen panic as the car crashes through the rail and plummets down the cliff toward the water.

The sound of her choking gasp woke her, and Gina opened her eyes to total darkness. Drenched in sweat, the quilt she had wrapped herself in when she fell on Luke's bed after the police had left, was suffocating her. Several local and state police officers had spent six hours tearing her house apart from top to bottom, following the orders of the three FBI agents who had stationed themselves in her kitchen. Gina had slept on and off for the better part of the forty-eight hours since their departure. She closed her eyes again, and tried to climb back into the ragged sleep, but the quilt was twisted around her midsection like a tourniquet. It increased the terrible pressure on her bladder, and she had no choice but to drag herself from her dead son's bed.

An overpowering emptiness had rooted itself inside her during those hours since she had identified her son's body. It was not vacuous, but a heavy growth, a weight, a burden. Once she escaped the strangulating quilt, she fell to the floor on her hands and knees, dragging the dense void with her. She had to crawl because she knew she could not walk. It would be impossible for her to stay upright while she carried this terrible hollowness. She kept her eyes mostly shut as she made her way to the bathroom. When she finished, she forced herself to stand. She held on to the walls and stumbled down the hallway, her legs quivering crazily, until she reached her own room and bed. Then she slept through Thanksgiving.

"Gina?" Days later, it seemed, she heard her mother's tentative whisper. She remembered that at some point her parents had come back from Buffalo with the kids. She lay still and pretended not to hear her.

Gina's relationship with her parents was complicated. When Pete had been sentenced to twenty years in a federal prison, it hadn't stopped the lawyer's bills from coming. Each month Gina came within mere dollars of being evicted from their city apartment. Her parents offered to help, but she refused, knowing well the high price of their generosity. Instead, she had moved to Langston, the small lakeside village where her parents had taken her during a rare week off from the store each summer, the happiest weeks of Gina's childhood. She applied for a job in the Hammermill lab and because of her Kodak experience, she was hired. The Claytons were in Langston one year before the paper mill began cutting back on its operations, and Gina was the first lab technician to be laid off. She walked into the Linwood Street Diner the next day and Linda hired her on the spot.

"How are you going to raise five kids on a waitress's pay?" her father shouted at her almost every time her mother handed him the phone during their Sunday night calls. The familiar realization that she had failed to live up to her parents' expectations threatened to bring her to tears once again. She took a deep breath and tried to assure her agitated father that they were fine, that she could do it. The cost of living in Langston was much more affordable than Rochester or Buffalo, she reminded him. She was getting plenty of hours at the diner and the tips were good, too. She was determined to prove to them that she could take care of her family on her own.

"My daughter, the scientist, working at a greasy spoon," he said, not even attempting to hide his disgust. She pictured him shaking his head, making eye contact with her worried mother. "How is the car running? You're getting it serviced, right? You know you can use that credit card I gave you if you ever need it."

"The car is running fine," she had lied. "I'm nearly forty years old, Pa. I don't need your money," she told him. What she did not tell him back then was that she still struggled. That she needed her kids to pull their weight, especially her two oldest. That once they were old enough to work, she depended on Luke's and Shelley's contributions toward the rent. This was Gina's reality, and after one of these angry exchanges with her father, some times with a kid or two within earshot, she felt wobbly and vulnerable.

Her mother gave up on trying to wake her and closed the bedroom door. Gina rolled over on her side. In the dim light she could make out a tray with a glass and plate on the bedside table. The sulfur smell of egg assailed her and she was sure that she would vomit. She placed a pillow over her head to smother the odor. She wanted nothing more than to creep back into the womb of sleep, but her arm and leg muscles burned and throbbed like a toothache and kept her awake and away from her desire for oblivion. She rolled over and the sheets scraped against her skin like sandpaper.

The door opened again. "Mom?" Shelley whispered to her. Gina opened her eyes. Her mother trailed her granddaughter into the room and left the door open behind them. The two stood beside the bed looking down at her, their faces backlit by the hall light. It was the expression on her mother's face that made her sit up for the first time in days. Deep concern with a dash of disapproval, Gina thought. How familiar it seemed.

"Honey, you have to get up." Gina could see that she was trying to be gentle, in spite of being on a mission. "We need to talk about funeral arrangements. The lab called and the body will be released tomorrow." The body. That's how Luke's grandmother referred to him now. She would never call him her "sweet boy" again. A familiar resentment bubbled to the surface as Gina listened to her mother's proposal.

"Daddy and I think that we should have a private wake and burial in Buffalo." Her mother was sitting on the bed now. Somehow she had managed to take Gina's hand. "Away from the locals and the reporters. We've already been in touch with John Fantuzzi from the old neighborhood. What do you think about that?" Gina wanted to scream, shriek, wail, so that her mother would stop talking. If she couldn't shut her up, if she wasn't able to stop her words, she knew that the future would be here, that Luke would be gone forever.

"That state policeman called this morning. He wants you to call him back so that they can schedule some time to talk with you again," her mother said. "He says it can wait until after the funeral."

Gina looked beyond her mother and was startled by the sight of her daughter's eyes, swollen from days of crying. She watched as they filled with tears again. "Mommy, what happened?" The name her daughter called her for the first time in a decade shocked her. Somehow, it was a call to action.

Gina shook off her mother's hand and stood. She reached out and wrapped her arms around her pregnant first-born. "I don't know, honey," she said, "but I'm going to find out."

Part II

CHAPTER EIGHT

THANKSGIVING

Adam Stoller moved around the old trestle table he had rescued from his childhood home in Chicago. Louie Prima and Keely Smith scatted in the background as Adam sang every other word of "That Old Black Magic," adding his own nonsense syllables. He was feeling good today, confident and purposeful - better than he had felt in weeks. He placed the last of the silverware where he guessed his mother would have put it on the rare occasions when company came to the Stollers' home for dinner.

From a high-backed dining chair he retrieved the box containing the paper-Mache turkey his tenant Diane had loaned him for today's celebration. He couldn't recall which of her kids had made it years ago, but each Thanksgiving the centerpiece graced the table of whichever friend was hosting. This year it was Adam's turn. One of the creature's googly eyes stared warily back at him as he carried it to the table. "What are you looking at?" he asked it. Adam cautiously placed "Plump," appropriately named by his young creator decades ago, next to the candelabra. He was careful not to knock off its construction paper hat. The faded black capotain, charmingly incongruous and glued in a jaunty angle to Plump's head, was about thirty years old. It would not do for him to rip the antique.

While Adam put the finishing touches on the table, he chewed a wad of Nicoderm like it was his last meal. When Rog and Tess had met him last night outside of Larry's, their favorite neighborhood pub, he heard Rog say to his wife as the couple approached, "He's a handsome bastard, isn't he, hon?" Her eyes traveled the length of Adam's body as she smiled and nodded in agreement. His friend knew Rog well enough to recognize that some serious ball-breaking was about to begin. "But he's rotten inside!" he told Tess. "All those muscles will disintegrate when the Black Lung gets him."

"Stop, Roger!" Tess said, making no pretense about her appreciation of their landlord and his physique.

Adam had been a wrestler throughout high school and college, and thanks to good genes, he had kept his youthful appearance. His 5'11" frame was muscular still and he had more hair than most guys his age, and that helped too. "He's trying to quit," Tess added, coming to Adam's defense. She and Rog watched as he ground out the Marlboro under his boot and threw it in the sidewalk trash can.

"Last one of 2015 - I mean, ever," he told them as they walked into the busiest night of the year at Larry's.

"The guy has quit smoking at least ten times since I moved in," her husband scoffed. It was true; gum, the patch, even Chantix had not cured Adam of the habit he had taken up when he was fifteen. It had happened during the two weeks at a summer enrichment camp for the arts he had attended. Most of the older kids in his writing workshops were smoking, and the coolness factor was undeniable. Even though he had to hide it from his parents and his wrestling coaches, he was hooked before he had turned seventeen. All these years later, he regretted ever starting, but he had never been able to quit for more than a month before some crisis, real or perceived, propelled him to the store for a pack of smokes. Maybe he would join all the other addicts who were vaporizing their nicotine these days. But as of midnight last night, he was back on the gum.

He picked up the half-empty glass of scotch off the buffet and drained it, standing back to appraise his work. He folded his arms. Satisfied, he took a deep breath. His apartment on the top floor of the brownstone was filled with delicious aromas. The smell of the roasting turkey stuffed with Diane's oyster and chestnut dressing was amazing.

For the past two days he had been happily distracted from his latest project by the necessary preparations for this day—after all, he reasoned, holidays are deadlines too. You can't delay, postpone, excuse yourself or you'll miss them entirely. He would get back to the book on Monday, he promised himself. The thought of his unfinished third novel caused him to chomp harder on the waxy gob in his mouth.

He really did not have a deadline, per se. To his publisher, he was a valued client; his editor had coddled him ever since he had sold his first novel to HBO. Adam had been hired to co-write the screenplay for the pilot last year. The ten episode *Notorious* was in pre-production right now and would be airing next fall.

"You're going to be famous, buddy," his agent had told him, "and maybe rich, too." Jesse Olson had been right about the money, anyway. When it had come on the market last year, Adam purchased the brownstone on Central Park West where he had formerly been a tenant. The advance from the network had made that dream come true, and the royalties from the sale of his three books, two novels and a short story collection, covered his living expenses. While most writers starved or moonlighted at jobs they hated, at age 40, Adam Stoller was making a decent living as an artist in America in the 21st century. He was a lucky man indeed, one who had many reasons to be thankful today.

Adam's father had returned home to Chicago after the Vietnam War and been hired by a small metal fabrication shop. He had hated the dirty work, but he had a family to support. By the time his son was a teenager he had saved enough money and quit the shop. He and Adam's mother bought a small bar on the Southside of the city, close to their home.

Adam had wanted to be a writer from the time he had attended that camp as a kid. Joe Stoller didn't understand his son's aspiration. Writing was not a job, it was a hobby. But his mother encouraged him to follow his passion, and he was accepted at Oberlin as a creative writing major. After having his first story published in *Tin House*, he left his job at a small magazine in Chicago to accept a fellowship in the MFA program at Syracuse. There he worked with the great George Saunders, who was instrumental in his development as a short story writer. Saunders had been generous with his time in helping Adam find a publisher for *Notorious,* too.

Within ten years of coming to New York, Adam had gone from being one step up from a squatter at friends' and acquaintances' apartments in Brooklyn to owning his own place in Manhattan. Diane, the food critic who had rented the basement apartment years before he bought the building, was a great tenant and she had become a good friend as well. Rog and Tess, actors with some Off Broadway credits, were somehow able to afford the rent on the second floor apartment. He never asked how they managed, but they always paid on time, and they were great sources of entertainment and friendship. Life was good, Adam had tried to remind himself during these past worrisome weeks.

So why this angst lately? Why did he sense the proverbial boom was about to be lowered as he sat in front of his laptop these days? The first three chapters of the new novel had come easily. He knew where he ultimately wanted to go with the story arc, but after he submitted those early chapters to his editor, he began to struggle in a way that reminded him of grappling with opponents on the wrestling mat. While he attempted to compose a scene or worked on introducing a character, he felt a resistance pinning him down and dragging him away. When he fought through it and managed to write a few pages, the next day those words seemed hollow, empty. There was a disconnectedness, an outright dishonesty about them, and ultimately, he worried lately, about him as their author.

Adam tried changing his writing routine. Instead of rolling out of bed at six AM when the alarm went off and relying on cups of espresso and a few cigarettes to rev him up, he tried sleeping in, getting up and going for a run in the park, showering as soon as he rose. When the change in his morning ritual didn't make a difference, he tried writing in the evening, but he seemed not to have a cohesive thought after 4 PM.

He decided to put the writing aside entirely for a few days. Instead, he reread *Notorious* and his second book, *Angelic*. Though neither sold many copies when they debuted, they both won some prizes and critical acclaim. As he read, Adam recognized in them the deceit, the artifice of his words. For the first time since he had started writing, he felt afraid. It was fear that was stopping the flow of creativity that he could count on until recently.

One dark October day, when once again no words would come, he took out his journal and gave himself permission to explore the root of this dread. An hour or so into the free flow of thoughts, he confronted what he had brushed aside these past few months for the sake of putting more words on the page. He rose and hurried out of the study, but the breakthrough haunted him from that point on. He had to face the fact that his life's work as a writer was a sham. He had pulled the wool over the eyes of his audience, and who were his readers after all? Agents, editors, publishers, critics, other writers, but *real* people—people like the ones his father had poured drinks for in his Southside bar—they were not reading one word of his. He was making zero impact on this fucked-up world.

The buzzer sounded and Adam called out, "It's open. Come on in."

"Hey, buddy," Rog said, handing him two bottles of prosecco as he moved quickly past his host. Adam observed the anatomically correct and aroused reindeer on the back of his friend's ironic Christmas sweater.

"You didn't have to dress up, you know," Adam said as he watched Rog disappear into his small study at the front of the apartment.

"What's he up to?" Adam asked Tess as she arrived a few moments later. She was a tall, brown-eyed blonde with a face perfectly angled for the camera, should she ever want to leave the stage and make films. She had told Adam last night that she was up for a temporary role in a soap opera. If she got it, it would be a lucrative way to indulge her passion for the theater.

"The Lions play today," she explained. "You can take the boy out of Detroit..." Tess headed to the kitchen with her casserole. "Damn! It smells wonderful in here!"

"What have you got there?" he asked, following her. He took some champagne flutes from the cupboard and began the cork-popping process.

"Lasagna. I know it's not standard fare for the day, but it's about the only edible thing in my repertoire," Tess said as she placed a dishtowel on the counter and set the pan on top. "How's the book coming?"

The buzzer sounded, saving Adam from telling the usual "it's coming" lie. He went to the door and in swept Diane Richir, paisley-print maxi skirt swirling around her ankles as she glided. She made a more dramatic entrance than the two actors had, Adam thought as she handed him what looked like a large picnic basket. "At your table today, Mr. Stoller, you'll have the only food critic in New York who can also bake a perfect sweet potato pie. There's apple for the traditionalists, too. I whipped some cream. Put that in the fridge, please."

Adam headed back to the kitchen and he and Tess exchanged smiles as they listened to the exclamations of the delighted Diane. "Ah, the table looks fabulous, Adam! Where did you get this beautiful china? Hello, Plump, darling!"

"EBay," Adam yelled back. "It reminded me of my grandmother's." He didn't add that lately he had been spending more time on EBay than on research for the book.

Tess carried two glasses of prosecco to the table and offered one to Diane. "Thank you, my dear," she said as they exchanged air kisses on both cheeks. It was a popular New York affectation in certain circles that the two of them loathed, so each time they met, they played the gesture out as if they were on stage.

"Are we only four today?" Diane asked Adam as he joined them.

"Yes, just we four," he said, attempting to stop that vein of conversation.

"So, I'm your date, yet again?" Adam looked at Diane's raised eyebrow and remained silent. "Adam, is it my imagination, or have we not seen you with a woman in months? I hope you aren't regressing to a mother complex. Is this book driving you that mad?" Tess laughed at her neighbor's boldness in addressing what she and Rog had wondered about, too.

"Don't encourage her, please," Adam begged Tess.

Diane continued the inquisition. "Is Dr. Twenty-Something out of the picture?"

Oh, God. Here it comes, he thought. He loved the woman, but she could be a total pain in his ass. Especially when she was right. He *had* stopped seeing the young doctor from NYU as of last month, and he couldn't explain what had made him do it or why he had been such a bastard about it. He had quit her like he wished he could quit cigarettes. Adam had employed the post-modern version of the Cold Turkey method; he had ghosted her. They had had a perfectly nice last evening together--dinner in the Village and great sex afterward. But then, he didn't know why, he couldn't make himself answer her calls or texts. A week went by and she actually came to his door. He hid in the study and pretended not to be home. What a shit he had been! When he thought about it, he felt very bad, but these days, he just couldn't deal with the pressure of a commitment. The book that refused to be written was enough for now.

Rog walked in and saved him from Diane's interrogation. "Hey, gorgeous. Happy Thanksgiving!" he said, as he planted a real kiss on her lips. "Is that for me?" he asked, taking a flute from Adam's hand. The four friends raised their glasses and a round of toasting began.

"Peace in my lifetime," Diane said for perhaps the fortieth time in her six decades on the planet.

"May a less-than-horrible script come my way. Soon!" Tess said.

"To the Lions making the playoffs!" Rog said.

The three turned to Adam who stood silently with his glass raised. After several seconds he said, "To having nothing to fear but fear itself."

They lifted their glasses and drank.

CHAPTER NINE

BREAKING NEWS

Adam poured coffee for the four of them in the kitchen while Diane presided over cutting the pie at the table. "Bring the cream, will you please, Adam?" Diane called from the other room.

His phone vibrated against the granite countertop. After his parents' morning call from their "prison," as his father referred to the expensive assisted-living facility they had moved to recently, Adam had muted it and left it in the kitchen the rest of the day. He glanced at it on his way to the refrigerator, and his agent's face stared back at him. What could Jesse possibly want from him on a a holiday? In spite of the four missed call icons on the home screen, he decided it couldn't be that important. He placed the cups of coffee and the cream on a tray and walked back to join his friends.

An hour later, Diane said her good nights. She had a deadline to meet and she would have to get up early the next morning. Rog went back to the study to watch the last game of the evening while Adam and Tess loaded the dishwasher and washed pots and pans.

His phone shuddered again. "Jesus, it's almost 9 o'clock! What does he want?" Adam said, picking up the phone and looking at the picture of Jesse Olson on his screen. "Sorry, Tess. I better take this." Adam walked to his bedroom and hit the Return Call button. A half a ring later his agent picked up. "Happy Thanksgiving, Jesse," he said.

Jesse Olson was perhaps the most sought-after literary agent in the country. The urgency in his voice shocked Adam. "Jesus! Thank God! I've been trying to reach you all day! I was just about to leave my in-laws' place in White Plains and drive over there. Have you seen the news?"

"I don't know what you're talking about." He could hear Rog speaking to Tess in the kitchen now, a clear exigency in his friend's tone.

"That school shooting in upstate on Monday," Jesse began.

"What about it?"

"The kid who did it was apparently a fan of yours. They found a copy of "Seneca Optical" in his pocket."

"What?"

Jesse spoke rapidly, as if he had rehearsed the words. "The FBI says that so far they've found nothing in the way of a manifesto or a suicide note. Nothing on Facebook or Twitter. The only thing they have in writing is your story. Ripped out of a copy of *Easy Listening* they found in his bedroom."

Adam's mind raced. "Seneca Optical" was something he had written several years before his short story collection was published. It originated as an exercise assigned by George Saunders in his Short Story Writing seminar. The challenge had been to contemporize a myth from an early culture. Adam had recently visited Ganondagan, the site of a Native American community near Rochester that had flourished throughout the seventeenth and eighteenth centuries. He had toured the bark longhouse and hiked some of the trails. In the gift shop of the museum, he had purchased a booklet on the Iroquois and the story of the Thunder Gods had intrigued him.

"Adam?" Jesse said. "Are you still there?"

"Yeah," he said as Tess and Rog tentatively walked into the room.

"So don't talk to the press. Let Marie and I take care of damage control."

Marie Lanphere was Adam's publicist. As soon as HBO had purchased *No-torious,* she had been diligent in getting his face and story out to any media outlet that would take it. Thanks to her, he was a minor celebrity, at least in New York. "Adam, did you hear me?" Jesse pressed him.

"Yes. I just can't understand how that story...how many did he kill?" he asked.

"Eight, counting himself. One kid is still in critical condition," his agent answered.

"Christ," he said. Tess and Rog stood watching him. He could tell from their shocked expressions that they had heard the news too. "I've got to go, Jesse."

"Okay, buddy. I'll call you tomorrow morning. Try to get some sleep. Listen, this could be a good thing for us. People are gonna want to read that story. *Easy Listening* sales are going to spike! How's the new book..." Adam hit End Call and set his phone down.

"How did you find out?" he asked his friends.

"At the end of the third quarter there was a news update. Jim Axelrod came on and said the kid had your short story in his pocket when they found him. There's speculation that it may provide some clues as to why he did it," Rog said. "He was supposedly the perfect kid until Monday."

"How can a few thousand words..." Adam's voice trailed off.

Tess answered, "It's never that simple, Adam. One story, one video game, one song does not make a mass murderer."

"You know what's really ironic about that particular piece?" Adam asked. "Even though I enjoyed writing it, I never really felt an ownership with it. It's probably the most formulaic thing I've written, but my publisher wanted an even ten for the collection, so I did a little revision on that one and sent it to him."

After Rog and Tess left him for their own apartment, Adam knew he wouldn't sleep. In his study, he read every news release and follow-up story he could find on the Lake Hinon School shooting. By two AM, he was looking through his journal from ten years before to find his pre-writing notes for "Seneca Optical." His beat sheets were scrawled below the quote he had copied from the prelude to Joseph Campbell's *The Hero With a Thousand Faces.*

"*A* hero *ventures forth from the world of common day into a region of supernatural wonder: fabulous forces are there encountered and a decisive victory is won: the hero comes back from this mysterious adventure with the power to bestow boons on his fellow man.*"

A half hour later, Adam opened the hardbound copy of *Easy Listening* and turned to the last story in his book.

CHAPTER TEN

TYPOLOGY

I t had been a few years since his final revision of the piece, and after he had chosen it by default for the collection and sent it to his publisher, he had not read the story again. It was better than he remembered. But a catalyst for a massacre? He couldn't fathom the connection between his words and the tragedy in upstate New York. After all, perhaps hundreds of people had read "Seneca Optical," but only one person had been found with it in his pocket after wreaking havoc in a high school. All these months of anguishing over whether or not his writing had any relevancy—was this the answer? Could his words actually have been the trigger for such an evil act?

He opened his laptop and googled "books that kill" and sure enough he read article after article that reminded him that "Seneca Optical" was not alone in this category. Years before, Stephen King had been horrified by a middle school boy's response to his book *Rage*. The kid had gunned down his algebra teacher and two classmates after quoting a line from the story. The boy told investigators that he had modeled his life after King's protagonist. The writer had called for his book to be taken out of print because of the crime it apparently had caused. Then there was crazy Robert Pierce's novel, *The Turner Diaries*, that Tim McVeigh claimed was instrumental in his carrying out the mass murder in Oklahoma City. The madman who shot John Lennon had a copy of *The Catcher in the Rye* in his room when the police arrested him. He signed the statement he gave them Holden Caulfield.

The notification ping from Adam's phone sounded. He picked it up and read a Breaking News alert from the Times. "*Eddie Gatto, Jr., first victim of Lake Hinon School shooter, who has been in a coma for the past two days, has died.*" "Oh, Christ," he said under his breath.

He pressed the video button below the headline. At a podium stood a grim-faced woman, an official of Rochester Memorial Hospital, the caption said, delivering the cause and time of death of the high school sophomore. From there, the video cut to still pictures of sixteen-year-old Eddie, riding a unicycle in his town's annual July 4th parade, wearing a suit and tie as he participated in a High School Quiz Bowl championship, sitting in front of a drum set in the school bandroom and smiling into the camera. The voice of Samuel Walters, Lake Hinon High School's band director, his voice breaking at times, explained to the viewer as the pictures rolled, that Eddie was a great kid, a terrific musician, a friend to all. Mr. Walters reminded the viewers that Eddie's life and the lives of all eight of the victims would be celebrated the next evening at a candlelight vigil to be held at the high school.

It was four in the morning by the time Adam climbed into bed, but when he closed his eyes he kept seeing Eddie Gatto's face. He wondered if, in some bizarre twist of fate, he was somehow responsible for this boy's death, for the deaths of the other seven victims and for that of the perpetrator, Luke Clayton.

He opened his eyes and stared into the darkness, trying desperately to turn off his thoughts. The last one he had before finally drifting off was that King's, Pierce's, and Salinger's demented readers, unlike their victims, had lived. Each had boldly announced in courtrooms and to the world that those works of fiction had inspired the violence they had visited upon innocents. The person who had caused the Lake Hinon nightmare had killed himself and apparently had left no word as to why he had chosen to commit murder and suicide while carrying Adam Stoller's "Seneca Optical."

As soon as Adam awoke late in the morning on Friday, his mind started to work on the puzzle that was Luke Clayton. In much the same way he had conceived of fictional characters, the writer began to imagine who this boy had been before he had been touched and transformed by evil. He sat up and grabbed his journal and the news releases he had printed and highlighted last night.

Sitting at the desk where dozens of characters had come forth from his imagination, he opened to two fresh pages in his current work journal. If Adam did any pre-writing at all it was in one of these small leather-bound books. He had a dozen or so filed away, their lined pages filled with his scrawl. They spanned his life as a writer, as far back as one an aunt had given him when he was in high school. Now he reread the news releases and noted in the journal the few facts that had been uncovered about Luke Clayton.

Adam hunched closer to the journal. This was his professional posture, the one that sent him to the chiropractor each month. There was so little there. The bare details about the kid only provoked more questions, which Adam furiously jotted down on the opposite page of his journal. He felt a rush, a burst of energy that had been missing in his life as of late. It was the urge to go beyond the few particulars about Luke Clayton and plumb deeper, to answer questions about his young fan that motivated the writer to put down the pen and open a new Word file. That potent connection to his creativity that had left him a few months back returned full force as he typed for two hours with barely a pause. A boy of sixteen, a stranger to him until now was coming to life in this small room. While his imagination fired, a dull headache gathered force and eventually barricaded his thoughts. A couple of hours after he had started, Adam rolled his desk chair away from the computer and massaged his temples. He realized he hadn't had caffeine nor any form of nicotine today.

In the kitchen he broke a piece of Nicoderm out of its plastic bubble and stuck it in his mouth while the espresso brewed. His phone vibrated against the granite countertop and a number he didn't recognize appeared on his screen.

"Mr. Stoller? Matt Richmond from *The Times*. I'm writing an article on the Langston shooting. I wonder if you'd care to comment about the role your short story may have played in this boy's actions."

"I would not," Adam said to Richmond and then to the six other reporters who called in the next hour. How the hell had they had managed to get ahold of his cell number?

When Jesse called to check on him, he assured his client that he had done the right thing in not weighing in on the tragedy. It would appear insensitive if Adam commented this soon after the incident, he told him. "Besides," Jesse said, "it will make the mystery even more alluring to potential readers if you have nothing to say."

"For Christ's sake, Jesse, this isn't about marketing a book!" Adam yelled into the phone.

"I get it, bro. You have scruples. But it's not your fault if this psycho ends up selling more copies for you," his agent said. "Who knows? Showtime or Netflix may come calling, too. By the way, how's the new novel coming?"

Adam hit the End Call button. Obviously, it had been Jesse, or maybe his publicist, who had given his number out to the reporters. His agent's cutthroat attitude sickened him. People had lost their lives and all he could talk about was the free publicity they were getting. He was shaking his head in disgust when his door buzzer sounded and interrupted his thoughts. He rarely looked through the peep hole, but spooked by the reporters' calls, this time he did. When he saw Diane standing on the other side, he unbolted the door.

"I came for some Black Friday leftovers," she said, heading to his kitchen. "And I made the mistake of turning on CNN after I posted my article. Did you see that that poor kid died?"

"Yes," he told her.

"I figured you might want some company. Is it too early for a drink?" He poured them each a beer and watched as Diane layered turkey, mashed potatoes, gravy, and cranberry sauce in a casserole dish. He was glad she had come—maybe she was the second mother he needed, especially now.

"So, what's Anderson Cooper's take on it?" he asked her.

"It's too early for the Silver Fox. Wolf Blitzer was questioning a panel of 'experts,'" Diane said, adding air quotes to her sarcastic tone, just in case he didn't catch it. "They were discussing the effects of violent video games and other media on the adolescent brain. Pure speculation, of course. But we Americans prefer these guessing games to any substantial facts during our twenty-four hour news cycle. *Much* more entertaining." She opened the oven door and slid the dish in. "By the way, the picture they had of you looked like it came from an FBI file." She wrinkled her nose in distaste at the memory.

"Great." Adam cringed at the thought of his friends and especially his parents seeing this, although his mother and father seemed to watch very little television these days. He made a mental note to give them a call later and explain it to them himself. "Do you want to take a walk while the casserole is baking?" he asked his friend. "I've been inside all day and I'm feeling antsy."

"Writing?" she asked.

"Kind of. I've been trying to figure out who Luke Clayton was."

"If I know you as well as I think I do, you've been trying to figure out how your story could have had that much influence over him--what your part was in this disaster, right?" Diane said.

"I guess so," he admitted.

"Sure, I'll take a walk. Let me grab my coat and scarf first. I'll meet you outside," she added as she opened his door.

The two walked into the November twilight. The skyline was all but faded when Diane broke the silence. "You know, Adam, they'll never figure this out for certain," she said confidently.

"How do you know that?"

"I have interests beyond new restaurants in Brooklyn, you know. My kids were in high school when Columbine happened. Ever since then, I've read everything I could find on these incidents. Tragically, there have been several a year since then," Diane said.

"How many of the perpetrators had an American short story on their bodies?" he asked.

"None that I know of," she said breathlessly as she tried to match her friend's longer strides. "That interview with Adam Lanza's father in *The New Yorker* was intriguing and horrifying at the same time. Did you read it?' she asked him.

"No." Suddenly Adam wanted a cigarette in the worst way. So far, the walk had done nothing to take the edge off.

"Of course, that kid was damaged goods. But the parents did everything they could to help him. Unfortunately, the mother thought target practice and owning an arsenal was useful therapy for him. But your boy." Diane paused. "He's a real enigma. Apparently, Luke Clayton was an angel before Monday."

"So what does your research tell you about a kid like that?" Adam asked.

"Well, Wolf's expert panel said that there are three typologies of school shooters. The psychotics—those kids typically stand out. They have horrendous brain disorders like schizophrenia. Their violence is almost organic. The voices or the demons tell them to do it," Diane said.

"So when they shoot up a school, it doesn't come as a huge surprise, right?" Adam said as the wind started to pick up.

Diane drew her scarf closer to her throat. "Right, just like the second kind of shooter, the sociopath. They're really scary because lots of times they can hide in plain sight, but they're ruthless. Eric Harris from Columbine was one. Sadistic. They're the ones who, as children, torture puppies. They're loners..."

"Couldn't Luke Clayton be classified as a sociopath?" Adam interrupted her.

"Let's see...helped his mother, and his siblings. Was a joiner. Worked part-time. I suppose he could have hidden behind that Boy Scout disguise. Pretty unlikely, though." She was silent as she concentrated on keeping up with Adam's long strides.

"So, not a sociopath?" Adam asked her as the street lights began to illuminate the familiar landmarks of their neighborhood.

"No, I don't think so. Luke Clayton, according to the panel, was more than likely the third kind of mass murderer. Traumatized. Somewhere, somehow, the kid was terribly hurt, damaged even, and just you wait," Diane assured him. "Somebody knows the story behind that massacre."

They turned the corner to their street. "And what about my story? What was it about something I wrote in graduate school that got inside this kid's head and possibly was the reason he killed? I can't stop thinking about that," Adam admitted.

"Hmm..." Diane looked pensive. She stopped at the intersection and looked up at her friend. "Maybe he thought in some twisted way that your story would tell his truth," she said.

"Have you read it?" he asked

"Not until this morning," she said. "As soon as I turned in my article, I took my signed copy of *Easy Listening* from the bookshelf. It was a damn good story, my friend," Diane said. "I imagine your fan base has increased tremendously in the last twenty-four hours."

"Jesus, that's what my agent says, too. Let's go in," he said as they stood in front of his brownstone. "I haven't eaten since yesterday."

CHAPTER ELEVEN

BLACKBIRD

Adam paced around the parameter of the small room that was his work space clutching a ceramic mug filled halfway with coffee. Since it was the only clean one available, he had grudgingly taken it from its place on the furthest reach of the kitchen shelf. The mug had been a gift from the last woman he had dated, Dr. Twenty-Something, as Diane referred to her. It was a nice gesture on her part, especially because he had not reciprocated in kind, but whenever he was forced by default to use the cup, Adam felt unsettled. In the first place, the size was wrong. It was so large that his coffee always got cold too quickly and he didn't own a microwave. Worse yet, the mug's glaring white color set off the bold black letters so that they were impossible to ignore. *"Today I Shall Be Epic,"* it gloated.

He stopped in front of the French door that led out to the small balcony. Rog called the converted bedroom where Adam spent the majority of his time "the cave," but typically by mid-morning the transoms admitted an hour or two of precious sunlight to the third floor apartment. That was not the case today, nor had it been for weeks. It was March 1st and the worst winter in the city's history would soon, according to the calendar, be coming to its long-awaited end. He took a swallow of his cooling coffee. A light snow was falling in spite of the date, and a sense of dread, the type that began in the pit of Adam's stomach, intensified as he stared at yet another dark gray sky.

He walked back to his desk and sat down. The calendar tucked into the blotter had no marks on it except for the large red circle he had drawn around the 15th with a sharpie. The Ides, of course. How cliché. Except it was not. His publisher expected to receive at least the first half of his novel by that date. Until he delivered it, Adam's advance money was in abeyance.

He did not have half a novel written. The truth was, he had made very little progress at all on the book. The Langston shooting and its mysterious perpetrator had lured him away from the project. When he should have been writing, he was instead reading every book and article, or watching every documentary he could find about school shooters. In Langston, the police investigation was still active, and the official word was that the authorities would share nothing until it was completed. The families of the victims had little to say to the media. A Facebook page memorializing the dead was mysteriously taken down. The national media had left the small town a month after the tragedy, and CNN seemed to have exhausted its speculations about the "Catastrophe in Small Town America," the tagline they used over and over again. They were on to the next disaster, and although Adam was from time to time haunted by the nagging question of what part his story played in Luke Clayton's transformation, how it may have contributed to his evil deed, he had no answers. The character sketch he had started to write was nothing but that. A piece of useless fiction. Just like Wolf Blitzer's experts, he was blindly speculating about Luke Clayton's motivation.

Then New Year's followed Christmas and he flew to Chicago to visit his parents. Although they were in their early 80's, they were generally well, physically that is. But during Adam's brief stay, his dad's short term recall was noticeably impaired. "So you're writing a book?" his father asked several times during his daily visits. "How much does that pay?" Adam knew the question had nothing to do with the fact that his son was spending a lot of money each month to keep his parents safe and secure in their beautiful assisted-living facility. His dad especially seemed to be oblivious to that fact.

When Adam returned to New York after the holiday, he tried to get back to work on the book, but the anxiety about his dad's failing health was one more thing that seemed to sap his creative energy. By February, he had to acknowledge first to himself, and later to Jesse Olson, that his writer's block was intransigent.

"Don't worry, buddy." Jesse had said. "Just as I predicted, *Easy Listening* has sold hundreds of copies and even more eBooks since the shooting, and once *Notorious* airs this summer, Adam Stoller will be a household name all over this country. Even in those houses that don't have bookcases!" the agent gleefully exclaimed. Adam often asked himself how he had ended up with this carnival barker, this spewer of hyperbole, as his representative. His feelings about Jesse spanned a wide spectrum - from amused admiration all the way to outright loathing.

"If the new novel drops within a month of the HBO thing, we'll be fine," Jesse said.

You'll be fine because *you* don't have to depend solely on my publisher's advance to pay *your* bills, Adam thought but did not say out loud. What would be the point?

So after the holidays he had tried to hunker down and focus on the book, but as he looked out on this bleak March morning, he felt hopeless. He pictured himself stepping out on the balcony and lighting a cigarette. He was about to reach into the bottom desk drawer to retrieve the crumpled pack of Marlboros he had thrown in there months before, when his phone vibrated. Providence intervening, he decided. Slamming the drawer closed with his foot, he picked up the phone.

"Hello, Mr. Stoller?" a voice he did not recognize asked. "This is Terry Graf. I'm the media editor at *Rolling Stone.* How are you?"

Adam knew who Terry Graf was. He was an alum of Syracuse too, and though they had never met, Graf was renown at the university as one of their most successful graduates. "Yes, Terry. I'm fine," he said.

"Congratulations on all your success. I'm a fan—I've read everything you've written. I'm looking forward to seeing what HBO does with *Notorious.*"

"Thanks, Terry. That's very kind of you." Adam was flattered but wary. This powerful guy from a media giant must have something else in mind besides complimenting him.

"So, Mr. Stoller..."

"Please, it's Adam," he said.

"Adam, the magazine is interested in having you do an assignment for us. The November shooting in upstate New York. So much about it, about the shooter, remains a mystery," he said.

"That seems to be the case," Adam said.

"And the fact that he had a copy of your story on him while he shot all those people and then himself...it's a fascinating piece of the puzzle. Would you agree?" Graf asked him.

"Yes. I've been beyond fascinated by it. But I really don't understand..."

Graf interrupted him. "We'd like to have you write an article for us, Adam. *Rolling Stone* would like you to go to Luke Clayton's hometown and do a personal exploration. We want *your* point of view—after all, you're the author of the short story that seems to have played some part in this insanity. We want you to try to figure out who this kid was before he committed this crime."

Adam was stunned. "You want me?" he asked. "But I'm a novelist, not a journalist."

"Yes, of course, we know that. But there's lots of precedence here at the magazine for this sort of thing. We've had other novelists do projects for us. Hunter Thompson and David Foster Wallace, of course, for starters." Adam was well aware of the work these giants and dozens of other great writers had done for the magazine.

"We're especially interested in the angle of how media—movies, music, and fiction might be a catalyst, the spark if you will, for some people, particularly kids who may be more easily influenced, to do harm, even evil. As apparently Luke Clayton was."

Adam's thoughts raced, chasing one another in a jumble. "You know, I wrote 'Seneca Optical' for George Saunder's workshop at Syracuse years ago. It landed in the collection by default." There was silence on the other end of the line. Adam continued to ramble. "I'm not a sociologist or psychologist, Terry, and I have no background in investigative journalism."

"We don't want someone with that kind of experience. There are plenty of those folks available if we did. We want you, Adam. We think it would be much more valuable to have the author of a story that might have pushed Luke Clayton over the brink write our article. We'd like you to go to the place where it happened. Meet his family, go to the school, feel out the community. Even talk to the families of the victims, if possible. It would be your observations and insights that would make this an amazing, unique piece," Graf said.

"Look, I've got a deadline to meet for my publisher," Adam started to explain.

Graf interrupted him. "Let me tell you the figure I've been authorized to offer you." The next words out of the editor's mouth silenced Adam. "Do you think that's fair?" he asked him.

He was stunned by the amount of money they wanted to pay him for writing a few thousand words. It was much more than the advance for the novel would be. "Terry, let me get back to you." Adam stuttered as he tried to get the words out. "I've got to think this over and call my agent."

"I've already had a conversation with Jesse Olson," Graf said. "He seemed to think your publisher would be happy to give you a month or two extension on your deadline, once you accepted our offer."

Of course. Adam should have known that Jesse was in on this. He felt his face growing hot at the realization that his agent knew and had not warned him. He must have figured that Adam would be more likely to accept the offer if it came from Graf.

"The article would run just before the first episode of *Notorious* airs. Your agent liked that idea very much. You still there, Adam?" Graf asked.

"Yes," he answered.

"Look, I've got to give our board an answer by Monday. I hope that's enough time for you. This could be an amazing opportunity to write something totally original. I'll call you Monday morning. I hope you'll come around to our way of thinking and that your answer will be yes," Terry said.

Adam put his phone down on the desk and walked to the balcony door, still in shock. He couldn't just take off for a month and leave his life and work behind, he told himself. But if he looked at Terry Graf's proposal as an opportunity rather than an interruption, there were advantages, he had to admit. There would be the chance to examine the people and circumstances in Luke Clayton's life, to find out if his own words somehow abetted the kid's crime. And he would be compensated well to do this; he could stop worrying about paying his parents' bills, at least for the rest of this year. He could take a break from this novel that was driving him crazy and it would be with his publisher's blessing.

Adam stepped out onto the small porch, breathing in the moist end-of-winter air. He looked up at the black branches of the trees. His peripheral vision registered a sudden movement from the top of the dormant oak in front of his building. An object, no, a shiny black bird, larger than a crow was free-falling from the uppermost branches. He watched in amazement as the creature landed on the roof of the news hut across the street. Offering no resistance, it slid in slow motion off the small structure. For a brief moment, the bird made eye contact with Adam before falling dead onto the sidewalk.

That evening Rog, Tess, and Diane met him at Larry's where he shared with his friends his plan to accept *Rolling Stone's* offer. On Monday morning, he gave Terry Graf his answer. By noon, Adam steered the rented Land Rover through the Lincoln Tunnel and headed west.

PART III

CHAPTER TWELVE

BACK TO WORK

Gina rolled up the sleeves of her uniform and began to scrub. All the counter stools at the Linwood Diner were empty. The first half-hour of the three-to-eleven shift was that peculiar time of day when no one wanted lunch anymore, and it was too early for dinner. Linda, the owner, and Freddie, the grill guy, were in the kitchen. Except for them and a middle-aged couple sitting in a back booth, Gina was alone in the place. She took a step back so that she could see how effective her efforts had been. The counter gleamed, but she decided to go over the surface with a dry cloth. The repetitive motion was numbing; for those few moments, she was insulated from thoughts and emotions that had overwhelmed her these past months.

Linda rushed past her with the canvas bank bag in her hand. "Be right back," her boss said as she hurried out the front door. In the four years that Gina had worked here, the two women had never been more than employer and employee, so Gina had been surprised to see Linda at Luke's funeral. She was one of the very few people who had driven the 120 miles to the service in Buffalo. After the prayer ceremony her parents had arranged, Linda had come up to Gina and put her arms around her. The woman spoke softly so that no one else could hear. "You know you have a job when you're ready to come back," she had told her.

A few weeks ago Gina had walked into the diner for the first time in months. Because she seemed to have little control over her emotions, it was one of most difficult things she had ever had to do in her life. Since that day in November whenever she was alone, without any forethought or warning, she would break down, unable to stop crying, sometimes for an hour at a time. When she got into the car to drive to work on her first day back, the sobbing started the minute she pulled out of the driveway. There was no prelude, no tearing up first. The sounds originated from her diaphragm, their crescendo wracking her body so badly that day, she had to pull into a gas station until she could drive again.

These sneak attacks of grief assaulted her at home, too, since she was often by herself in the house during the day. Shelley was at work and her parents had been successful in convincing Gina that Johnny, Tom, and Lisa would be better off with their grandparents in Buffalo. "Just until school's out for the summer," her mother had said. "It's been hard on them too, Gina. You can't possibly expect them to go back to the place where their brother murdered people and killed himself."

It surprised her that the kids had not argued when the plan was shared with them. So Gina yielded to her mother and permitted her three youngest children to move away from her to a city where no one knew them, where no one knew that they had had a brother. She missed them terribly. After Shelley would leave for the bank, Gina frequently found herself wandering back and forth between the twins' room to the girls' room, compulsively picking up and then putting down their things, burying her head in each of their pillows, searching for the essence of each of her living children. When she called them every couple of days, they seemed fine, especially her troublesome twins. On the weekends, they Skyped, and although Gina from time to time noticed a sudden look of bewilderment on Lisa's face, the boys smiled and joked throughout these sessions.

Gina's grief paralyzed and imprisoned her throughout that winter following Luke's death. Most days she couldn't eat and most nights she couldn't sleep. When she did manage to doze off for an hour or so, she would often awaken to a sensation of being submerged so deeply under water that she could not get back to the surface, no matter how hard she struggled. There were other times when she awoke in the dark with a manic burst of energy, and her thoughts would immediately rush to the families of Luke's victims. They were living in the same hell she resided in, their child, mother, father, spouse, brother, sister ripped from their lives with no warning. In this anxious state, she made elaborate plans to write long letters to these survivors; no, on second thought, she would go to their homes. She would tell them to their faces how sorry she was, that she understood what they were going through. But these people despised Gina, she knew. They held her responsible for the terrible void they now lived with, and she knew they were justified in their hate. They loathed her as she loathed herself.

As difficult as it would be to face the hostile outside world, she had to go back to work. Shelley's baby was due in April, and the bank allowed only a six-week unpaid maternity leave. Gina would be supporting both of them until Shelley could return to work. She sent a weekly check to her parents, but so far not one of the six had been cashed. When she had the strength to deal with them, she would insist that her parents take her money, even if she had to drive to Buffalo and leave the cash somewhere in their house.

That first snowy morning when she had walked back into work, head bent as though she must examine each tile on the floor, she was still distraught from the crying that had overtaken her and fearful of what she might face at the diner. She hurried back to the small staff room behind the kitchen where the waitresses hung their coats and put their purses into the small lockers Linda had found at an auction. After shoving her coat and purse into her space, she went into the bathroom and held a wet paper towel under her swollen eyes.

A knock on the door startled her. "You okay in there?" Linda asked quietly.

"Yes," she said, balling the paper towel up and tossing it.

When she opened the door, Linda stood there in boss mode with Gina's Linwood Diner shirt in her hand. "I want you on the counter for now," she said as she handed it to her.

"The counter?" Gina felt the alarm rise in her. The counter meant twice as many orders and fewer tips, compared to serving the tables and booths.

"Yes. Just until people get used to you being back. One-time customers are more likely to sit there. Folks who aren't from the area, who get off the Thruway to go to the lake. And the regulars who sit there, well, I can see and hear what's going on from the kitchen, in case any of them decides to be an asshole. Besides, if anyone on the stools doesn't want to be waited on by you, they can get up and walk to a table or booth," she said. "Or they can turn around and leave."

"Okay, thanks, Linda," Gina said.

Her boss looked her up and down. "Freddie fixed you some eggs and toast. Eat before you head to the counter."

The other waitresses on Gina's first shift back seemed to be divided in their reaction to her being there. Half of them were cool, ignoring her completely whenever it was possible. The others were downright patronizing in their exchanges with her. Not one of them mentioned Luke or the shootings.

As the days and then the weeks passed, the regular customers' reactions to her varied too. Most coldly ignored her on their way into the main dining room. But then there were the disgusted glares she received from patrons who rushed through the front door to the hostess station. Sometimes, however, their disapproval was more blatant than a dirty look. On several occasions when she turned from the kitchen serving ledge to the counter, she would notice a finger pointing at her from a nearby booth. And as Linda had predicted, a few people turned around and walked out when they saw Gina.

In the world outside of the diner, as well, she faced the angry stares of people who she didn't recognize, but who obviously knew who she was. Whenever she had to be out in public in Langston or Jamesburg shopping or paying bills, which was becoming more and more necessary as Shelley's pregnancy kept her from running errands, people often whispered behind their hands or silently glowered at her.

One day as she shopped in Kohl's for her future grandchild's wardrobe, she caught the tail end of a woman's conversation with her husband. "That's the *monster's mother!*" she said to him. The remark had taken Gina's breath away. So had several death threats left on her answering machine, including one that started with a friendly voice saying, "*Merry Christmas, Gina! I'm glad your son killed himself. Why don't you do the same?!*" The bastard would probably be thrilled to know that sometimes when she startled awake in the middle of the night, she envisioned ways she would do exactly that. But she would not do it on the advice of this anonymous coward. She had cancelled her landline service that day.

By March, her presence no longer caused a stir with the regular patrons of the diner. For whatever reason, at this point people sensed that the restaurant was a neutral zone. It may have been the fact that they were caught in the glare of Linda's warning gaze whenever they showed signs of disrespecting her best waitress. "After Easter, let's get you back out in the dining room," she said. "I think we've seen the last of the rubbernecking."

Linda knew that Gina wasn't happy working the counter. What Linda did not know is that Gina had another job. When she was not at the diner, on the days and nights when the sobbing did not take over, she was putting every ounce of effort into finding out what had happened to her son. To understand what had changed Luke, what had transformed him and made him capable of committing atrocities, this became her compulsion. How had he managed to mislead the world, to deceive his mother, who thought she knew him?

On those mornings, when before she opened her eyes, Gina felt the heavy blanket of grief weighing her down, she battled the urge to stay in bed forever. She had a purpose, a mission, she told herself, so she must get up. The police had not come up with a motive for Luke's rampage; she had not heard from them in weeks. Maybe they were satisfied to call the catastrophe a "random act," but Gina refused to believe that her son had somehow "snapped."

Although the local press and even some national outlets had called her wanting interviews, she spoke to no one. She refused to be a party to the post-mortem profiling of her son. She could not completely avoid the headlines, however, assaulting her from a newspaper box or a scroll line on CNN. "*Good Son or Bad Seed?*" "*Lake Hinon School Killer An Enigma*" "*Luke Clayton—Quiet Student or Brooding Killer?*" "*Lake High Killer—A Dark Riddle.*"

She began her pursuit for the truth by searching her house again for a sign, something that the police had not found when they had ripped the place apart. Looking through his books and his notebooks from school, she spent hours in Luke's room. She went through every pocket of every article of his clothing. She read every page of everything she had found on his search history. It all seemed benign. The only subject that she found that was at all related to the shooting was the Wikipedia page of the author Adam Stoller.

After days of hunting for clues, Gina had to face the fact that she had exhausted her quest for the truth within the four walls of their home. She rarely went out except to go to work, but she steeled herself to venture outside of the house to find some answers to the dozens of questions about Luke that haunted her.

The Smith and Wesson that Luke had used was traced to the grand-father of his closest friend, Travis Worthing. It was legally registered, the police had told her. Luke had managed to take it and a couple of clips of ammunition, along with the man's camouflage gear from the locked safe in the Worthings' garage, apparently without Travis knowing it. Gina had questions for Mr. Worthing, but her ultimate objective was to find out what Luke may have confided to Travis. She needed to understand what Luke had been thinking that morning when he had ended the lives of eight peo-ple and then taken his own, and she hoped that Travis would be able to tell her.

The Worthings lived on the outskirts of the village of Langston on a road where neighbors were few and far between. Although she had met Travis' grandparents when they introduced themselves to her at the one football game that season that she had been able to make, she hadn't known where they lived until she looked up their address today in an old phone directory. A sob caught in her throat as she realized that although he spent a lot of time at the Worthings' home, she had never asked Luke where his best friend lived.

Once again she felt a groundswell of guilt that, too late, made her ques-tion herself. What kind of mother didn't ask her teen where he was going, to what address, what adult could she contact if need be? Why had she not been more vigilant, more protective, when it came to her son? The answer was always the same. Because Luke was a different kind of teen—trust-worthy, mature, independent. Her other kids acted out often. On any given day, one or more of them was angry, moody, disrespectful. In these ways, Luke's siblings demanded her attention and scrutiny. Their single mother worked long hours at the diner and when she wasn't there she was busy with the everyday emergencies that seemed to be a constant occurrence in the Clayton home. Maybe Luke had sent her some signal of his inner turmoil, but because she was preoccupied with the chaos that surrounded her, she had not seen it. For Christ's sake, she had never asked him where Travis lived!

Gina drove slowly up the dirt driveway and gazed at the dark-timbered A-frame. A neat stack of wood was piled next to the side door and smoke drifted from the chimney into the early spring day. At the edge of the woods that bordered the house, a dozen or so sparrows and chickadees crowded around the seed in a tall feeder. On the large front windows of the home were green gingham curtains. A grapevine wreath hung on the bright red front door.

As Gina stepped out of her car, she heard birdsong and nothing else. In spite of her nervousness, a calm came over her. No wonder her quiet son liked spending time here, a place so different from his own hectic home. In the back of the house stood the unattached garage. Gina's heart began to pound as she recognized the place where Luke had stolen the gun that had terminated nine lives.

She took a deep breath and walked up the steps of the spacious porch. Wooden Adirondack furniture added to the rustic beauty of the place. Gina walked to the front door and lifted the brass knocker. Almost immediately, it was opened. A tall woman in her late sixties stood at the threshold. Alice Worthing looked as though she were seeing a ghost standing before her on her porch.

"Hello, Mrs. Worthing. Do you remember me?" Gina asked.

The woman smiled uncertainly. "Yes, of course, Mrs. Clayton. Come in," she said, leading her into the expansive space of the living area. The wooden paneling and beams gave the room a lodge ambience. Gina tried not to stare at the antlered creatures that hung over the huge stone fireplace mantel. She had grown up in the city, and her father had not believed in owning a gun, never mind killing animals with one.

The cinnamon aroma of something baking intensified as she followed Mrs. Worthing to the kitchen. The older woman stopped and turned to face Gina. "I've wanted to call you to tell you how sorry we are for your loss, but I just haven't been able to pick up the phone."

Gina had not heard those words enough, and she felt the woman's genuine sympathy. She had not been able to fully share her grief with her parents or her children. They needed to be protected from the blackness that often overwhelmed her. Pete had been denied a leave from prison for their son's funeral, so they had spoken only once since Luke's death. She heard the devastation in Pete's voice, and instead of telling him about the pain that was tearing her apart, she listened to her bereaved husband.

"I can't stop thinking about that Saturday before the shooting," Pete had said. "That was the last time I saw him. He seemed so serious, so intent on…" Gina had gone over and over in her head what Luke had been doing in those days leading up to November 23rd. Her son had told her that he was going with the Worthings to a Sabres game in Buffalo on that Saturday afternoon.

"What are you talking about, Pete? I brought Luke and the other kids to see you in October for your birthday," she interrupted.

"He took the bus by himself that day."

"What?" She couldn't believe what she was hearing. Luke had lied to her about where he had been. Gina felt a keen sense of betrayal. She knew this reaction was absurd, given the circumstances, but she had trusted her son implicitly.

"He said you got called into work at the last minute." Pete began to sob.

"What did he say to you, Pete? Did he seem upset?" She tried to sound calm, but her heart was racing.

"No. Like I said, he seemed…I don't know, solemn. The kid was an old soul, you know? We always said that about him from the time he was a baby."

"What did he say, Pete? Did he tell you anything about …" she hesitated. "About what he was planning to do?"

"No. I asked him about school, about football, and he said everything was going fine. He told me that you all were doing great. Shelley was feeling good and that you were working a lot. That Lisa and the twins were behaving…mostly." Her husband was silent for a few moments and then he said, "He just seemed super intense."

Her heart seemed to stop. "What do you mean, Pete?" she asked him.

"When I play that visit back in my head, and I have, dozens of times, it was all just the usual small talk between us. But from the beginning, I sensed something different in him, and when he stood to leave, I took his hand in mine and pulled him in for a hug, you know? And then he whispered in my ear. 'I understand why you did it, Dad. It was for us.' And then just like that, he was gone." Gina listened as he broke into heaving sobs. So her son's mission that day was to say goodbye to his father and forgive him for messing up their lives. Of course he wouldn't share that with her.

"I've fucked up so badly, Gina. I couldn't even make it to my own kid's funeral," he told her as she tried to console him.

"Thank God," she remembered her father saying when he found out that Pete would not be at the service. "The last thing you need is to have that loser around the kids."

Now a woman she barely knew had offered her a heartfelt condolence and Gina was grateful. "Would you like some coffee?" Mrs. Worthing asked her. "I just finished brewing a pot."

As the two women sat at the round kitchen table, their heads bowed over their coffee cups, Gina said, "I want you to know how much I appreciate you letting me come in. I have so many questions about my boy." She looked into the older woman's eyes. "Did you know him very well?"

"I would say we spent more time with Luke than any other friend of Travis'. Your son was a nice boy—very respectful and polite whenever he visited. He was a good influence on our grandson." The woman paused and took another sip of coffee. "Travis came to live with us the first time when he was in elementary school, you know. His parents had trouble with drugs. They didn't, or I should say, couldn't take care of him. So we took him in for good when he turned twelve," she explained.

Gina had never known the circumstances of Travis' coming to live with the Worthings, but then she had never found the time to ask Luke about it, either. As she listened to the boy's grandmother, she realized that of course Luke and Travis had a lot in common that most likely accounted for their friendship. Two young boys, uprooted from their homes, both of their lives shattered by their parents' involvement with drugs. Luke's dad, in jail and missing from his life from an early age, and Travis without either mother or father.

Mrs. Worthing continued. "It was one thing when Travis was a little boy, but it's tough to keep up with a teenager when you're our age. He was a real challenge in junior high school. Maybe Luke told you that he has ADHD?" she asked Gina.

"No, I didn't know that," she answered.

"But his grandpa never lost patience or gave up on him. Travis was picked on, once kids found out about his parents, and he acted out a lot back then. Kids can be so cruel, you know," she said.

"Yes, they can," Gina agreed.

"His grandfather was all for it when Travis told him he wanted to go out for football. He was a skinny kid, and I was afraid he'd get hurt. But my husband thought he needed the challenge and the discipline that came with the sport. We were glad when Luke went out for the team, too. We knew Travis would follow Luke anywhere." She realized what she had admitted and paused for a minute, looking at Gina to determine if she should go on.

"We felt that your son was a good influence on him, as I said before." The woman took a sip of her coffee. "Travis has been devastated by Luke's death. He's just not the same kid, and the worst part of it is, we can't get him to talk about it, about how he's feeling about all of this. We're trying to convince him to go back to the counselor he saw when he was younger. "For a moment, Mrs. Worthing seemed at a loss for words. "Did you know Travis quit the football team after...what happened, even though they were going to States?" she asked.

"No, I didn't know that." Gina's voice shook as she broached the question that had brought her to the Worthings' home. "Luke had never been around guns, Mrs. Worthing. As far as I knew, anyway." Gina lowered her eyes. She didn't want the woman to think she was challenging her. She quietly asked, "Do you have any idea how he could have known about that safe in your garage?'

"Yes. My husband took the boys target shooting in our back woods a number of times this fall. They would go about a quarter mile from the house and set up bottles and cans. Luke never told you about it?" she asked.

"No, he didn't." Gina kept her voice even, although she felt like screaming. Why hadn't these people felt like they needed her permission before they let her son shoot a gun?

"But my husband never gave him the combination to the lock that was on the safe, just like he told the police. Luke must have watched him carefully when he was putting the guns away. And that morning..." Mrs. Worthing's voice trailed off as she glanced out the side window of her house.

"Yes? What about it?" Gina asked.

"Luke had called that Sunday night and asked Travis if he could catch a ride to Lincoln with his grandpa on Monday on his way to work. When Jack picked him up at your house the next morning, he said later he'd never seen the boy so excited; he was usually such an even-keeled kid." The woman didn't seem to register that she was explaining the nature of a child to his mother.

"He told Jack that he had just passed his driver's test, that he needed a ride to Lincoln so he could pick up your car," she said and paused for a moment. It was mind-boggling, in light of the horror her son had been responsible for that day, that Luke's lie about having a license rattled Gina. It had bothered her when the police told her the Worthings' account and now as Travis' grandmother explained it.

"I never gave it a second thought when he pulled into our driveway and knocked on the door an hour later," Mrs. Worthing said. "Travis had gotten up late that morning. I went upstairs to tell him that Luke was here. I thought that Luke had gone back to the car to wait for him, but according to the police, that's when he must have gone into our garage and taken Jack's old camouflage gear and the handgun." The older woman looked close to tears now.

The kitchen door flew open and both women jumped as Travis Worthing entered. No longer the lean boy Gina remembered, he was taller and broader. He had the scruffy look that was so admired by Lisa and her friends—shaggy hair and unshaven sprouts where a mustache and beard would grow one day. He shot a wary glance at Gina. "I saw the Pontiac in the driveway." The kid was pale and shaking. Gina wondered if he had expected to see his friend Luke sitting in his kitchen instead of her. As if this was all one big nightmare that he had woken up from.

"Travis, it's 1:30! What are you doing home already?" his surprised grandmother asked.

"There were no classes after lunch. It's Wellness Day, which is a ridiculous waste of time," the boy said in the tone that condemned all adults for being so lame.

"How did you get home?" his grandmother asked.

"I walked," he stated flatly. "I'm going upstairs."

Gina stood up as the boy started to leave the kitchen. "Travis, I'd like to talk to you about Luke. You were his best friend..."

"I was his *only* friend, Mrs. Clayton," Travis responded. Gina could see that the boy was agitated by her presence.

"Okay, his only friend. Would you please sit down and talk with me?" she asked gently.

"I'm not feeling very good. And I don't want to talk to you," Travis answered over his shoulder as he bolted out of the room. The two women listened to the boy's footsteps as he took the stairs two at a time. Even though he was only in her presence for seconds, Gina sensed that Travis knew something, something he had not shared with the investigators. She needed to get him to open up to her about Luke.

"You should probably go, Mrs. Clayton. My husband will be home in a half hour and I'm just not sure how he would feel about your being here with Travis," Mrs. Worthing said.

"Of course. Well, thank you so much for talking with me, Mrs. Worthing. I really appreciate it," Gina said as she walked toward the front door.

"You're welcome, Mrs. Clayton."

"Please, call me Gina."

"Gina. And again, I'm so very sorry for your loss."

"Thank you." Gina stood on the front porch and faced her. "Do you think I might be able to come and talk with Travis when he's ready?"

The woman looked doubtful. "Let me talk it over with my husband," she said.

"Of course," Gina said.

Once she was behind the wheel of the Pontiac, Gina looked up at the A-Frame. A movement in one of the second story windows caught her eye. Travis Worthing stared back at her for a second and then pulled the curtains closed.

CHAPTER THIRTEEN

VIGIL

Adam had stopped only once during the six-hour drive from the city, and by three in the afternoon he was steering the Land Rover under the sandstone portico of the historic Lakeside Inn in Jamesburg. The cold wind blowing off Lake Hinon penetrated his suede jacket as he pulled his bag from the back of the car.

The night before he had read about the conversion of the nineteenth-century Italian Villa building. According to the Inn's website, the mansion had been constructed as a family home for Swedish immigrant Kidda Peterson. Within a few years of boarding a ship at Gothenberg, Peterson bought hundreds of acres of woodland in the region. During his lifetime and after, his company, Jamesburg Wood Products, supplied the lumber for dozens of homebuilders throughout the Northeast. As the business grew, Mr. Peterson hired a team of furniture designers, and that enterprise brought even more revenue to the already successful company. The most famous furniture customer was President Woodrow Wilson. He and first lady Edith had purchased several JWP pieces that were fixtures throughout rooms in the White House up to this day.

The picture of the inn with its red brick exterior and square tower had appealed to Adam. *The Rolling Stone* had reserved a suite at the Lincoln

Marriot for him, but he cancelled it after the receptionist at the Inn told him they were rather slow at this time of year. He would be able to book one of their eighteen guest rooms for a week at a time, she assured him.

Lamps were being turned on in each of the dozen or so arched windows as a bellman opened the massive carved door for Adam. "Welcome to the Lakeside Inn, sir," he said, as though Adam had made his day by showing up. Tall cherry columns and panels gleamed as he rolled his suitcase on the marble floor of the lobby. He turned to look behind him at the imposing stone fireplace and the inglenook surrounding it. The Inn's website had boasted that all of the rooms throughout the mansion featured a fireplace as well as a different genus of wood from each of Central New York's indigenous trees.

"Good afternoon. Can I help you?' The woman at the reception desk smiled warmly at him. Like the bellman's, her demeanor, a kind of genuine focus and engagement that he never found in New York or Chicago, reminded Adam of the small town sincerity that he had experienced during his time at Syracuse. As she handed him the key to the Mahogany Room she said, "I'm Mary Beth. If there's anything you need to make your stay with us a great experience, please let me know, Mr. Stoller."

He unlocked the substantial door to his room with a real key—no electronic pads had replaced the locks—and turned the ornate brass knob. On a large desk in the corner of the room, a green glass-shaded lamp glowed. He set his suitcase on the luggage rack and switched on the other three lamps that were located in each corner of the spacious room. Adam saw that the fireplace mantel and the bed's massive headboard were made from the same exquisite dark timber. A bank of three windows framed Lake Hinon, and as Adam stared out at the thawing body of water, he watched as a few lights came on along the distant shoreline.

He set his laptop on the desk and sat down. He draped his jacket over the back of the chair and from the pocket he pulled out the pamphlet that Mary Beth had given him. *Lake Hinon Life* described area restaurants and attractions that "no tourist would want to miss." Adam opened to the map of the lake and the communities surrounding it. He pulled out a sharpie from his bag and circled Langston. Luke Clayton's hometown was on the opposite shore from the Inn.

During the drive across the state, Adam had thought about who he would need to talk to in order to understand what had been in the shooter's head that November day. "Seneca Optical" was a derivation of an Iroquois legend, and this area was rich in Native history. Adam's guess was that the kid may have been assigned the story in school. The Lake Hinon School District was high on Adam's list of people and places that might help him uncover Luke's affiliation, perhaps his obsession, with his short story.

He had another reason for wanting to get into the high school. Adam had read every article written about Luke Clayton. The general consensus of the media was that he was mostly liked by his schoolmates, but that he had very few close friends. Up until now, not one of these kids, whoever they were, had talked to the press. Adam would have to find them. He would have to discover a way to get them to talk to him about Luke.

It was also essential, Adam reasoned, to track down the mother. The father, he had read, had been out of the picture for years, incarcerated by the time Luke was twelve, according to the media. Adam tried not to pre-judge the mother, not to hold her accountable for the horror her kid had caused. But he could not help but conclude that she must be a real loser. How could she have been so out of touch with her own kid? He would have to find her and eventually ask her that question.

An hour later, showered and changed, he sat at a table in the Oak Room, an "intimate dining space overlooking the lake", as the website had promised. Originally it had been the formal parlor in the Peterson home.

A striking feature of the room was the wide honey-colored oak beams on the ceiling. Adam counted seven round oak tables, each with four place settings. A couple sat at one and a woman sat alone at another. In the center of the room under a Tiffany chandelier was a large tiger-oak trestle table.

A young waitress greeted him. Her name was Katie, she told him. "Will anyone else be joining you?" she asked. She couldn't be more than seventeen, Adam thought.

"No," he told her. "It's just me tonight. This is a really beautiful place," he added, as she poured ice water from a crystal pitcher.

"Yes," the teen answered. "Our boss says we're the best kept secret in this part of the state. Most people travel to the Finger Lakes to vacation, but we think Lake Hinon is just as beautiful as any of them and not as crowded during the tourist season."

"I'll bet once people find this place, they come back," he said looking out at the bay.

"Yes. Quite a few people return every year." She lowered her eyes as she set the pitcher on the table. "Of course, this year might be different with what happened at the high school..."

"That was a terrible thing," he said softly.

"What sounds good to you today?" the girl asked, resuming her cheerful tone.

Adam looked up from the menu and took a chance. "Were you there that day?" Katie glanced around at the other diners. It was obvious she did not want to be overheard having this conversation.

"The daily specials are listed at the top of the menu. I'll give you some time to look it over," she said cordially.

A few moments later she took his order. He was finishing a glass of a local Shiraz when she brought his dinner. "Yes, I was in chorale practice," she said, as if he had just asked the question. "The police said he walked right by the music suite where I was that morning and went to the training center. He shot Mr. Harrison, Mr. Davis, and my friend Ryan." She paused. "I went to elementary with Ryan." A young adult seconds before, the waitress devolved to a child before his eyes.

"I'm so sorry," Adam said. "Did you know Luke Clayton, Katie?"

Waitress and writer were startled by the maître de who suddenly appeared at the table. "How does everything look, sir?" he asked.

"Great," Adam replied.

"Fresh yellow perch caught right out here in our beautiful lake. Good choice. Enjoy!"

Adam watched as the man followed Katie into the kitchen. By the time he had finished his meal, an older waitress came to his table and asked if he would like dessert or coffee.

"No thanks," he answered. "What happened to Katie?"

"Oh, her shift ended. The boss tries to schedule the high school kids so that they can get home at a decent hour on week nights," she said.

"I see," Adam said. "You'll be sure she gets her tip then?"

"Of course," she answered with a smile.

It looked like the Lakeside Inn staff had been instructed not to talk about 11/23, which was the succinct label the catastrophe had been given initially by the media. It seemed that the local residents had adopted it, however. Once he got off the Thruway and began driving through the outlying small towns toward Jamesburg, Adam had passed a Dairy Queen, a car dealership, a hot dog stand, a credit union--all with signs that stated similar sentiments: *Pray for Langston and Jamesburg, Pray for the Victims of 11/23.*

As he walked to the Land Rover, Adam wondered about the taxonomy of tragedy. Years, and in some cases, decades after a calamity occurred, dates alone could evoke their horror. He quickly checked off a list of them in his head: the beginning of his grandfathers' war: December 7th, 1941, the end of the Camelot era: November 22nd, 1963, Columbine: 4/20/99, the attack on the homeland that changed everything: 9/11. Now Central New York's day of infamy was memorialized in six syllables: 11/23.

Dusk would surrender to night within moments at this time of year, but Adam was determined to get the lay of the land as soon as he could. He dictated his destination to the rental car's fancy navigation system: "Lake Hinon High School, Langston, New York." As the sun sped closer to the lake, the confident British woman's voice instructed him to head east out of the parking lot.

On the drive, as promised in the pamphlet, he saw acres of tree-lined lots with beautiful nineteenth and early twentieth-century mansions. Once he was directed to turn away from the lake, Adam left the impressive estates behind as he drove through Jamesburg's more modest neighborhoods.

By the time he turned left onto Main Street, the thoroughfare that eventually connected Jamesburg to Langston, the light rain that had been falling on the windshield was replaced by wet springtime snowflakes. On upper Main, residences were intermixed with commercial buildings and through the steady back and forth of the wipers, he saw an electronic sign in front of a small stone church. He slowed down to read it. *Prayer Vigil for the 11/23 Victims and Survivors 7 PM tonight*. He checked the dashboard clock; it was 6:30. Adam turned left into a driveway and then headed back in the direction of the church. A small parking lot behind the building was already full and the side street was lined with cars. Adam drove to the next intersection and parked on the near-empty street.

By the time he entered the small church, every pew was filled. The back wall was lined with people leaning against it. A man pointed him in the direction of the stairs that led to the choir loft. "There are still a few more seats up there," he said.

From this high vantage point, Adam looked down at the congregation. In the midst of dozens of men and women, he saw a solid block of black and red. Six boys with Lake Hinon High School varsity football jackets sat together. They stood up with the rest of the congregants as a young man, dressed in faded jeans and a black blazer, walked to the podium. From behind Adam, the organist began to play and sing a hymn he did not recognize. It was no wonder—he had been raised Catholic, but he could not remember the last time he'd been inside a church.

"Welcome, everyone," the minister said when the hymn was over. "Please be seated." The man didn't look much older than thirty, but he commanded the attention of the room as he spoke. "A full season has passed since evil came marauding amongst us." He paused and walked slowly toward a window on the right side of the altar. The echo of his heeled boots on the tile floor emphasized his words. "Ladies and gentlemen, the promise that spring brings is on its way. For some in this room, through God's mercy, the healing has begun." He paused meaningfully and then walked back to the podium as he spoke. "For most of us, though, the pain that Satan has wrought is our daily burden to carry." Adam looked around at the people in the choir loft. Every man, woman, and teen was focused on the minister.

"Before we begin to pray together, as we do each time we meet, we will offer the opportunity to anyone who would like to share his or her experience, their thoughts and feelings, with the group." He turned his head slowly and looked over the podium to one side of the church and then to the other. "We were two separate communities before this tragedy, but now we are forevermore connected," he said. "Most of us knew somebody who was struck down that day. Or perhaps we know someone or live with someone who survived, but who still suffers." A sob drifted from the back of the choir loft and merged with several more that rose from the pews below. The sounds of sniffling and coughing echoed throughout the space.

From the front of the church, a short man dressed in a tight-fitting suit walked slowly down the center aisle and into the congregation. In his right hand, Adam could see a wireless microphone. "Thanks, Ray," the minister said to the man's back. "Ladies and gentlemen, boys and girls, we come together tonight, as we have each Monday night since the terrible events of 11/23 to share our pain. To ask God to help us to heal." He looked out at those in front of him and then up to the people in the loft. "Raise your hand if you'd like to say something, and Ray will come to you."

Adam watched as a woman in the third row rose to her feet, took the microphone, and turned to face the congregation. He could see the circles under her eyes from his place in the loft. "I'm Joan Foster. Our only child, Kelly, was in that English class." She paused for a moment. Her voice trembled when she spoke again. "Our daughter had to lie on the floor while her teacher and friend were slaughtered...and it could have been her!"

The man next to her, probably her husband, Adam thought, stood up and put his arm around her as she continued speaking. "We've always been protective parents. Some would say, overprotective. We wouldn't allow our daughter to go on the 6th grade field trip to the Forest for two nights," she said as her husband took a handkerchief from his back pocket. "She's seventeen and she's only been allowed to have overnights at our house, and now she's headed to college, where we won't have any say in what she does or where she goes. I can't sleep at night thinking about how close we came to losing her. How powerless we are to protect her." Many heads nodded, either in agreement with Joan Foster or perhaps as a gesture of compassion. Adam, a stranger in the midst of this communal grief, had no way of knowing which sentiment was being expressed.

Ray took the microphone from Joan Foster and continued his mission. Another woman across the aisle from the Fosters had signaled to him that she would like to speak. "Hello," she said, as she rose from her seat. "For those of you who don't know me, I'm Jane Murphy. My husband and I have been neighbors and friends of the Johnstons, who lost their only child, Ryan, on November 23rd. I wanted to say a few words about him tonight, and I'm going to try not to cry." Adam saw her pull a tissue from her coat pocket, just in case.

"I remember clearly the day that Judy and Gary first brought Ryan home. Many of you know that he was adopted as an infant," she said, looking up and down the pew. Again, Adam saw the nodding of many heads throughout the church. "It was the happiest day of their lives, they always said." She cleared her throat and continued. "Ryan was such a good kid. I always knew that about him. So it didn't surprise me or my husband when we learned about his heroic actions in the training room that morning. As most of you know, he was a dedicated athlete and a state contender in wrestling. He had gone in during a free period that morning to work out, his parents were later told. Coaches Harrison and Davis were in their offices in the back when the killer opened the door. Ryan bravely risked his life to protect the coaches. He didn't run or hide. He confronted the evil that was in front of him. But a barbell is no match for a pistol." She paused and looked at the people seated to her left and then to the ones on her right. The congregation had grown silent. "Mortally wounded, he managed to call the office and alert them that there was a killer loose in his school. We should never forget that Ryan Johnston, on November 23rd, just three months short of his eighteenth birthday, died a hero." Adam realized he had been holding his breath during most of Jane Murphy's speech. He watched as the woman passed the microphone back to Ray and sat down.

Ray walked to the midway point of the chapel and stopped when he saw a hand go up. He gave the device to a tall man who stepped into the center aisle. His ball cap and jacket shared the same logo. Adam squinted until he could read the words *Wallace Farms* embroidered in the center of the image.

"I'm Al Wallace," he said. "Most of you know that Scott was my cousin John's first-born. What happened that day has ripped our entire family apart. My eighty-year-old aunt and uncle, Scott's grandparents, are devastated. Scott was my cousin's pride and joy. He was a great kid, with a great future. But his family and friends will never get to see that." Adam watched as dozens of heads nodded.

"Like Joan, I haven't slept more than three or four hours a night since November," the man continued. "Right after it happened, one word would be in my head when I woke in the middle of the night. Why? I asked myself that, over and over again." Al Wallace turned and looked to his left. Adam couldn't be sure, but the man seemed to be looking at the block of football players.

"But lately when I open my eyes at two or three in the morning, two words haunt me. *What IF? What IF?*" He stopped again. But the echo of his words stayed with everyone in the room. "*What if* there had never been a merger between the two schools? *What if* there were no jealousies on the football team—jealousies about which kids from which town started? *What if* everyone here had voted *NO*?" Ray's tentative look toward the minister and then back at Al Wallace signaled respectfully that his turn to address the murmuring group was over.

Adam struggled to grasp what the man meant. Was Scott Wallace's uncle saying that nine people died that day because of a school merger? Luke Clayton, he seemed to infer, acted out of jealousy. If Wallace was right, then what did his short story have to do with the catastrophe?

The next speaker was below the loft, out of Adam's line of sight. From somewhere in the back of the church, the microphone crackled and a man said, "Hello. I'm Ron Byers. I teach at Lake Hinon High School. This is the first Monday that I've attended a vigil." A man's partially audible whisper came from behind Adam. The words "*Langston teacher*" was what he heard.

"Janet Shelkowski was my mentor, my colleague, and my friend," Ron Byers said. "I've had all of the deceased kids as students in my classes at one time or another. Luke...the shooter...was in my class that first semester." The small hairs on the back of Adam's neck stood up. He watched almost everyone sitting in the pews below as they twisted and turned toward the speaker.

"I love teaching," Byers said. "I know there's been a lot of controversy about our new district, but tonight I'd like to say something to the grown-ups here." He paused for a moment and then he said, "Lots of times we adults don't realize the impact our opinions and judgments have on kids, especially teenagers." The sotto voice behind Adam whispered something about the guy "*preaching.*"

"But we need to listen to our kids." Adam could not see the teacher, but what he heard in his voice was genuine passion. "They need to be able to trust that they can talk to us. There's a possibility that if even one adult had paid more attention to something that their son or daughter or student said..." The teacher stopped short of saying the tragedy could have been averted.

"*Blaming the victims...*" a woman sitting next to the whisperer said under her breath.

"And I'd like to say to the kids here and throughout our two towns, I know how hard it is to be you, how much you must hurt. But please know you're loved by your communities, by your teachers, by your parents. If you have a friend who's troubled, who's angry...tell an adult. I know that's difficult, but please trust us. Trust that we will do our best to help."

Ron Byers must have handed the microphone back to Ray, because a woman's voice began to speak about how the reputation of the community had been damaged by this event. She went on to say that businesses, including her own, were suffering and would continue to lose money through the summer tourist season and maybe would never recover.

Adam was barely listening. He needed to get to Luke's teacher, but how would he be able to recognize a stranger in a church full of strangers? He rose from the pew quietly and tiptoed down the loft stairs and leaned into an empty space along the back wall.

The minister began to lead the group in a prayer. Adam bowed his head, but he couldn't concentrate on anything but finding Ron Byers. From the back of the church, he looked at the people in the rows that had been hidden from his view in the loft. He counted the backs of heads. There were thirty-three men to choose from. He could eliminate the one wearing the Jamesburg Police Department jacket and perhaps another four or five white-haired men. The teacher's voice had sounded youthful.

"Please know that if you need to talk, I am here," Adam heard the minister say. "We will come together again next Monday evening. In the meantime, let us pray that as the days pass, God's love will continue to heal our wounds. Go in peace," the minister said, and the organist began to play something that Adam thought sounded close to *Morning Has Broken*.

As people began to vacate the back pews, Adam attempted to make eye contact with every man who walked toward the door. He tried to imagine what Ron Byers might look like, but how could you tell a teacher from a plumber? It seemed futile. Suddenly, the urge for a cigarette supplanted the heaviness he had experienced in the midst of this collective pain. He walked out the door with every intention of stopping at the first convenience store or gas station where he might get a pack of smokes.

"Adam Stoller?" Shocked to hear his name called in this place where he was a stranger, he turned around and saw a young man's face illuminated by the church's electronic sign. On the streets of New York, Adam was hardly a public person. After all, he was a writer, not a soap star. How did this guy know him?

"You're the author, right?" the man asked as Adam approached him. "I thought I recognized you when you came in tonight."

"Yes," Adam answered. "And you're...."

"Let's walk," he said, as the congregation flowed out of the small church. Adam followed the stranger down the sidewalk. "I'm Ron Byers," he said as they walked. "I teach Myths and Legends at the high school. It's an English elective."

Adam stopped and reached out his hand to Ron Byers. "I heard what you said tonight," Adam told him. "It made a lot of sense. You must be a great teacher." The handshake ended, and the two men resumed their walk.

"I assigned "*Seneca Optical*" to my class, the class Luke Clayton was in," Ron Byers said.

"Jesus," Adam said.

"I assume you've come here because of your story?"

Adam decided in that moment that he would not mention the *Rolling Stone* article. He wanted to hear what Ron Byers had to say; he didn't want to scare him off by admitting that he was on a work assignment. Besides, the fact was that he had mainly come here to find out the truth for his own peace of mind. "Yes, that's true," he said to Ron Byers.

"I've been a fan of yours for years, and I was familiar with the short story," the teacher said. "It fit perfectly into my *Hero With A Thousand Faces* unit. Plus, with our lake being named after the deity..." The sound of a cellphone buzzing in the teacher's jacket interrupted him.

"Yes, honey. Diapers. Got it. See you soon," he said. He looked up at Adam as he tucked the phone back into his pocket.

"But what can you tell me about Luke?" Adam asked. "Why do you think he had my story..."

The teacher stopped him. "Look, Mr. Stoller..."

"Adam, please..."

"Adam," the young man said. "I have a wife and a newborn at home." The two men stood alone in front of the church as the sound of dozens of cars starting filled the night air.

The door to the church opened again and they heard the minister call out, "Good to see you here tonight, Ron. Say hello to Trish for me."

"Will do, Reverend," Byers said.

When the two men reached the church parking lot Adam asked, "Can I buy you a beer or a cup of coffee?"

"I've got to get home, but thanks," the teacher said, unlocking his car door.

"When can we get together, Ron? I really need to understand why or how this kid was influenced by..."

Ron Byers turned toward Adam. There was a look of resolve on his face. "Come to the high school this Thursday. After classes. Around three ten. Will that work for you?" he asked.

Adam was relieved. He had stumbled upon this treasure, a person who knew his story *and* Luke Clayton. He was thrilled that Ron Byers seemed open to meeting again. "Absolutely! Thank you, Ron!" he said.

The young teacher nodded and climbed into his car. Adam rapped on the window before he could pull away. "Can you tell me anything about the mother? About where I might find her?" he said when the window opened.

"I've never met her, but I know she works a lot. That's what Luke said, anyway. Rumor has it that she's back to work again, which figures. She's raising a bunch of kids on her own, you know."

"Do you know who she works for?" Adam asked, as the teacher began to roll the window back up.

"Before the shooting, she waited tables at the Linwood Diner in Lincoln, but I'm not sure if she's still there. Look, Adam, I've got to go," he said.

"Sure, Ron. Thanks so much. I'll see you at the school on Thursday." Adam stepped away as Byers steered his Town and Country out of the lot. As he watched him go, he saw the brake lights come on and he heard the driver's side window open again. He jogged to catch up to the vehicle.

"Don't go to the main door on Thursday. There's a back entrance by the loading dock. Be there at three ten. I'll be there to let you in," the teacher said.

Chapter Fourteen

STRANGER

"He's here," Gina told Linda who was setting salads on the serving counter.

"Okay, come on back," Linda said, untying her cook's apron.

The two women had made this plan yesterday after the stranger had come in at dinner time and sat at the counter for two hours. He had had the dinner special, a fish fry, which he told Gina was the best thing he had ever eaten. The large portion of pie-ala-mode he ordered for dessert was followed by three cups of coffee. When he was her only customer left at the counter, it was obvious that he had been biding his time to gain Gina's undivided attention.

"Wow! This is a beautiful area," he said, while she attempted to clean the counter around him. His tone implied that Gina was responsible for the allure of the place.

She smiled politely and said, "Yes, it is."

"I took a drive today around Lake Hinon. It looks like it's thawing along the shoreline and in the bays. I'll bet everyone around here is glad to see that," he said. It was more of a question than a statement.

"Yes, it's been a long winter," she said. The worst one of her life, she added to herself. "How about where you're from? Did you have a miserable one too?" she asked the stranger, trying to be amiable.

"Oh, yeah," he answered.

"Where are you from?" she asked.

"New York, the city." He sounded apologetic. "But I spent a winter in Syracuse, so I know how brutal it can be in this part of New York."

She knew that she was supposed to ask what he had been doing in Syracuse that winter, but there was something about him that caused Gina to resist carrying on the pleasant customer service small talk that she was very good at. For one thing, he was too intense. He had tried to maintain eye contact with her throughout the mundane conversation. For another, he was too good-looking. The blue cashmere scarf he wore perfectly matched his eyes, and by the look of his trim body when he took off his gray suede jacket, that Dutch apple pie he had eaten was probably his first in years. Why would such an attractive, most likely well-off New Yorker be in the Linwood Diner in early March? And why was he being so attentive to a waitress there? She moved down the counter away from him.

"I'm in the area for my job," he added without having been asked.

She moved the cloth back up the counter toward him. She was about to ask him what he did for work when he said, "How about you, Gina? Have you lived in the area long?"

She felt prickles erupt on her scalp and the tiny hairs on the back of her neck stood up. How had he known her name? She wasn't wearing a nametag or anything that would have given it away. And why was he so interested in her? Suddenly she knew why—the bastard was a reporter! She quickly moved back to the opposite end of the counter with her polishing cloth.

"Yes, quite a while," she said and disappeared around the corner into the kitchen. Linda had her coat on and was heading out the back door. She turned to say something to the cook when she saw Gina standing there.

"What's wrong?" she asked when she saw the look on Gina's face.

"I'm not sure. There's a guy at the counter—I'm not certain why, but he's freaking me out a bit," Gina said. "He's acting a little too friendly, and he knew my name."

From her cover behind the serving counter, Linda stole a look at the man. "Definitely not a local," she observed.

"No, he says he's from New York City," Gina said.

"Kind of looks like a cop," Freddie the night cook added as he peered out toward the front of the diner.

"I don't think so. The cops I've talked to haven't needed to see me at work. I've been in the Jamesburg Police station at least a dozen times. Except for that day at the troopers' barracks and that first night when they came to the house, that's where they've interviewed me," Gina said.

"So who do you think he is?" Linda asked.

"A reporter, maybe? I've turned down at least twenty offers to be interviewed since November, including Jim Andrews from *AM Jamesburg*."

"Thank goodness," Linda said. "The guy's a windbag and a gossip."

"I cancelled my landline so that I wouldn't have to hear them begging for a meeting every time I listened to the messages on my answering machine," Gina said. She didn't tell Linda and Freddie about how she had decided to listen to all of the saved messages, including the death threats she had received, before putting the device up in the attic with the other obsolete miscellany of her life. Her boss and co-worker didn't need to know that she had forgotten about the November 23rd emergency dispatch from the school, that it had caught her completely off guard when it came on. It was much worse than the anonymous voices that called her a whore/bitch and wished for her demise. Even though she turned it off before it played all the way through, the shock of it had sent her back to her bed for the day.

"None of them have come to the house yet?" Linda asked.

"Not since early December. They haven't dared—that would probably

141

be harassment. But I guess it was just a matter of time before they started showing up here. It's a public place, after all," Gina said.

"He's putting his jacket on," Freddie said from his post at the serving ledge.

"Don't worry, Gina. If he shows up again, we'll put you in the kitchen, and I'll deal with him," Linda assured her.

Linda had her back, of that Gina was sure. Her boss had more than proven it. She had let Gina come back to work when most people in her position would not want her within ten feet of their place of business. Even though Gina could not explain how she was "doing," each time Linda inquired, even though she knew now that grief was a place she lived in, not a passing emotion, she appreciated her boss' genuine concern. Thank God she had one person in her life who she could count on to be on her side, no questions asked.

When Gina returned to the counter, the stranger was gone. She picked up the receipt and the small pile of bills underneath it. The twenty dollar tip he had left her was one more sign that he was definitely not from around here.

At 5:30 the next day, the man once again walked into the Linwood Diner. He smiled and waved to Gina and turned to hang his expensive jacket on one of the hooks on the wall behind him. By the time he sat down on the stool he had occupied yesterday, Gina had escaped to the kitchen and Linda was standing in front of him. After he left, her boss told Gina that he hadn't had much to say to her.

"He ordered a salad and when I brought it to him, he asked where the other waitress had gone. I told him you were in the kitchen, that we rotated our positions every few nights," she said. "And that was the last time he said anything to me. He ate his food, payed, and left."

Maybe she had been wrong about the man. He might have been one

142

of those people who came to a restaurant for more than a meal. Maybe he was simply someone alone in a strange place, someone looking for conversation before heading back to a lonely motel room. But if that was the case, how had he known her name?

Gina decided it wasn't important. She had too much on her mind to worry about the possibility that the stranger was a reporter. Yesterday, she had found the strength to call the school and make an appointment with Bob Walker, the principal. Travis Worthing, at least at this point, would not talk to her about Luke. But perhaps her son's principal, and with their boss' permission, Luke's teachers, might.

It was obvious that Mr. Walker's secretary had been shocked when Gina had told her who was calling. She was on hold for close to five minutes before the principal got on the line. He sounded very reluctant when she told him why she had called, but he had agreed that he would see her at four the next day when most of the students and staff would be gone. Linda had said she could come in late tomorrow if she could make up the time after her shift ended.

As she drove home from work, her mind wandered through a maze of potential questions she would ask her son's principal. What did his attendance record look like? Was he tardy many times? How about discipline reports? She would save the most important question for last. Would Mr. Walker permit her to speak with Luke's teachers? Gina knew that these were routine questions that most parents would be comfortable asking. But her son was a murderer; he had committed suicide in a classroom, so she was not like most parents. The anxiety she felt as she thought about the meeting began to cloud her logic. She would get up early tomorrow morning when she would have more clarity and make a list of questions for Mr. Walker, she told herself as she turned onto her street.

The Clayton house was dark. Shelley had been exhausted throughout her third trimester and during these last days of her pregnancy she had been going to bed long before her mother came home from the diner. Her daughter was the only person with whom Gina might have been able to share her grief. Her oldest child had lost her closest sibling, and her mother knew she was suffering, too. Gina accepted the likelihood that the two of them were purposefully avoiding one another to keep the pain at bay before the baby's arrival. It was easier for both of them, she reasoned, to dodge rather than to confront the truth and the pain.

As she began the left turn into her driveway, the Pontiac's headlights shown on a red Land Rover parked in front of old man Simpson's house. Gina knew immediately that something wasn't right. As she got out of her car, she heard a man's voice come from out of the dark night. "Mrs. Clayton, please don't be alarmed." A car door shut.

For a moment, she had no idea who he was. But the interior light of his car had exposed the gray suede jacket. "Did you follow me?" she asked, trying not to panic. He was walking on the sidewalk toward her. "You'd better leave, or I'll have to call the police," she warned him.

"I just want to talk to you about Luke," he said.

The overhead light on the neighbor's porch came on, and old man Simpson walked out his front door. "Do you need help, Gina?" he asked her. She was shocked to hear the cantankerous man sound so solicitous. He had never called her by name, first or last, in the four years they had been neighbors.

"No, thanks, Mr. Simpson. This person was just leaving." Under her neighbor's watchful eyes, she locked her car door and walked up the steps to her porch stoop.

"Please, Mrs. Clayton," the man on the sidewalk pleaded, "I just want to talk with you about your son."

She turned the key in the lock and pushed the stubborn front door open. Before she stepped into the dark house, Gina whirled around and saw him standing at the bottom of her front steps. "Why would I talk to a perfect stranger about Luke?" she said, shutting the door behind her.

His voice was muffled through the closed door, but she could still hear the man's reply. "I'm Adam Stoller. I wrote the story..."

Gina ran up the dark stairs and into her bedroom so she would hear no more. The writer's appearance in front of her home had triggered an adrenaline rush more powerful than caffeine. By the time she had brushed her teeth and put on her pajamas, she could no longer hear Stoller's and Mr. Simpson's muted voices in front of her house. She lifted a slat on the blinds and peered out. The shadows cast on the sidewalk by her neighbor's porch light had disappeared. She climbed into bed and turned off her lamp. As she lay in the dark with her eyes wide open, she couldn't get Adam Stoller and the short story Luke had carried that day out of her head.

Luke had been an avid reader from the time he could read chapter books. As a little boy, he would throw himself on the nearest carpeted space, a book opened in front of him, and assume an impossible pose, body bent from the waist almost to the floor. Pete had called him his Swami and had taken a picture of his son in this crazy posture. Gina knew which album the photo was in, but she couldn't bear to look at it.

At the top of her son's Christmas list each year throughout his childhood was the title of a book he wanted. Unable to sleep, Gina tried to recall some of them now. Of course, like the majority of his peers, the current edition from the *Harry Potter* series had been on the list each year. Like most boys his age, he was a fan of the Percy Jackson books by the time he was in sixth grade. He had read and reread the Tolkein triolgy that year, too. But after Pete's arrest, there had been no more Christmas lists. Gina tried to give herself the benefit of the doubt; perhaps that was why she had had no idea what Luke's reading choices were as a teenager.

From the time of the birth of her first child, Gina herself had little time to read, and when she did, her choice was not fiction. It was no wonder that she had never heard of Adam Stoller before November. The little research she had found on Luke's computer revealed that he was an award-winning novelist, but that did not answer her question—what was the significance of Stoller's writing for Luke? Why had he committed murder and suicide with that story in his pocket?

Gina had sent Shelley to check out a copy of *Easy Listening* from the Lincoln Library late in December. It was public knowledge that the book was a part of the tragedy. Every press release and news report about the shooting had highlighted the fact that Luke had carried "Seneca Optical" with him on his horrible mission. Her daughter would be less conspicuous borrowing it than she would be, she rationalized, especially from the large city library.

On that snowy New Year's Eve, with Shelley visiting her grandparents' home in Buffalo for the holiday, Gina opened the book to "*Seneca Optical*" and tried to read it, but she couldn't do it. Not yet. She wasn't ready to deal with any answers the story might give her about Luke and what he had done. Nor was she ready to face the possibility that the story might not give her any answers at all.

She turned the lamp back on. The book was still in the drawer of her bedside table, months overdue. Adam Stoller's "visit" had jolted her out of her resistance. She was ready. She opened the drawer, pulled the book from it, and began to read.

CHAPTER FIFTEEN

Easy Listening, Short Stories by Adam Stoller
SENECA OPTICAL

Why me? *What was so special about me, you want to know. Even as I look down at you from miles above, I'm not sure how to answer that question.*

What I do know for certain is that two weeks before I turned eighteen, I was Chosen. On that day, I, Eric Conley, was imbued with a preternatural omnipotence and righteousness. I, who have been abandoned, unwanted, deemed evil, cast out—on that day I was selected and gifted with a Power that changed me, and then I used it to change the world.

I remember very little of my childhood. Everything up until one bright July day in my twelfth year comes back to me in fragments, in bits and pieces, and only when I concentrate very hard. It seems that I woke up to my life in the front seat of a rusty, idling Plymouth Voyager. Woozy and nauseous from the exhaust fumes wafting in, I turned my head away from the open window. My mother's latest boyfriend—Lee, or was it Sam, sat in the driver's seat.

"Here, take this," he said, shoving a five-dollar bill into my hand. "Get out of the car," said the man, whoever he was, pushing me and my Power Rangers backpack up against the door.

Where was your mother, you might ask. A few days before, I had woken up and opened my eyes in time to watch her walk out of the apartment where

147

the three of us had been crashing for the night, black garbage bag and purse slung over her shoulder. She was leaving Lee/Sam and her only child, me, behind. What I didn't know then, but have figured out since, is that all of her sources in the city must have dried up. She was leaving for good in pursuit of the HIGH.

When Sam/Lee woke up that morning, I told him that she had left us. "Get your things together. We're leaving," he said. I had no idea where we were going, but now, it seemed that we were there.

I clung to the door handle and looked out the window at the huge old house. "What is this? Where are we?" I asked the boyfriend. I was trying not to cry. I knew how that would aggravate the man and make things worse for me.

"Get out," he repeated as he shoved me up against the door again. "Tell them you're an orphan." Before my left foot landed on the curb, the mini-van was pulling away, blowing blue smoke into the humid air as it sped off.

I stood on the sidewalk, stunned. There was a signpost on the lawn in front of the place. Montgomery County Juvenile Center. I read it over and over again while the continuous stream of traffic heading into D.C. whizzed by me. The day was hot, but my teeth chattered as I walked toward the gigantic front porch that wrapped around the house. Dragging one foot after the other, I finally reached the door and lifted the brass knocker. A large man opened it and filled the doorway.

Because I had not committed a crime, had not officially entered the youth detention system through the courts, the man who was the director of the home told me from behind his huge desk, they could not take me in. He would call the police. They would look for my mother, he said, thinking that this assurance might stop the hyperventilating kid before him. I ran out of his office to the porch and stumbled down the stairs. I did not and would not miss my mother. You don't miss what you never had.

The next two days were a blur; I wandered around the neighborhood during the daylight hours, buying sandwiches and Pepsis from a convenience store where no one spoke English. When the dark came, I snuck back to the detention center and slept in a corner of the huge porch. No one seemed to notice that I was there.

On the third morning of my new life, I heard a woman calling my name as she shook me awake. When I opened my eyes, I saw a lady and a cop standing beside her. "Eric? Please come with us." The director must have told her my name. I followed her inside the old house to the director's office, and the cop followed me.

The lady told me to sit down. She was a social worker, she said. I didn't even know what that meant at that point in my life. "This is officer Kutz. He has some bad news, I'm afraid."

They had found my mother, the cop told me. She had died last night; she had been run over as she stood hitchhiking on a dark Virginia highway. He could have said, "It's supposed to be hot today," and I would have had the same empty feeling. The cop asked if I knew of any relatives in the D.C. area, and I told the truth. "I never met any and I never heard of any."

"We'll keep searching. Don't you worry, Eric. In the meantime, Mrs. Loomis here will find a safe place for you to stay temporarily."

With those words, I, Eric Conley, became a ward of the state of Maryland and began living my life inside the system. That day I was sent to another group home in the county where abandoned or orphaned juveniles were housed for a short time until they could be placed in a facility or in a foster home. It wasn't horrible or anything. You have to understand that for a kid who had squatted in abandoned buildings and lived in a parked Plymouth Voyager for a couple of weeks, having a bed and three meals a day was not the worst experience I had ever had.

My first foster home was with a single mother. I watched Ms. Joan closely *through those first months, fascinated by her determination to keep her own three little kids safe and secure. She was so different from my own sorry excuse for a mother. She struggled each day with the responsibilities and hardships of her life, but she was kind and steady. She was the first adult in my life who I felt I could 100% trust, and she had been honest with me from the beginning—my real home could not be with her. It was a temporary shelter, she said. I would be safe while I was there, she assured me. "The right people could come along any day now," she said. "A couple who can provide better than I can, who would love having a son like you." As honest as I believed Ms. Joan was, at that moment I knew she was telling a lie. We both knew better. My own mother had known better. I was not lovable, I was not worth keeping.*

For one thing, I had always been a sickly little kid. Even though I had been born at a time when most infants were vaccinated, my mother's drug habit always came before everything else. I could not remember ever having been to a doctor's office until Ms. Joan, afraid that my chronic runny nose, fevers, and coughing fits would infect her kids, took me to a pediatrician during our first month together.

"With no health records, I've got to make an educated guess," the doctor said to Joan as he examined me. "It's quite possible that Eric has had chicken pox, whooping cough, maybe the mumps, too. We'll give him some boosters, but you're probably going to find that his immune system isn't great." The doctor looked into each of my ears. He told Joan that the left one had so much scar tissue, he guessed that my hearing was impaired significantly. "I'll give you a referral to an audiologist, and let's have his vision checked out, too, before school starts."

Joan took a day off from work so that she could go to both appointments with me. The hearing test proved the pediatrician's theory. I had a 30% acuity in my left ear. The specialist told her I didn't need a hearing aid at this point, but that in school, I should always sit in the front of the classroom. My vision test results were just as bleak. Two weeks after the eye exam, I was fitted with thick-lensed glasses. They were ugly, square-framed and tortoise-shelled.

The day I got my new glasses, I stood in the bathroom, staring at my face in the mirror. I was so ugly, and my improved vision made that clear. I examined the dark circles under my eyes, the nose that bumped out abruptly from the rest of my features, a bubble of snot threatening to drip. My upper lip was outlined with wild peach fuzz, darker than the hair on my head. Skin the color of milk, even in the summer. Tight blond curls and large ears too big for my narrow skull. As if my face wasn't enough of a handicap, throughout that summer my body began to morph grotesquely. That fall in the endless, lonely halls of middle school, my long limbs appeared fragile and easily breakable to my predator classmates as I suddenly grew to my six foot height.

In spite of my outcast status with my peers, I really liked school. I was a curious and cooperative student. And I loved to read. I read everything that was assigned and everything else that the librarian Mr. Hamann suggested. I often stayed up all night reading under the tent of a thin blanket with a flashlight aimed at the pages. Because of that nocturnal habit of reading with very little light, I added a constant squint to my visage, another aspect of my appearance that my peers were happy to ridicule.

By the time I started high school, I always sat in the front of the room, vulnerable to physical and verbal attacks from the back. As I had expected them to, my classmates loathed me, for the dark circles, the newly flourishing acne, my skinny scarecrow frame.

In the summer before my junior year, Ms. Joan accepted a job transfer to North Carolina. She told me that I would not be coming with her. You might think I was devastated by this news, but I was only grateful that I had met her and experienced what a real mother's concern, if not love, felt like. I didn't want to have to transfer from my school. Luckily, I was sent to a group home for a few weeks, which was really not so bad. Next came several temporary placements with families, and by temporary, I mean for a week or two at a time. All of them were in the same neighborhood as my school, so I was not really too upset about all the moving.

Eventually, I was placed in a home with a couple in their fifties, Mr. and Mrs. Sampson, who had two other foster kids living with them in their bungalow in the north eastern part of the city. As I had dreaded, I would have to transfer to a new school. This one in Brookland had ten times the number of kids as my old school. But as it turned out, where I went to school would be the least of my worries.

"Hey, asshole, come in here." I was carrying my stuff through the upstairs hallway to the tiny bedroom the Sampsons had told me would be mine. I stopped and stared at each of the framed paint-by-number pictures of Jesus that lined the dark paneled walls. Looking up from one that depicted in gruesome detail the damage the crown of thorns had done, blood dripping down the Savior's face, I saw Carl, pale blue eyes and albino complexion. I was struck by how much he looked like a white rat from biology lab. He was holding his bedroom door open just enough so I could see his rodent face. He was much shorter than me, but it turned out he was my age. I dropped my bag on the floor and as I walked into the room, Carl closed the door behind me. Sitting on one of the beds in the small room was another boy, obviously younger than Carl and me.

"This is Johnny. He's my real brother." It didn't seem possible that this normal looking kid with dark hair and eyes could be this cretin's brother. Before I could express my doubts, I felt Carl's arm roughly encompass my shoulders. A cold steel blade was on my throat. "And if you ever touch him, this is what you're going to get."

Over the course of the next year in the Sampson's home, Carl would keep these threats coming on a daily basis. He would sometimes hide in the closet in my bedroom for a full half-hour and then jump out, wielding the hunting knife or a baseball bat, or some other weapon. As for Johnny, he rarely spoke or looked anyone in the eye. Maybe he was autistic, I don't know, but he was just as creepy in his own silent way as his psycho brother. And then there were the Sampsons.

The pictures of Jesus on just about every wall of their cramped home had been painted by the dour-faced Mrs. Sampson. As the five of us ate dinner at the cramped kitchen table that first night she bragged, "Did those in my ceramics class." I realized she was talking to me. I had been staring at the figurines that sat on a small shelf. "My favorite saints and martyrs." She could have been speaking a foreign language for all I knew about religion.

"Now, boys," Mr. Sampson said, "let's bow our heads." I followed suit as my new "family" closed their eyes. "Johnny, let's have you lead us in the thanks," he said. As soon as the mumbling was over, Johnny and Carl picked up their spoons and began shoveling food into their mouths.

The old man turned to me. "Have you been saved, Eric?"

"Sir?"

"Have you been baptized in the blood of our Lord Jesus Christ? Your caseworker don't seem to find no record of it, your poor mother being dead and all." I had no idea how to answer him, so I said nothing.

"Don't worry, son. It's not too late. You three boys have ended up here with us for a reason." His voice was always shaky, but Mr. Sampson's tone had a certainty that could not be denied. He rambled on and on, as the steam rose off the food in front of us, and then just as suddenly as he had started questioning me about my "own personal Savior," he stopped.

He switched the subject to something as a foster kid in and out of facilities and other people's homes I was much more familiar with. He began to lay out the RULES of this house. Carl and Johnny slurped chili off their spoons and ignored him. I guessed they had heard it all before.

The Sampsons' rules mostly had to do with time--being on time for meals, for curfew (during school days and nights, weekends, too) and spending time in the ways that the Sampsons deemed acceptable. There would be strict time requirements for the use of computers, phones, and TV. Sunday, all day, was the time to attend church, and each night at dinner, which was always at 6 o'clock, there would be time set aside to contemplate a verse from the Bible.

"Tonight, we'll be talkin' about this one from Proverbs 22:15," he said as he reached for the small red leather bound Bible next to his bowl. As he opened it, Carl snorted and said something that sounded like, "umf," and Mr. Sampson shot him a warning look.

""Folly is bound up in the heart of a child, but the rod of discipline drives it far from him,'" he read in his juddering voice.

The "discussion" that night and every night at the Sampson's dinner table was in fact a lecture given by the old man. "What the Bible is saying here, boys, is that children are stupid, silly, ridiculous even. That's why God approves of discipline, physical discipline. Now since you are not our natural born sons and the state forbids us to strike you, we will instead make sure that your ignorance of the Lord will change to knowledge and love for him through our nightly talks."

As he rambled on, I stared at Mrs. Sampson's little china saints. One was tied to a stake, while the yellow and red flames licked at his body. Next to him was a female saint. One breast had been cut off. Mrs. Sampson had painted the blood that poured from the wound a pale orange.

And so began my time with the Sampsons and the two idiot brothers who were my "foster siblings." My new high school in Brookland was 90% black kids, so at first my blond curly hair and stick-skinny frame were beacons for daily ridicule. I had been right to dread the transfer. But by winter, I was no longer a novelty, and the jeers and threats I had encountered on a daily basis, diminished. I was mostly left alone like an alien from an intergalactic exchange program might have been. My teachers were nice enough, and I was happy that there were so many classes to choose from. By the second semester, I had almost all of my core requirements for graduation completed, so I enrolled in two electives that interested me, Forensic Science and an Art Appreciation class.

For the first time in my life, I was attending church every Sunday—all day. The two hour service followed by a two hour Bible class, then the hour-long prayer session, during which I mainly prayed to stay awake. It was late into the service and the afternoon. I had failed to open my eyes when the rest of the congregation did. On that Sunday in December, I came to understand just how deeply Mr. Sampson's belief in "the rod" was.

When we got home, he sent me upstairs, even though Carl and Johnny headed right to the dinner table. He said I needed to think about my "tranz-gression" against not only he and the "missuz," but "Jezuz" Himself. I heard his slow footsteps on the stairs shortly after I had gone up, huffing and puffing until he reached the top and then stopping outside my bedroom door. He opened it without knocking. His weird smile, more than the bamboo cane that appeared from behind his back, unnerved me.

It must have been close to midnight when I heard a soft rap on the closet door. Still standing, as the old man had instructed, I opened it. Mrs. Sampson set a bowl of cereal and a piece of notebook paper on the table next to my bed and left without a word. I was grateful to her, not only for the first bit of food I'd had since morning, but for her silence. The crushing headache that had started during the old man's rant had gotten worse throughout my hours in the closet.

I wolfed down the Cheerios and then picked up the paper. In a barely legible scrawl were written the words the old man, pacing back and forth the length of the room, had shouted over and over again. "Because the sentence against an evil deed is not executed speedily, the heart of the children of man

155

is fully set to do evil." He had ranted and raved for what seemed like hours, and I swear, at one point, he started speaking in a foreign language. Then suddenly he was silent. He pointed to the closet with the cane he had been swinging throughout his tirade.

You're wondering if he hit me with it, made welts rise and blood flow. No, he didn't, not that night anyway. That's why, when my caseworker checked in on me every few months, I could get away with the lie. "Everything is just fine," I would tell her, and my good grades, clean clothes, and, with the exception of my worsening vision, my stabilized health, reassured her that I was a well-cared for teenage boy who would very soon be graduating from high school and aging out of the foster system. This was all the proof she needed that this home was a successful last placement for her client, Eric Conley.

But as the months passed in the Sampson household, as much as I tried to avoid his wrath, the number of times I had to go through this ritual with the old man increased. The stack of papers with scribbled Bible verses piled up, and the bamboo cane came ever closer to making contact. Why didn't I say something, you want to know. The answer is simple. The only constant I had in my life, the only thing I looked forward to was school. I did not want to have to move again. If I told my caseworker what was going on, I would be sent to a group home and more than likely I would have to settle for getting a GED. At my high school, I was a loner, but I was used to that. My teachers cared about their students, and the classes were interesting. I could put up with the crazies at the Sampsons' home, as long as I could finish high school.

Two weeks before my birthday, I took the Metrobus from the stop near my high school and got off at Union Station. My caseworker had made an eye exam appointment for me, something I hadn't had since my time at Ms. Joan's. Union Station was a trip, as usual. Leaving the teeming pandemonium of commuters, shoppers, and the homeless behind me, I walked out the terminal's huge doors to a narrow cross street. It was strangely desolate compared to the rest of this hectic part of D.C. There was little traffic on its one-way street. As I walked, I looked down at my phone to double check the address. Yes, this was it, although the cardboard sign set on the window sill inside looked temporary and homemade. SENECA OPTICAL, it read.

I opened the door to a small, empty waiting room. A bell jangled over my head. There was no one in the glass-encased receptionist's area, either. I glanced around the tiny space where no one was waiting. Three metal folding chairs were the only furniture. What the hell? Where had Maryland's welfare system sent a seventeen-year-old ward of the state to get glasses?

I wrote my name and appointment time on the sheet. I waited a few seconds, but no one came out from the dark interior to greet me, so I sat down. The space was missing the usual outdated magazines found in most doctors' offices. On the wall opposite from me hung the only artwork in the place - three framed paintings hinged together. I had learned about this form in my art class. A triptych told a story in three sections. Setting my bag down on the chair, I took the few steps to the pictures and squinted at the blurry images until they came into focus.

The first panel depicted an old time Native American in breechcloth and leggings, a bow and a sheath bag full of arrows slung over his shoulder. The native appeared to be floating above a pine forest, looking down from the clouds to a large body of still water. In the next panel, the same man, still in the sky, was surrounded by other natives, one of whom was obviously the chief. This man appeared to be rubbing something into the brave's eyes. In the lake below, a huge scaly monster, dragon-like, was climbing out of the water and onto the steep bank. The third panel showed the hunter looking down from the sky as he drew his bow. He was taking aim at the wounded serpent who had fallen into the lake. It seemed as though the brave was about to deliver the final death blow to its arrow-ridden body. The water was red with the monster's blood, and the chief and the rest of the men looked upon the kill *in obvious admiration.*

Below the painting, there was a brass plate. I squinted so that I could read the engraving: 'Hi'nun and the Lost Brave.' As I stood there, I studied the panels over and over again, enthralled. I was lost in the story the paintings told, trying to discern their meaning, when a deep voice from behind me broke the spell. "Eric Conley?"

I turned, and saw the face of a Native American man who could have stepped out from the images behind me. His dark complexion and chiseled features gave him a noble, unearthly quality. As I looked at him, I had a weird realization. Of all the foreigners on the streets of Washington, D.C., this indigenous American would stand out as most alien in a sea of foreign faces. His black hair, grey at the temples, was gathered in a ponytail that fell between his shoulder blades. The white lab coat he wore, totally out of sync with his native features, was embroidered with the company logo: Seneca Optical. Below it, a paper nametag was stuck to it, the words "Dr. Jack" scrawled in red marker. The man stared at me like he was trying to figure out what species I belonged to. "How long have you had those?"

"What? Oh, these." He was referring to the glasses that hung slightly askew on my nose. "Three years? Maybe four."

"When was the last time you had a vision exam?" he asked.

"About five or six years ago."

"Okay, Eric. Come on back."

I followed him into a small examination room. I got the impression that the entire place was empty except for me and Dr. Jack. Smiling, he directed me to the chair opposite from where he would eventually project the eye charts that would prove that I was a few degrees away from legal blindness. "Please put your head back against the rest, Eric," he said. "I'm going to administer some drops before doing your exam. This first one will enlarge your pupils so I can get a look at the lining of your retinas."

I leaned my head back and tried to keep each eye wide open as he dispensed the liquid that instantly stung. "One more time. This one will help me to see what that squinting habit of yours is all about. Good," he said, as he sat down in the chair in front of me and brought the examination scope up to my face. But before he turned out the lights in the room, he said, "Do you always squint when you are looking at something up close? You were studying the paintings in the waiting room from about two inches away."

"If I really want to make out words in a book or on a board in school, yes. I have to get very close and squinting helps me to isolate letters. And that painting was so cool, I wanted to see every detail."

Dr. Jack turned off the lights and turned on the projector. "It depicts an important myth in the Iroquois culture," he said. "Can you read the letters on the top line for me?"

I did my best, and then I gathered my nerve and asked, "Are you Iroquois?"

"I am. I'm from the Turtle Clan of the Seneca," he said. He moved the lenses on his machine, bringing the top line into focus. "How about now? Read it again, please."

I felt my own tribelessness at that moment. I belonged nowhere and to no people, really. I saw the chart line more clearly and did as he instructed. "So, can you tell me more about those paintings?"

"They tell the story of the god Hi'nun, the chief of the Thunders, who were also deities." Throughout the telling of the myth, Dr. Jack continued my eye exam. "One day, a hunter became lost in the forest. He was weak with hunger and he became more and more confused about finding the way back to his home and his people. Despondent, he sat down under a tree, thinking he would fall asleep and give himself over to the wild animals and weather. He grew drowsy and then suddenly, he heard a mysterious voice coming from above him, in the clouds. As he looked up, he had the sensation

159

that he was rising skyward toward the voice. He was soon floating above the canopy of trees and then he was in the company of Hi'nun and the other Immortals. Hi'nun asked him to look down at the lake below. 'Do you see the water-serpent?' Hi'nun asked the man. 'He is the monster who roams the earth and pollutes humanity with evil.' But the man saw nothing in the lake. Then Hi'nun anointed the hunter's eyes with a sacred ointment, which gave him the power of supernatural sight. Now the hunter was transformed into a warrior. When he looked down into the lake, astounded, he could see the creature. Without hesitating, he drew his bow back and took careful aim. The gods and the brave watched as a terrible commotion arose in the lake below. The bloody serpent climbed the banks of the lake, writhing in pain. They watched as he fell back into the lake and died, sinking to the bottom."

Throughout the telling of the Hi'nun legend, Dr. Jack continued to slide different lenses in front of my eyes, attempting to find the best combination. "How's that one? What about that one? And now?"

I answered his questions, even though, as his story built to its climax, I was barely breathing. "So what happened to the hunter?" I asked.

Dr. Jack continued to click various lenses in and out of his machine. "Hi'nun rewarded him for removing evil from the world and saving the human world below. He was safe at last in the Afterworld of the Thunders. Okay, so try to read the bottom line for me again."

After the exam, Dr. Jack led me to a small fitting room in the back of the office and I picked out a plain black frame. "Your glasses should be ready next Friday," he said. "How blurry is your vision right now? You can sit out in the waiting room until the drops wear off, if you want."

"No, thanks, I'm fine. I've got to get going," Being on time, keeping my curfew had proved to be my greatest failure, as far as Mr. Sampson was concerned. "See you next week." Ever since Dr. Jack related the Seneca story of Hi'nun, I could feel my heart pounding in my chest. Before I closed the

door behind me, I squinted one more time at the final panel in the triptych. I walked back to Union Station, the image of Hi'nun anointing the brave's eyes so clearly imprinted in my mind, I wanted to get back to my little room at the Sampsons as fast as I could and open my sketchpad before the details faded.

The Metrobus to Brookland was delayed for some reason. It was crowded with end-of-work commuters when it finally did pull up, and I had to stand for a few minutes until a seat opened up in the very back. I closed my eyes and thought about everything that had transpired at Seneca Optical, especially the painting and Dr. Jack's retelling of the Hi'nun myth. When I opened them, I noticed something very strange--not only had the blurriness cleared, but my focus—in spite of the glasses Dr. Jack had said were useless--was incredibly sharp. I proved this transformation had taken place with several experiments. First, I could read every word of the ads posted in the front of the bus. Looking down, I stared at a freckle on my hand and followed its jagged outline as though it was under a microscope. In front of me sat a middle-aged man bent over a newspaper. Before I even realized it, I was reading an article over his shoulder, word for word. I turned my acute focus from the paper and stared at the back of the man's neck. What had at first looked like a terrible sunburn was growing redder and more deeply scarred with crisscrosses as I gazed at it. The longer I concentrated on it, the more transformed the skin became, until I was staring at crimson, mottled scales.

I reached for the buzzer over my head, amazed and terrified by the power of my vision. As the back door of the bus opened, I jumped down the steps, two stops away from the Sampsons' house. I knew there would be hell to pay because I was so late—and I was right.

"Eric, where have you been? Don't lie to me. At least show that much respect for me," the old man said with that twisted smile he put on whenever he was about to make me pay for my transgressions. I could tell I was really in for it, no matter how truthful I was. He would be speaking in tongues before

161

the night was over, I thought. Again, I was right.

By midnight it was over. For good, I decided. I was leaving this shithole. This time the old man had not spared the rod, and angry welts had been raised all over my ass and thighs. I had no plan but to get away; living on the streets until I turned eighteen would be better than living with these creepy psychos.

Everything I owned fit into my backpack, but I would need to "borrow" one more thing in order to survive on the streets. Just before daylight broke, I opened the door to the brothers' bedroom. I silently crawled to Carl's bedside and reached under the box spring; the leather scabbard was in my hand and I was out the door in seconds.

For the next two weeks, I lived in the shadows of D.C. I slept in various parks and recreation centers, botanical gardens, and along the river, in and out of places that tourists frequented. I even dared to go back to my high school a couple of days that first week. I was working on a painting in my art class when the phone rang. "Eric, they want you in the office," Mr. Cook said as he hung up.

I grabbed my bag from my locker. Up until now, it seemed that no one at school had been aware of the fact that I had run away from my foster home. But as I walked past the main office, there stood my caseworker talking to one of the secretaries. Thankfully, the surveillance cameras at the front doors had been vandalized so many times, I knew they wouldn't record my exit. I flew down the steps and never looked back.

The huge downtown branch of the D.C. library became my new school, and at the same time, my shelter on days when the weather was lousy. Anyone, even a homeless person, could spend hours there, in the stacks or on the computer, and as long as the staff was sure you weren't sleeping or using drugs in their facility, you could stay until they closed the doors at night. I spent most of my time in the art section, looking at masterworks and reading about the lives of the artists. I spent a day in the Native American collection, researching the mythology of several tribes. I think I read everything they had on Iroquois legends, especially the myth of Hi'nun and the Lost Brave. It seemed strange that I couldn't find any reference to a drawing or painting that captured the story.

I had been homeless for one week when I went to my follow-up with Dr. Jack at Seneca Optical. I wrote my name and appointment time on the sheet, as I had that first visit. Again, the place was strangely devoid of other patients or staff. But there was the triptych, and as I squinted at the paintings trying to find an artist's signature, I heard Dr. Jack's low voice behind me. "Eric? Come on back."

He led me to the small room where I had first learned about Hi'nun. As he fitted my new glasses, I noticed the two bottles of drops behind him. "Let me give these a final polish," he said. He took the glasses off my face. "Be right back."

I looked at the vials on the table and suddenly, a powerful wave of certainty swept over me. I stretched and grabbed, both involuntary reflexes, like blinking. The moment I shoved one of the vials into my pocket, I was filled with an intoxicating infallibility. I didn't understand the source of it, but I wholeheartedly accepted this new consciousness, this Gift.

When Dr. Jack came back into the exam room, he didn't seem to notice that one of the bottles had vanished. He walked back to the waiting area with me. When he put his hand out, a shiver of panic rushed through me. Maybe he had noticed that I had taken the drops after all. But instead of demanding that I give the bottle back he said, "Good luck, Eric," and shook my hand.

That night, as the sky lit up with heat lightning, I decided I would have to sleep inside. Union Station, with its multiple floors of benches and restrooms and its gigantic food court was one of the best places in D.C. to spend a stormy night. It was almost impossible for the security guards to sort out the home-

163

less from the city's tourists and its thousands of commuters. As thunderbolts cracked the sky, I staked a claim on a bench in the narrow hallway outside of a men's restroom.

I had been there only minutes when a familiar voice called my name. The sound overrode all the noise that came from inside and outside the station. For the second time that day, I was overcome with an impulse to act. I seemed to be watching myself from a distance as I reached into my pocket and took out the small plastic bottle. I read the label—Cyclopentolate—and did not hesitate. I took the cap off and tilted my head back. I felt the familiar sting and closed my eyes.

When I opened them, I saw a blurry form walking down the corridor toward me. The man hesitated and then sat down on the bench across from me. He began to chew his fingernails, seemingly oblivious to my presence just a few feet away. But, as my vision cleared, I could not turn away from him. I focused first on the large crown of spines that grew out of his bald head, the two in the center longer than the others. A huge dark spot erupted on his neck as I watched. Reddish brown scales covered what had been his face, and the hooded eyes slid back and forth peripherally. He slowly rose from the bench onto feet that seemed child-sized and too delicate to carry his weight. I watched, fascinated, as he lumbered, then skittered away, his long tail dragging on the floor until he entered the men's room.

I waited and watched anxiously for the lizard man to return. And then, I heard my name called again. Without thinking, I took the knife out of its leather sheath, put it in the inside pocket of my jacket, stood up, and went in pursuit of the serpent.

As soon as I opened the door, I heard the child's voice crying for help from inside a bolted stall. Climbing onto the back of the toilet in the next compartment, I scaled the wall into the lizard's quarry. The kid scrambled under the door to freedom as I jumped onto the reptile's back. Reaching into my pocket, I clutched the knife, sure of what I was about to do. There was nothing human about this creature now, except for the shredded clothing it wore. Before my eyes it inflated with air, its head ballooning to double its original size. The monster opened its mouth, hissing, trying to bite at me. At the same time, from the corners of its eyes, blood sprayed out and hit me in the face. I plunged the knife into its flesh over and over again. It let out a raspy shriek and fell on its back to the floor, motionless. Ripping his shirt open with the knife, I stared at the smoother scales on its belly, as I kneeled over its lifeless body.

I rinsed the knife in the sink and then cleaned off the blood from my hands and face. Calmly walking through the commotion of the boy, mother, and cops, I took the escalator to the main part of the terminal and found a bench in a Metro waiting platform. I put my backpack on the seat and was asleep before my head hit the makeshift pillow. The noise of the storm had subsided and I slept peacefully until the morning light came through the huge arched windows.

I sat up and stretched. Breathing deeply, I felt a serenity that I had never before experienced. I watched for a while as hundreds of people moved past me, on their individual paths to their separate destinations. I was surrounded by them and completely alone at the same time, but I felt righteous. I had been Chosen.

Throughout my life, I had moved through the world unnoticed, and this invisibility seemed to prevail during my homelessness. D.C. cops rarely hassle street people, unless they are bothering the tourists. I had enough money to eat fast food for a few more days, and when my cash ran out, I could go to any one of numerous soup kitchens and food pantries located throughout the Capitol district.

I chose places to sleep during the next few days that were somewhat off the beaten path. That's why I happened to be in West Potomac Park watching *the sunset on the river as it moved directly in line with the Washington Memorial—and that is when I heard my name called once again.*

I waited until I could see no runners coming along the path. I sat on the bench, removed my glasses, and tilted my head back. The Cyclopentolate leant the sinking sun a prism. "Eric." In the midst of the chorus of toads and cicadas, I heard the voice of Dr. Jack. I picked up my bag and jogged toward the sound.

A solitary scream followed by a second muffled shriek came from the deep pines that lined the track. I ran toward a thicket of underbrush, and pulled the knife out, hacking at the untamed growth until I found what I had been summoned to discover. In the waning light, a slimy, olive green sheen. Its flattened head and body, stretched out to six feet, looked like a crushed, gargantuan worm. A pair of single gill apertures the size of dinner plates on each side of its brown-spotted neck opened and closed in rapid succession. The enormous hellbender's stubby legs pinned the woman down beneath it, her running shoes flung aside in the struggle.

Six thrusts of the hunting knife, each one deeper into the level midsection of the enormous salamander, rendered it lifeless. I rolled the monster off of her, and the terrified woman ran shoeless back toward the river. I stared at the creature's smooth belly for a second and then tore it open from its head to its venter.

The next morning, I walked from Union Station, where I had again spent the night in order to avoid the possibility of being identified by the runner at the park, to the cross street where Seneca Optical was located. I was anxious to see Dr. Jack. I didn't know if I would tell him everything I had experienced in the last 48 hours. I felt almost certain that he already knew. Turning onto the narrow street, I could see the demolition workers tearing into the small brick building. I stood in front of the sawhorses and the yellow tape with the word 'Condemned' printed all over it. The front window was still there, and so was the raggedy sign. But I knew that I would never see Dr. Jack again.

I walked the few blocks to the Southeast Neighborhood Library. It was my favorite of the several branches I had been to—a place where I could easily hide in plain sight from the Sampsons and the police, although I had no indication that they were looking for me. The library on this morning, like all the other times I had been there, was bustling. In the sunlit foyer, signs were posted advertising all kinds of activities: "Audubon Society of D.C. meeting," " Zumba With Your Toddler," "Daddy and Mommy Lap Time with Your Baby," all were taking place here this morning.

Heading toward the dozen or so computers that lined the far wall, I found an empty chair. Sitting in front of the monitor, I immediately clicked on the morning's edition of the Post. In the City Section, a headline below the banner read, "**Does DC Have A Serial Killer?**" My heart pounded as I read the article.

"**For the second day in a row, Metro police have reported a stabbing death in the Capitol district. Last night's victim was found by a jogger in the deep underbrush of West Potomac Park. 'He looks like he's been gutted,' Charles Rice told the 911 dispatcher. Mr. Rice told police when they arrived at the scene that he had left the running path to relieve himself and passed a 'kind of weirdo looking young guy' walking in the opposite direction. 'He was definitely not a runner. He had curly blond hair and old-timey glasses. I can't be sure because it was dusk, but his hands looked like they were covered in blood. I continued to walk a few more yards and then I saw the body.'**

Detectives had a similar description of a man who emerged from the restroom at Union Station, shortly before Thomas Danver, of Minneapolis, was found brutally stabbed to death on the floor. DC Police ask anyone who sees a man matching the description of the suspect to call 911."

I felt strangely calm as soon as I finished reading the article, and I headed to the art section where I could spend the daylight hours reading and people-watching from a leather chair in the corner of the sunlit room. I had been nodding off over a biography of Salvador Dali, when I heard Dr. Jack's voice. "Eric." It was coming from the direction of a gathering of toddlers and parents. I leaned my head back against the chair and applied the drops.

In seconds, the blurriness transformed to a laser focus. I watched as a young guy skulked around the outside of the happy circle. He stopped at one of the marble columns that divided the meeting room from the huge center section of the facility. The children's librarian lead the gathering in one more song, and soon the moms and dads were standing up with their babies in their arms and heading in several directions.

I focused on the man as he followed a young mother into the children's library. He touched her on the shoulder to get her attention, but she turned abruptly away, clutching her young toddler's hand tighter. Suddenly, she picked her child up and began to walk quickly toward the main door of the library. I watched as she stopped at a rack in the foyer and put the smiling baby in a stroller.

Again, Dr. Jack called my name. I stood up and began to follow the guy who was in pursuit of the mother and child. The four of us emerged into the warm D.C. day. The man took the stairs and walked alongside her as she pushed the stroller down a ramp. I was right behind him and I heard his demand. "Just listen to me, bitch!" he insisted, but instead, she began jogging behind the stroller.

As they crossed the intersection into a small park, I followed just a few feet behind. The man jumped in front of the stroller, grabbed the woman by her wrist, and dragged her away from the baby and the path. As he pulled her toward the bushes, I again felt the certainty and righteousness of what I was about to do. I pulled the scabbard out of my bag and had the knife in my hand in seconds. Running past the abandoned baby, I rushed toward the sound of his mother's screams.

The wide head on the skinny neck was positioned above the woman. The vertical slits of the viper's eyes were flanked by the characteristic heat-sensitive pits. They were trained on the terrified woman. As she screamed, the creature rose above her, and showed its enormous fangs. The dry, horny segments of his tail shook, buzzing and rattling.

I circled behind them, unnoticed. The copper-colored cross bands of the serpent gleamed in the tree-filtered sunlight. I was on it in seconds, stabbing first at its mid-section and then at its head. I lost track of the woman and of everything else, methodically stabbing over and over again, calmly decapitating the monster.

"Drop the weapon! Drop the knife! Now!" I turned away from the snake's carcass, and saw the two cops, guns drawn and pointed at me

Again, I heard the low voice calling, this time from the treetops. "Eric." I had no choice but to follow it. I heard the guns explode as I went toward the voice, but now, I was rising, floating above the park, the library, the city.

I looked down as I ascended. There they all were, sliding on their slimy bellies, skidding and skittering on their undersized legs, moving unafraid in the midst of the humans that surrounded them. I watched them crossing through busy intersections, waiting in line outside of the Holocaust Museum, climbing up the wall of the Vietnam Vets Memorial, sunning themselves on the steps of the Capitol, clambering up the black iron fence in front of the White House.

From the heavens above me, I heard the flapping of enormous wings and the pounding of thunder. I flew higher and higher toward the voice calling my name, but below me I could still see them so clearly—amphibians, and reptiles in all their variations—frogs, toads, turtles, crocodilians, salamanders, lizards, and snakes.

It was true. It could not be doubted. I, Eric Conley, for my short time on Earth, had been Chosen by a higher power to destroy the evil in the world.

Dark Riddle

I rose higher and higher toward the sound of the great thunder and still my focus was crystal clear. My voice rang out over the city and up to the skies as I shouted.

"I SEE YOU! I CAN SEE YOU ALL!"

Chapter Sixteen

AFTER SCHOOL

As she read, Gina could see why Luke might be engaged in this story where the main character was a teen, a teen whose life was tough. His magical transformation and the evil creatures that he slaughtered in the name of justice most likely reminded her son of the books that he had loved as a kid. She could certainly see why he might have been entertained by Stoller's story. But Gina had anticipated so much more. Her hope that some particular words on a page would unlock the secret of her son's jaded heart faded away as she closed the book. Again, she was left with more questions about her son than answers.

Now one more piece of this nightmarish puzzle had stood in front of her house tonight. What did Adam Stoller want from her? Thank God Shelley had slept through the commotion, but Gina had tossed and turned for more than an hour after she had finished reading his story. Just when she had convinced herself that she had to get up and do something about her insomnia, a ragged sleep took over.

Shelley's alarm went off at seven, and Gina sat up in bed as soon as she heard it. Seconds later, she planted her feet on the cold floor and threw on her bathrobe.

"Mom, what are you doing up this early?" Shelley asked. As her daughter walked into the kitchen, Gina looked up from her work at the stove. She was struck by the beauty of her oldest child. She was taller than her mother and she had inherited Pete's long limbs. Her deep blue eyes, jewel-like from the day she first opened them, still startled Gina with their exquisiteness. The sunlight coming through the small window over the sink highlighted the luster of the young woman's auburn hair and her pearlescent skin. How long had it been since Gina had allowed herself to simply feel this love for a child?

She had been a mother for two decades, but most of that time was taken up with the hard necessities of life: the cooking, cleaning, laundry required for a family of three, four, six, seven. Early in her kids' lives, her part-time job at Kodak typically took her away from them in the evenings. Then the over-time hours she worked in the lab after Pete's arrest so that she could pay the rent and the bills kept her from them much of that year. The months it took to find a refuge from her husband's criminal legacy, the move itself exacting all of her concentration. Once they settled in Langston, she had had to spend the majority of her kids' waking hours working first at the Hammermill lab and then at the diner.

Her hectic life had distracted her; she couldn't afford the time to indulge herself in this pure emotion of love. Exhausted more often than not, she had told herself she was doing this for her kids. She was steadfast in her refusal of her parents' offers to help. This was her journey; she had made the lousy choices that had led her here. She had not wanted to be bailed out by nor indebted to her mother and father.

She was sure that Luke had been aware of her struggles, financial and otherwise. He had witnessed her stubborn resistance when her parents had tried to intercede. Had Luke needed her help somehow, too, and not asked for it? Did he not reach out to her because she had taught him, by her example, that he should handle his problems by himself? Was he his mother's son in this way? As she stood in her kitchen this morning, she realized the high price she might have payed for her autonomy. It may have cost her son's life, as well as the lives of his victims.

"I'm making breakfast for my daughter and grandchild," she said, wielding the spatula expertly to flip the omelet.

"Amazing." Shelley smiled as she poured herself a cup of coffee. For months Gina had tried to hide the disappointment and fear she felt for her daughter's future. Shelley was following in her footsteps, except that unlike her mother, she would not be marrying her baby's father. Dan Kelly was a high school boyfriend who had not maintained Shelley's affection beyond their graduation from high school. He had wanted to marry her, but Shelley did not want that and had broken it off with him shortly after she had found out she was expecting. He was away at college now, and she was a teller in a bank, pregnant and making just a little bit more than minimum wage. Her mother was bitter about this, Shelley knew. But she herself had accepted it. She was happy about becoming a mother.

She sat down at the table, obviously pleased with her mother's efforts on her behalf. "It won't be long before this baby will be joining us on his own," she said.

"*His* own?" Gina repeated.

"Yes." Shelley's smile lit up the kitchen. "I was going to wait to tell you, but the secret will be out soon enough."

Gina crossed the room to hug and kiss her oldest. She had not done this enough with any of her kids. She was always working, always rushing. She would push the guilt away, telling herself that there would be time to show them and tell them how much she loved them one day, but Gina had found out in the cruelest way possible that she had been wrong about that.

"Boys are wonderful," she said now as she stood over her daughter and wrapped her arms around her. A sob caught in her throat. Shelley stood up and held her mother in her arms. "I'm sorry," Gina said. "I didn't sleep well last night."

"Mom, you don't have to apologize for feeling sad. We're all sad. And we all miss him, too," her daughter said.

For the first time since Luke's death, Gina opened up to her daughter. Shelley and Luke had always been close, and up to this point Gina had been careful not to upset her by questioning her and adding to her grief, but she realized in that moment as her daughter held her that Shelley was a grown woman, about to become a mother herself.

"Shell, what did I miss? What do you think was going on with your brother leading up to that day?" She took a step back and looked into her daughter's eyes that were filled with tears. "Did you notice anything? Did he tell you that something was bothering him?"

"Mom, I've asked myself those same questions over and over again." She put her arm around her mother. Guiding her to a chair, she sat down across from her. "Our life since Dad's arrest, since the move here, has been hectic, you know. The little kids were freaked out by it all. The twins have acted out from the beginning and Lisa has been pretty fragile." Shelley rubbed the tears from her eyes and kept going. "I wasn't crazy about the changes, either, but Luke seemed to adjust better than all of us. He was younger than me, so I guess it seems weird, but I always could depend on his, his…." She searched for the word. "Steadiness."

"Yes," Gina said, "So could I. What do you think changed?"

"Since I started working full time, I hardly saw Luke. The only difference I can say that I noticed when I did spend time with him was that he was quieter."

"Did he ever tell you that he was having trouble in school?"

"No. I did notice that he was spending a lot more time with Travis Worthing. As far as I knew, that was the only kid he really hung with before…" Shelley began to tear up again. "It makes me so sad that Luke didn't come to me, Mom. I would have done anything to help him."

She reached across the table and held her daughter's hands. "Shelley, you were a good sister to Luke. You weren't in any way responsible for what happened," Gina said.

"Then who was, Mom? Who was?"

After Shelley left for the bank, Gina cleaned up the kitchen and sat down at the table with her journal. She needed to organize her thoughts. Although her body ached for more sleep, her mind was clear. The four o'clock appointment was what she must concentrate on now. Mr. Walker was a stranger, but he was in charge of the place where Luke had spent the majority of his days. It was important that she ask the right questions. What was Luke's attendance like that first semester, she would ask. Did he have any run-ins with teachers or other students during that time? Did Mr. Walker have any discipline reports on Luke? Had the principal noticed any problems between any of the victims and Luke? As she wrote, it struck her again that she had been a terrible mother, that these were questions she should have asked her son while he was alive. She wracked her brain, trying to recall. Had he ever attempted to confide in her, she wondered now. Had she been too busy, too distracted, to listen to him?

Her noisy sobs filled the empty kitchen as she thought again about their last moments together. She had slept almost the whole time that Luke had driven around the lake. Was she asleep at other times when her son had needed her? And she had not responded to his last words to her. "Thanks for the driving practice, Mom." Had she not listened closely or responded to him at other times, as well?

If the windows had been open, the neighbors would have heard the sobbing. But Gina did not attempt to stifle them. She was at the point in her grieving where she would allow these sneaky "aftershocks" to consume her.

She had learned from experience that it was best not to try to fight them or the next event would be a seven-point quake.

When her weeping subsided, Gina went to the sink and splashed water into her eyes. She had to be able to think straight. She wrote for an hour more and then copied her questions for Mr. Walker again on a clean legal pad. It was noon by the time she headed back upstairs. Before she knew what she was doing, she opened the door to her dead son's room. As she had done that day in November, she lay down on his bed and slept.

Two-and-a-half hours later, she woke refreshed. The eyes of the Thunderbird stared back at her as she glanced around her son's sparse bedroom. She read the bold words scripted below. ***Power, Transformation, Unquestioned Authority.*** A fleeting thought, like gossamer, came and went before she could grasp it. Standing up, she shook her head to clear it. Her focus needed to be on the meeting with Luke's principal. Gina closed the bedroom door and headed to the bathroom.

After her shower, she extended her usual five minute regimen in front of the mirror, taking the time to use the flat iron on her hair and then applying mascara and lip gloss. She wanted to represent Luke in a positive way today. She put on black slacks and a blazer over the turtleneck and packed her jeans and long tee-shirt that she would wear under her Linwood Diner smock tonight.

With sleep and preparation on her side, Gina drove to her appointment with Mr. Walker with a sense of confidence and resolve. By four o'clock when she turned into the school, there were only a dozen or so cars in the parking lot of the beautiful new campus. She pulled into the space that was furthest from the entrance to the high school. A wave of vertigo came over her as she stepped out of the car, but she fought it. The last time she had come here, it was to identify her son's body. Unbeckoned, the memory of her son's face, one side intact and recognizable, threatened to overwhelm her. Inhaling deeply, she pushed the memory aside. Today, she needed to be clear-minded and strong for Luke's sake. She grabbed the legal pad and locked the car.

As she came closer to the entrance, Gina recognized the uniformed policeman standing inside the glass foyer. On a few occasions when she had been questioned at the Jamesburg station, this same officer was present in the interview room. He never spoke, but he had looked familiar to her. Maybe he had been a customer at the diner, she thought then, as she sat being questioned about her son. Now, she remembered exactly when she had first seen him. The man had stood next to her and the state trooper that day as the coroner had revealed her son's mutilated face.

What was he doing here today? All of the determination she had felt about her session with Mr. Walker melted away. She watched anxiously as the cop pressed several buttons on the door's security pad. It buzzed and he pushed it open. "Come in, Mrs. Clayton," he said. "We've met before. I'm Joe Gloss. I work for the Jamesburg Police Department, and I'm the school resource officer here.

"Yes," she said, trying not to sound nervous. "Is something wrong?"

"Oh, no. I'm here most days during the school day and a couple of days a week on after-school duty. I still work for the town part-time," he said, as if she had asked the question. "Mrs. Levy asked me to buzz you in." She followed him through the door and into the lobby. Gina stood still for a second. The last time she had been here she had been surrounded by police officers and dead bodies.

She felt like Joe Gloss could read her thoughts as he took her arm and guided her to the main office door. "Mrs. Clayton is here," he announced. She listened to the echo of his footsteps as he walked down the long, empty corridor. Wendy Levy stood up from her desk and crossed the room to the tall counter. Gina could see by the apologetic expression on the woman's face that this would not go the way she had hoped.

"Mrs. Clayton, I'm so sorry! I tried to call you so that you wouldn't go out of your way, but apparently your phone number has changed," she said. In the glare of the fluorescent lights, the woman looked exhausted. She was probably Gina's age, but the lines around her eyes and mouth made her look much older. "I'm afraid Mr. Walker won't be able to meet with you today. He was called away on a family emergency," she said.

Gina did not expect the tears that suddenly welled in her eyes. "I see," she said. "Well, when *can* I see him?"

Wendy Levy walked back to her desk and looked at her computer monitor. Gina watched as the secretary moved the mouse around for several minutes. "With Spring Break starting next week, I'm afraid it will have to be sometime next month," she said. "Would you like me to make an appointment for you then?"

Gina took a tissue out of her purse and dabbed at her eyes. She rarely cried in front of anyone, but she had gathered all her strength to face Walker. Her expectations had been high and the disappointment and frustration made her feel vulnerable in front of this stranger. "I'll have to check my work schedule and get back to you," she told the woman.

Wendy Levy rose and moved to the front of the office. Gina was shocked when the woman reached across the counter and covered her hand with her own. "I'm so sorry for your loss, Mrs. Clayton. Luke seemed like such a good kid."

"You knew Luke?" she asked.

"Of course. I know all of the high school kids. I deal one-on-one with them more often than their teachers do. That's why I have such good relationships with them, for the most part," the woman said. Gina could hear the pride in Wendy Levy's voice.

"So, how often did you see Luke?" Gina asked.

"Oh, a few times a week. Not because he was late very often or in trouble, like some kids are. I don't believe I had to write more than a few passes for him this semester. And I can only remember a couple of times this year that he had come in to see Bob...Mr. Walker. And Luke had requested the time with him. It wasn't for disciplinary reasons." Gina was holding her breath as she looked into the woman's eyes. "Like I said, your son was a nice boy. He would stop in from time to time just to say hi..." Suddenly, Wendy glanced up and over Gina's head. The secretary let go of her hand. When Gina turned, she saw Officer Gloss standing behind her. She had not heard him come in.

Wendy Levy's compassionate demeanor had disappeared by the time Gina turned back to the secretary. "Yes, so when you know your schedule, just give me a call and I'll set up another appointment with Mr. Walker," she said, businesslike once again. "Joe, will you please show Mrs. Clayton out?"

The police officer wished her a polite, "Good afternoon" and buzzed the main door open. As she walked slowly out into the approaching March dusk, it suddenly struck Gina—she had been set up! Mr. Walker never had any intentions of seeing her, and more than likely, Wendy Levy and Joe Gloss were his minions. She got into her car, her head reeling. At least Travis Worthing had been honest with her. He did not want to talk to her about Luke and he told her so. But these people had strung her along, making her believe that they would cooperate with her, giving her some hope that she might get some answers about her son. She started the car, but she was so angry, she sat there with the motor running for a few minutes, trying to calm herself. Staring straight ahead, Gina made an effort to recall everything Wendy Levy had said that was not formal and obviously scripted. She took the legal pad and a pen from her purse and began to write.

The lights in the parking lot came on as the daylight faded for good, and Gina looked up. The main entrance door was again being held open by Joe Gloss, and she watched as a man emerged. Her eyes followed his progress as he walked through the parking lot toward the new Land Rover.

Gina pulled up alongside the red car just as the man was climbing in. He turned toward her as she rolled down her passenger window. "Mr. Stoller?" she said. "Let's talk."

Chapter Seventeen

FIRST NAME BASIS

In a small booth tucked into a back corner of the Cliffside Cafe, Adam Stoller sat across from Gina Clayton. He had followed her Pontiac out of the school parking lot for thirty winding miles to this place, as she had instructed. She narrowed her eyes and leaned across the table toward him. In spite of the low-lit room, he could see that the look on her face was totally unlike the aim-to-please countenance that she had worn at the Linwood Diner a few nights ago.

"Why are you here, Mr. Stoller?" she asked. "What do you want from me?" He could hear, in spite of her unwavering tone, that she was making an effort to keep her composure. "And what were you doing at the high school today?"

"Look, Mrs. Clayton, the last thing I want to do is upset you," he said. "But your son carried my story with him when..." He didn't want to alienate her any further, so he struggled with his words. "That day. November 23rd. Everything changed for me." He turned away from her for a second and his face flushed with embarrassment. Across the table sat a woman whose life had obviously been destroyed by her son's horrific actions.

The woman's icy stare was not encouraging, but Adam had no choice but to push through his explanation. "After I found out about the....the events of that day, I tried to go back to writing, to living my life, but I couldn't. All I could think about was: who was this boy? What role did my story play in this horror? So that's why I'm here. In order to figure that out, I need to know who Luke was before 11/23."

Gina squared her shoulders. She placed her elbows on the table and folded her hands in front of her. "So do I," she said as she looked him squarely in the eyes.

He stared back, mystified. Before he could ask her what she meant, their waitress materialized out of nowhere. "How about a warm-up, folks?" she asked.

Once she had poured the coffee and left, Adam waited for Gina to elaborate, to say something more. When she didn't, he said, "I need to understand what responsibility I might have for the tragedy."

"So do I," she said again.

Once more he waited for a further explanation from her, but none came. The space between them grew heavy with the silence until Adam broke it with an answer to another of her questions. "I was at the school today because Luke's teacher, Ron Byers, who assigned the story for his class, agreed to talk with me."

"That's interesting," she said, narrowing her eyes. Her even tone was now tinged with scorn. "Since I, Luke's mother, couldn't get past the front office today." She shook her head and looked down. "You need to understand, Mr. Stoller..."

"Adam..."

"Mr. Stoller, that I am not able to tell you who Luke was on November 23rd." The woman's head was still bowed, but she was speaking in earnest. "I can tell you about how sweet-natured he was as a little boy. I can tell you that when his twin brothers came along, he had to transition overnight from being a toddler to being a big brother, and he has always taken that job very seriously." She looked back up at him and he could see that she was on the verge of tears. "I can tell you some things about him as a teenager: that he played football, that he was an avid reader, that he had a part-time job that helped to pay our rent. I can tell you that in a houseful of rowdy kids, he was a quiet, responsible teenager. His brothers and sisters called him Problem One. They heard me say again and again that he never gave me problem one." She closed her eyes and shook her head again, as though the irony of the nickname still was difficult for her to bear.

She took a deep breath and continued. "Luke was self-reliant. As a matter of fact, I depended on him more than he depended on me, especially after his father went to prison." Adam listened to the woman's sincere explanation. He thought about how his own hard-working parents had indulged him, their only child, from the time he was born and even through his rotten teen years. It seemed that Luke's life had skipped ahead from childhood to adulthood without the benefit of the bridge afforded most adolescents.

Gina sat back in the booth. "I took for granted that I knew my son, but believe me when I tell you, Mr. Stoller, I did not. I don't know who he was, what was in his head that day in November—what motivated him to murder people. I don't know why he did not want to live any longer." She lowered her eyes and pressed her lips together. When she looked at him again, there were no tears. Adam recognized that he was in the company of one tough person.

"So you see, even though you're a perfect stranger, you and I appear to be on the same mission, Mr. Stoller. To find out who my son was. Except that you've made some progress during your short stay. Much more so than I." She looked into his eyes again. "You're looking at the monster's mother. Gina Clayton is a pariah. No one wants to talk to her. Not Luke's best friend, not the high school principal. No one."

Her phone rang and as Adam listened to the one-sided conversation with Gina's boss, he tried to analyze the shift in judgment he was experiencing. Before he had packed his bag and left his apartment in the city, he had made his mind up about this woman. Luke's mother had to be a nut, or abusive, or both for her kid to do what he did, he had been certain. But in this brief time spent in her company he could see that she was not culpable for her son's actions. No, he was sure that Gina Clayton was one more casualty of the November 23rd atrocity.

"Yes, Linda," she said into her phone. "The meeting went okay, but I've got the start of a migraine. I'm not going to make it in tonight. Tell Claire I'll cover her day hours tomorrow." She paused a moment. "Okay, I'll do that. Thanks again."

As she returned her phone to her purse, she looked across the table and a hint of a smile flitted across her face. "It must be nice to be an independently wealthy author. Do you call yourself when you can't make it to work?'"

Adam knew that he would have to reveal that his reason for coming here was not simply a personal mission to discover the truth. He would have to level with Luke's mother and tell her that he was working on an article for *Rolling Stone*. He was being paid to write about this place where Luke had lived and died, about his family and friends, about how "*Seneca Optical*" factored into the tragedy. But as he looked across the table at her, he decided he couldn't tell her, not yet. He was just beginning to gain her trust, maybe. That would have to happen before he could tell her the whole truth.

"Look, Mrs. Clayton, I want to help you," he said. "Maybe we can help each other. I met Luke's teacher at a prayer vigil I stumbled into the other night, and he agreed to talk with me." He could see that Gina was now locked into his every word. "I think Ron Byers is a valuable link to understanding Luke's attachment to that story. Today Byers told me that Luke was an outstanding student in his Myths and Legends course. Did your son ever tell you about that class?" He noticed that Gina's face looked flushed in the small arc of light cast by the candle on the table.

"Not that I can recall," she admitted. "I knew he liked English."

"From what I could gather, it's a very popular class at Lake Hinon High. Byers is a teacher who obviously cares about his students, and I'm sure that's part of it. But people, especially young people, love archetypes. Pure-hearted heroes and rotten-to-the-core villains are more fun to read about and easier to understand than complex human characters, especially for kids. Mythology is still 'trending' in today's world," Adam told her.

"Kind of similar to the way fairy tales hold their value throughout the ages, right?" Gina said.

"Exactly," he said. "And every nation and culture has its own set of stories and archetypes. Ancient people turned to their tales of gods and goddesses and mythological creatures to figure out the meaning of their own lives." He paused in his explanation. The last thing he wanted to do was make her think he was talking down to her. "Am I making any sense?" he asked.

For the second time today he saw a glimmer of a smile on her face. "Mr. Stoller, have you ever thought that perhaps even waitresses might have gone to college?" she said. "I took an intro course in Greek drama my freshman year. It was for science majors, but still, I'm following you."

His face reddened. "Of course, I'm sorry if I sounded arrogant, but I love this stuff. As a grad assistant, I had to teach the Greek Classicists for a semester. But Ron Byers goes beyond the Greek and Roman mythologies in his course. He teaches the kids about the hero's journey based on Joseph Campell's theory. Do you know Joseph Campbell?" he asked.

"A little," she answered, leaving out the fact that she had discovered Campbell in just these past couple of months. She had picked up Luke's copy of *The Power of Myth* one evening and was halfway through it. She had also discovered some DVD's in his room of Bill Moyers interviewing Campbell, and she was slowly working her way through them.

"Okay. Well, Ron Byers gets into George Lucas and Marvel comics in his class, based on Campbell's idea of the hero, but he also brings in the mythos of the Native people of this region. That's why he assigned 'Seneca *Optical*.' When I wrote it, I was attempting to contemporize..."

She interrupted him before he could finish. "I read your story last night after you left," she said. "I knew the lake was named for the Iroquois deity Hinon, but I didn't know the legend of the lost brave until I read 'Seneca *Optical*.' Did Mr. Byers tell you anything about Luke's reaction to the story?"

"Not specifically. I wanted to ask him that, but as it turned out, I didn't have the chance. He did tell me that for the first few weeks of the class, Luke seemed very involved and enthusiastic about the discussions and activities of his course. He would often hang around after class to talk about what they had been reading. He described your boy as one of the deepest thinkers he had ever taught. Until the shooting, he didn't really give much thought to it, but in looking back, Byers could see that for a couple of weeks before it happened, Luke had been closing up. Kind of disconnecting from the class and from Byers, too."

For the hundredth time, Gina chastised herself for failing Luke. She had tried to recall any change in her son's habits or behavior during the weeks leading up to the shooting that might parallel what his teacher observed, but she could not. Football practice, homework, football games, work at Sumner's Grocery, trying to get a driver's license; to his mother, Luke's life seemed to revolve around the typical interests of a "normal" sixteen-year-old boy.

"Just recently, Byers decided to look at what Luke had written in his class journal," Adam continued. Gina felt like she had been punched in the chest. Could she have heard Stoller correctly?

"What did you just say?" she asked and held her breath as he answered.

"Byers assigns response journals in his classes," he repeated. "He uses them in several ways. If the kids have questions or reactions to the assigned reading, he'll have them write them in their journals as a starting point for their class discussion. He told me that typically he would have the kids write in them at the end of each class, too. They could record anything that was on their minds."

Gina was stunned. "I looked through everything in Luke's room. I didn't find this journal. And neither did the police," she told him.

"That's because the journals stay in the classroom, or rather in the computer lab adjacent to the classroom. Byers has a plastic bin where they're kept until the class ends in June," Adam said.

"Do the police know about this journal?" Gina asked.

"I don't think so; Byers told me he still has it."

"I need to see that journal," Gina said as she slid halfway out of the booth.

"Hold on, Mrs. Clayton! I was just about to ask Byers if I could look at it today when the principal came to his classroom door," he said.

"Damn it!" Gina said and sat still again. "I knew the secretary was lying when she told me Walker wasn't there today!"

"He was there, alright. And there was a cop standing out in the hallway behind him. Walker called Byers out and closed the classroom door, but I could still hear raised voices. When the teacher came back in a few minutes later, he seemed pretty flustered, and he told me I would have to leave. He said he was in trouble for not signing me in at the main office. The cop stood in the doorway the whole time," Adam explained.

Gina watched as Adam Stoller reached into the front pocket of his shirt. "When I got up to leave, Byers shook my hand, and in his palm was this." He passed a miniscule scrap of notebook paper to her.

"A phone number," she said.

"Yup. Even though I was shown out of the school by the cop, I think I, *we*, have an ally in Ron Byers, Mrs. Clayton."

She slid back into the booth until she once again sat directly across from Adam Stoller. She stared into the writer's eyes for several seconds. Then she spoke. "Please. Call me Gina."

PART IV

Chapter Eighteen

HELLO CALLER

On his way back to the Inn from the CVS where he had bought some bottled water and shaving cream, Adam looked at the audio choices on the dashboard screen. During his drive upstate, he had listened to the newest Jonathan Franzen novel, and he hadn't needed any other distraction for the six-hour ride. Now, he tentatively pressed a finger to the car's touchscreen.

The lessee before him must have been a fan of AM radio. Before he could switch to the Sirius choices, he heard a voice utter a name he recognized. "Janet Shelkowski," the man said, and within moments, Adam was again bearing witness to the emotional turmoil that Luke Clayton had left as his legacy. He turned up the volume.

"Hello, Caller," a saccharine voice said. "What's your name, please?"

"I'm Tony Brown. I teach English at Lake Hinon School."

"Welcome to *AM Jamesburg*, Mr. Brown. Now what did you want to say about your friend…"

Tony Brown abruptly interrupted the sappy-voiced host. "Mrs. Shelkowski was not my friend, and that is something I regret deeply. I behaved very badly once we were combined with the Langston faculty." Adam heard the man take a deep breath. "I highly resented the administration's decision to reassign me to the middle school. I had taught high school for twenty years in Jamesburg."

"Well, that does seem unfair," the moderator replied.

"No, Jim, not really. Janet had her doctorate and she had taught longer than I. It was a fair choice the district made, and it was a solid one for the kids' sake, too. I regret being too stubborn to say these things to Janet while she was here with us. But I want to say them now."

"Go ahead, then, Tony," the show's host said.

Tony Brown inhaled deeply again and continued. "Janet Shelkowski was a master teacher. I don't say that because of her kids' Regents scores or their AP test results. I know it because so many of my former students from Jamesburg would stop by and see me. They told me how tough a teacher Janet was, but they also added that they loved her class. As they talked, I realized that Janet engaged her students in literature and language because her teaching style was so passionate, and the kids knew she cared about them. She always intertwined their lives into her lessons, and because of that, I know that they read more and wrote better."

"Well now, folks, we can all agree that those are good things. Well said, Tony," the moderator said. "Is there a final thought you might want to share with everyone before we move on the the next caller?"

"Yes," Tony Brown said after a few seconds of silence. "It was a terrible thing that happened to us that day. To have Janet and the others ripped out of our lives like that, and many people have expressed this better than I can. But here's my point today. I'd like to remind your audience that keeping an open mind in the face of change, as Janet did and I did not, is a better way to live your life. And life is precious. Don't take the time you have left for granted. That's it."

"Mr. Tony Brown, thank you," the cloying voice said. "Who's our next caller?"

The angry voice that answered the host startled Adam. "This is Patrick

Dean. Now listen, Jim, I hope you and all your listeners can agree with me when I say this community has had just about enough!" The man was hoarse, as if he had been shouting for a long time. "After what happened here in November, it should be crystal clear to everyone that the merger was a colossal mistake! But enough idiots voted for it, and here we are!"

"Okay," the host interceded, trying to calm his caller down. "Now, Patrick, this is an emotional topic, I know, but let's try to keep this discussion civil. No name-calling, please."

Patrick barely skipped a beat after this minor reprimand. "The last thing taxpayers need to be reminded of is that psycho killer every time we get a piece of mail from the school, every time we go to a basketball game or a parent-teacher conference! Hell, we don't even have to walk into the building and that *thing* is staring at us from that expensive electronic sign they put in front of the place, reminding us of 11/23! Why should we have to look at *that*? I'd like to urge your listeners who feel like I do to get themselves to a school board meeting and tell these people that the mascot needs to go! "

Even though Adam was not a local, he understood the intent of Patrick's rant. Beyond reporting the scant details of Luke Clayton's biography, the national media, like a dog with its only bone, had chewed over and over again on the irony of the school mascot—the fact that it was designed by the killer and now represented the very institution that he had bloodied. Just as Adam turned the volume up, the host, whose folksy Southern accent seemed totally incongruent with the typical flat "A's" of central New York, cut the raspy-voiced caller off once more, this time to break for a commercial.

After the annoying jingle for Langston Hardware had ended, the moderator returned. "If you're just tuning in, this is *AM Jamesburg* with Jim Andrews. We talk about all manner of things that concern our lake communities, and wow, folks, the phones have really lit up over this topic that Patrick has introduced! We're talkin' about the Lake Hinon School mascot and whether it should be removed and replaced. It seems the majority of you out there might believe that should be the case, considering its origins. We've got time for one more this morning. Hello, Caller. Welcome to *AM Jamesburg*. What's your name, and what's on your mind?" Ten seconds of dead air was the response. "Are you still with us, Caller?" Jim Andrews, back in carnival barker mode, inquired.

A young woman answered tentatively. "Yeah. I'm here."

"Go on," Andrews prodded. "We're running a little short on time, but we can always use a female perspective. What's your name, honey?"

"Kathryn," she said.

"Go ahead, dear," Andrews said.

"I'm calling about the mascot. I don't think it should be taken down. I think the school should keep it."

"Oh? And why is that, Kathryn?" Andrew's saccharine tone was sickening, and Adam was ready to turn the radio off.

But when she spoke again, he realized the woman's voice was familiar. "Because it represents who we are," she said. Adam turned the volume up and pulled into the parking lot of the Inn. He left the motor running and continued to listen.

"Now there's where a lot of today's callers might disagree with you, sweetheart," Andrews continued in his transparently patronizing way. "But go ahead, do tell," he continued.

"Well, those of us who were raised here have been taught about Hinon from the time we started kindergarten. He represents the first people of the area. He's a symbol of courage, bravery, wisdom…"

Andrews interrupted her. His tone had changed. "But what about the person who designed the mascot? What does he represent, in your mind anyway?" he said, all business now.

194

Silence for a moment and then, "I don't think that Luke was pure evil like so many people have been saying this morning," came the soft reply.

"Did you know him, Miss Kathryn?" Andrews persisted now like he was cross-examining the witness in a courtroom. Adam listened, enthralled, as he stared ahead at the columns on the gigantic porch of the Inn.

"No one is all bad," the woman replied, ignoring the host's question.

"Well, folks, you heard it here first. Someone who has destroyed hundreds of lives in our area is not 'all bad.' That's the beauty of free speech, I guess. Everyone is entitled to his or *her* own opinion, right?" A discernable click interrupted his editorializing. "Well now, I think our benevolent caller just hung up on us," Andrews said with mock alarm. "That's unfortunate, isn't it listeners? But as it turns out, we're out of time for today. Tune in on Monday morning for another edition of *AM James...*" Adam cut Jim Andrews short as he turned the car engine off.

He took the case of water out of the back and headed toward the Inn. From around the opposite side of the gigantic porch came Katie, his waitress that first day in the Oak Room. She didn't seem to notice him as she slipped her phone into her jacket. Suddenly, Adam knew where he had heard the caller's voice before.

Chapter Nineteen

THE JOURNAL

Adam sat at the mahogany desk in his room, a glass of scotch in his hand, and read over the notes he had made in his journal on this morning's revelations gleaned from the *AM Jamesburg* callers. On his list of To Do's was a new item; he would seek Katie out and ask her more about her relationship with Luke Clayton. He put his pen down and pushed the chair back from the massive piece of furniture.

He wondered about the previous residents and guests who had stayed here during the three generations of the property's existence. Who else had sat at this very desk, perhaps to conduct business or to dream? An unexpected wisp of a recollection floated in as he sat there. His laptop was on the desk, and Adam had the sudden urge to open to his novel, to test his ability to get in touch with the muse, the spirit, the demon, whatever it was, that up until a few months ago, had transported him to the interior of his imaginings. Was it ready to return to him, like muscle memory, after all this time? He put the glass down and reached for the laptop just as his phone rang. Diane Richir's face appeared on the home screen.

"What's wrong?" he asked, visualizing the ashen remnants of the brownstone.

"So nice to hear your voice, too, Adam," she said. "I'm not calling to report any disasters. I've been worried about you, that's all. How's it going?"

"It's going well, I think. Each day that I'm here, I learn more about Luke Clayton."

"Really? Have you found the mother yet?" she asked.

"Yes. It took a few days, but she finally agreed to talk with me," he said.

"How horrible is she?" Diane asked.

"Not horrible at all. The woman is intelligent, hard-working, and as far as I can tell, she was a loving mother. She seems to have been genuinely confounded and devastated by her son's actions."

"I don't understand how that's possible." Adam could not miss the hard edge in Diane's voice.

"She's a single mother with no real support from anyone. If she's guilty of anything, as far as I can see, it's of working too much. Of not paying enough attention to a troubled kid who seems to have flown under everyone's radar. But I think she deserves credit for picking herself up and trying to figure it out, in spite of her pain and grief." As he spoke, he realized just how deep his admiration for Gina was.

"So she's open to your turning over rocks and looking for the answers about her infamous kid? She's okay with you writing an article about your experience there?" Leave it to Diane to get to the heart of the matter, he thought.

"Yes and no," he said.

"What does that mean?" she wanted to know.

"Yes, she understands that I feel a responsibility for what happened. She's open to my trying to uncover the truth. I've proven that I'm able to move around in the shadows to an extent that she can't. Just about every person in the area knows she's Luke's mother. In general, everyone in the two communities blames her for what happened."

"Of course they do. It's the easiest justification for simple minds," she said. "It's always the mother's fault." Adam realized that it had not taken long for Diane to change her mind about Gina. "But you haven't told her about the *Rolling Stone* article, right?"

"No, I haven't," he admitted.

"And why not?" Diane asked.

"As of yesterday, she no longer thinks of me as a stalker. We've agreed to be partners in figuring out Luke's transformation from dependable son to mass murderer. I think she trusts me, or wants to anyway. I seem to be her only alternative," he explained.

"What about the police?"

"According to the research I've done and what Gina has told me, the investigation is still open, but they've had nothing new to report in months."

"I raised my kids in Essex County," she said. "I know what small towns are like. What's the talk on the street?"

"Everyone is pretty tight-lipped." As an afterthought he said, "Unless they're testifying in church or calling in to a local radio show." Adam shared with Diane the highlights of what he had witnessed at the prayer vigil and heard on *AM Jamesburg*. For some reason, he didn't tell her that he had met the young lady who had defended Luke over the airwaves.

"So, when will you tell Gina Clayton the whole truth about why you're there?" There was more than a hint of accusation in her tone.

A soft knock on the door startled him. "I've got to go Diane. I'll give you a call in a couple of days."

Before he could cut her off, Diane said, "Take care of yourself, Adam."

"I will," he answered and walked to the door as he hung up.

"Good afternoon, Mr. Stoller," Mary Beth, the desk receptionist who had seemed omnipresent during the course of his stay at the Inn, smiled brightly in at him. "This came for you a few minutes ago. A young lady with a darling baby dropped it at the desk and asked me to be sure you got it," she said as she handed him a large brown envelope. Adam noticed that it was sealed with a couple of layers of tape securing the flap.

"Thanks, Mary Beth," he said.

"You're very welcome, Mr. Stoller. How are you enjoying your stay?" she asked.

"It's been fine," he assured her.

"Great! Let me know if you need anything."

"I will," he said, closing the massive door.

After his meeting with Gina last night, Adam had called Ron Byers and asked him if he might be able to have a look at Luke's response journal. Byers had been silent for a few seconds and when he spoke again he said he would have to think about it. The young teacher must have decided that Adam could be trusted. It seemed that he had enlisted his wife's help, too.

Adam sat down at the desk and used the heavy brass letter-opener to tear the flap. Reaching inside the envelope, he pulled out a slim bundle of pages stapled together. A loose piece of 8X10 copy paper lay on top of it. Scrawled across it were the words: "Hope this helps. R.B."

The photocopied pages of a murderer's journal lay before him. His hands trembled slightly as he began to leaf through it. The first thing that struck him was Luke Clayton's neat block print. From the black and white marbled cover of the composition notebook where he had written his name on the first line and "Myths and Legends" in the space below it, the handwriting signaled a careful, meticulous nature. Unique for an adolescent male, Adam thought.

As he scanned the thirty or so pages of the journal, he saw that the entries were typically three-quarters to a page in length. Luke had dated each of them in the left margin. Every day's chosen topic was underlined precisely. The boy tended to make bullets in front of each of his succinct observations. Rarer than these comments were more freestyle reactions to focus topics, more than likely generated by the teacher.

Adam read each entry carefully. Byers had told him that he had assigned Adam's story to his class sometime near the end of October. Glancing at the dates, he found what he was looking for on the last pages of Luke's journal.

10/22/2015 – Response to short story "Seneca Optical" by Adam Stoller

What I liked:

- Original Iroquois myth from area
- Lake named for deity Hinon – researched him for my mascot
- His description of reptiles was cool (why do these creatures always get a bad rap as being Satanic?)
- Evil humans are "seen" by the protagonist
- Eric suffers. He is alone
- He wipes out the evil that he sees

QUESTION: Does fate/God choose who will "see"? Who will punish the evil doers?

Adam had to admit that it was exciting, no, if he was being totally honest, it was flattering as well to get inside the head of a reader this way. The kid certainly "got him" and the essence of his story. But in light of the events of November 23rd, the question Luke had asked at the end went beyond the scope of an objective reaction to literature. It was the ultimate goal of most writers of fiction to have their works move the reader to reflect on his or her life. The question of whether his writing mattered in any meaningful way to his readers is what had plagued Adam and blocked him for months. Could what came from his imagination motivate a reader to reflect on his own life? Now he had to face the possibility that his art may have moved Luke Clayton to do that, and in so doing, to commit an atrocity.

The next entry, written weeks later dispelled any doubt that Luke had indeed internalized the story. A chill ran down Adam's spine as he read.

11/15/2015 – <u>More on "Seneca Optical"</u>
Reptiles <u>still</u> roam the earth

- **Bullies**
- **Cowards**
- **"Whether you call someone a hero or a monster is all relative to where the focus of your consciousness may be." Joseph Campbell**

The next page was not a part of the journal, but a single sheet with a photocopy of a Lake Hinon High School hall pass. It was dated November 15, 2015, the same day of the entry Adam had just read.

For: Luke Clayton
From: Study Hall
To: Mr. Walker's office
Time Leaving: 10:25
Time Returned: 11:00

Two signatures appeared on the bottom: Mrs. Bradley and W. Levy. Why had Byers included this, he wondered.

Adam turned to the last two sheets in the bundle. One was written thirteen days before the shooting. The final one was entered on the Friday before. The last day of Luke Clayton's life as a "normal" high school student. He had dedicated a separate page to each entry, in spite of their brevity.

11/17/2015

LOST BRAVE

11/20/2015

I CAN SEE YOU ALL!

Adam read the final line of his own short story out loud. These were perhaps the last words that Luke Clayton had written before he ended several lives, including his own. He stood up and lifted the page closer to his eyes. He stared at the boy's sketch of the Iroquois deity. Just as Jim Andrew's angry caller had asserted that morning, it was a ubiquitous reminder of not only the Iroquois myth, but of Luke and his ideals. Adam had seen it everywhere in the school yesterday when he had gone to meet with Byers, and now here it was drawn neatly in black ink and set off with the last words from "*Seneca Optical.*"

A loud pounding on the door interrupted his thoughts. He hurried to open it. Gina Clayton stood on the other side of the threshold, fist still clenched and ready to pound some more. Her face was flushed and her eyes were wide. Before she uttered a word, he could see that she was seething.

Her shout bounced off the high-ceilinged hall and reverberated throughout the Inn's long corridor. "You son-of-a-bitch!"

CHAPTER TWENTY

THE OVERLOOK

For the first time in months, Gina woke up in the manner that most people did, her mind gradually transitioning from deep slumber to dull consciousness to full wakefulness. Since Luke's death, she more often than not startled awake from a dark dream or thought that clutched at her in the middle of the night and stole restfulness away. This morning when she sat up and looked at the clock on her nightstand, she realized that she had actually slept through the night.

Was it Adam Stoller's pledge to be her cohort in this quest for the truth that was giving her some comfort, some ease? From the time of Pete's arrest, she had been alone in handling every decision and crisis that life threw in her path. But Adam seemed genuinely invested in this pursuit, and so she would allow herself to trust him. They were meeting later today at the Lakeside Inn to outline a strategy that they decided would include making a list of people who might be able to help them. Gina wasn't sure how many of them would speak with her, but as she headed to the shower this morning, she had every intention of talking with one of them today before she met with Stoller.

It seemed to Gina that Wendy Levy had stepped outside of her watchdog role for a few potent moments in her office yesterday. She said that

Luke was a good kid, that she had chatted with him more than once during the fall semester. Gina would never have known about the appointments her son had with Walker if the secretary had not mentioned them. It was not the norm for most high school kids, and it was certainly not likely that her reserved son would want to drop in for a casual conversation with Mr. Walker. Gina had met the principal only once before. A janitor had caught Johnny smoking behind the school, and she had been called in for a conference. From his handshake that day to his avoidance of eye contact with her, Walker had struck Gina as a cold fish.

Her hunch was that Wendy Levy might know the reason for these encounters between Luke and Walker. She would cover Claire's shift at work as she had promised, but when it ended, she would go back to the school and try to get Wendy Levy to elaborate. After all, she paid her school taxes, and her other kids, when they returned from Buffalo, would be students there once again. She had every right to enter that building, she told herself. What a difference a day, no, Gina had to admit, Adam Stoller had made in her attitude.

At three-thirty that afternoon, Gina turned into the school just as the secretary's car was idling in the line at the red light waiting to turn onto Main Street. Gina performed a quick three-point maneuver and beat the school bus behind her to the signal. Wendy was a couple of cars ahead by the time she pulled onto the street. Gina wasn't sure exactly what she would do once she caught up to her, but she had thought of little else but their encounter yesterday. Soon she was pulling into a spot in Wegman's parking lot, a few rows away from Wendy Levy's car. She watched as the woman opened her hatchback to retrieve some shopping bags.

"Hello, Mrs. Levy," Gina said as she stood behind her.

"Oh! Mrs. Clayton. You startled me," she said as she turned and faced her.

"I'm so sorry. But I needed to see you again. Can we talk for a moment? I just have a couple of questions. About Luke," she said. "I was heading to your office, but I saw you leaving the campus."

"Yes, I leave at dismissal time on the Friday before a Monday school board meeting. I have to take notes at the one coming up next week," she explained. Wendy's eyes scanned the lot. It was obvious to Gina that she did not want to be seen out in public with her. What Gina could not see was that Wendy Levy, too, had been thinking of little else but their exchange yesterday. Her guilt at having let Luke into the building that morning was certainly part of it, but as a mother herself, she knew that Gina was hungry for any reassurance that Luke was the boy his mother had thought he was.

Although Joe Gloss, Bob Walker, and Superintendent Graves, and her own husband had warned her to keep her distance, Wendy felt genuine compassion for Gina. After all, she was not on school property at the moment. She had every right to speak with this woman.

"Okay. But not here." She unlocked the car doors with a click of her key fob. "Please. Get in," she said to Gina.

They did not speak as Wendy drove toward the lake. When she turned into the beautiful overlook rest stop, hers was one of just a few cars parked there. From this hillside vantage point, the whole span of the lake could be seen and the contentious towns of Langston and Jamesburg were simply land points outlining its majesty. "Look at that," Wendy broke the silence they had shared on the drive. "The ice is almost gone."

"Yes, it is." Gina turned to face the woman. "Thank you so much, Mrs. Levy..."

"Please. I'm Wendy to the kids and pretty much everyone else," she said.

"Wendy. Thanks so much for talking with me," Gina said. "Most people avoid me these days. They think I'm responsible for Luke's actions, and they may be right."

Wendy turned to face Gina. "I'm not sure what you think I might know about Luke that you didn't," she said.

"But you see, as it turns out, I knew very little about my son. You may have spent more time in his company than I did this past year," Gina said.

"Until November, I thought he was a lovely boy," Wendy said. "He was respectful and pleasant." The kind words about her son from this stranger threatened to bring tears. Gina put her shoulders back and took a deep breath to stop them. Wendy seemed unaware of the effect she was having on Luke's mother as she continued talking. "As far as discipline, we saw more of your Johnny in the office than we did Luke," she told her.

"That doesn't surprise me," Gina said. "But you mentioned yesterday that Luke had been in Mr. Walker's office a couple of times."

"Yes, he came in with Travis Worthing. I think it was late in October, just after the school day had ended. Luke asked if the boys could see Mr. Walker," Wendy said.

"Did he say what it was about?"

"No. Just that they needed a few minutes with him before football practice," she said.

"Did Luke seem upset?" his mother asked.

"No, but Travis did," she said. "Although that wasn't unusual for Travis. He was kind of a nervous kid in general, needy, I guess you'd say. He's left the district, you know."

"I didn't know that," Gina said.

"Yes, just this week. His grandmother told us he'll be completing his sophomore classes online," Wendy said. "I guess school just got to be too much for him, his being Luke's best friend and all…"

"So what about the next time?" Gina asked.

"The next time?

"That Luke came to see Mr. Walker?"

"Oh, yes. He was with Travis again. Again, it was after school. Travis was a wreck. I could see that his face was very flushed. The boys had to wait a few minutes in my office because Bob was on the phone. Travis sat in the chair in front of me clenching and unclenching his jaw, shaking his leg."

"What about Luke? Did he seem upset?" Gina asked.

"No, Luke was calm, at least on the way in. The boys must have been in there for fifteen, twenty minutes. When the door opened, they came out with Joe Gloss, our resource officer, walking behind them," Wendy said.

Gina could feel her heart pounding. "What was the officer doing there? Had he gone in with them?" she asked, doing her best not to sound alarmed.

"No. Mr. Walker's office has a second entry from the corridor. I hadn't seen him go in through my office, so he must have used that one. Joe stopped at my desk and told me to write the boys a pass to football practice," Wendy said.

"Do you remember how Luke seemed after that meeting?"

"He seemed…distracted. I thought it was because his friend was so upset. It looked like Travis had been crying," she said.

"Did you see Luke again after that day?"

"Yes. There were at least two times in November that I can recall. He had a pass each time. Luke was all business those days. I tried to kid with him a little, but he was pretty serious," Wendy said. "I believe that was the last time I saw Luke before…" She stopped talking and both women watched as another car pulled into the overlook.

"Wendy, do you have any idea what the boys, or what Luke, spoke about with Mr. Walker?"

"No, I honestly don't. It's not my place to ask, and Bob…Mr. Walker never discussed it with me. I'm sorry I can't help you more, but that's all I know." She started the engine and backed out of the space.

"Wendy, thank you so much for talking with me," Gina said when they pulled into Wegman's lot.

The secretary shut off the engine and turned to face Gina. "Look, I've told you everything I know, so please don't contact me again, Mrs. Clayton. I could get into trouble at work if anyone found out."

"Of course," Gina said, unfastening her seat belt.

"And you understand that everything I've said needs to be off the record, don't you? I could lose my job if any of what I told you is published and attributed to me," Wendy said.

"Published?" Gina said, not understanding.

"In the article that Adam Stoller is writing."

Wendy unfastened her belt and looked at Luke's mother. As she opened the door, she could see by Gina's astonished expression that the woman had no idea what she was talking about.

CHAPTER TWENTY-ONE

THE LIE

Gina pushed past Adam Stoller. Before he could close the door, she was shouting at him. "What kind of a slimy bastard are you? How dare you worm your way into my life and pretend to be my ally, when all you are is a low-life journalist!"

Adam was speechless as he faced her wrathful sarcasm. "You were on a personal journey to try to understand my son, to figure out how your story impacted him, you said."

"But that's true, Gina, I…"

"You can stop lying! Wendy Levy told me that you're working for a newspaper…"

"Magazine." The woman's face turned crimson as he added, "Rolling Stone." He looked down at her clenched fists and waited for her to slug him. When she didn't, he said, "I was going to tell you about it, but until yesterday, I didn't think you would understand." As he stammered through the rest of his explanation, her stare burned through him. "Look, Gina, I told you the truth when I said my reason for coming here was personal. The possibility that my short story was an impetus for Luke's actions was something I couldn't shake from the moment I heard about it. For months, the thought destroyed my attempts to write. I had to find out the truth."

"So you decided to go public with what you found and make a pile of money doing it, right?" Her accusation filled the space between them.

"The editor came to *me* with the idea, and yes, the fact that they would pay me to write the article was certainly something that made it more appealing, but..."

"But nothing!" Gina said. "You're just like all the rest of the bloodsucking media! You want to expose and exploit my kid and his life, my life..."

"That's not true! I would never do that, especially not to you and your kids," he said. "I won't lie. Before I came here, I thought for sure that Luke must have had a terrible home life – a dad in prison and a mother..."

"Exactly – an awful woman who..."

"But from the moment I met you, I knew that you were not that person. I can see how much you've suffered and the price you've paid for what you wrongly believe to be your fault. Gina! You are *not* the reason Luke shot and killed those people and himself! I know that, and I'm getting closer to being able to prove it," he said.

"What are you talking about? What proof?" She was still furious with him but his last words had piqued her interest.

He walked to the desk and picked up the photocopied pages. "This," he said, holding out the journal to her. She took it and stared at the cover.

"Where did you get this?" she demanded.

"From Ron Byers," he said. Gina was amazed. He had been here for only a few days, and yet in that time Adam Stoller had uncovered what the police, the FBI, and Gina herself had not.

"The journal was a class assignment, but in the final entries, Luke reveals that it became more than that for him. Look at the last four pages," he said. "Read the Joseph Campell quote. Was Luke thinking about the main character in the story as a hero or monster, or was he thinking of himself?"

Gina read for a few moments. "Reptiles. He thought that people were evil, like the creatures in the story." She was thinking out loud, as if Adam had left the room. "But why?" she asked as she turned another page. "A hall pass dated the 15th. Wendy Levy told me he had asked to see Walker a couple of times before…"

"Wendy Levy?" Adam interrupted.

"Yes. I just came from talking with her," she said.

"What else did she say?" he asked, forgetting for a moment that Gina despised him.

"If I tell you, are you going to put it in your *Rolling Stone* article?" She practically spat out the words.

"Gina, please, let's sit down," he said as he steered her toward the two high-backed chairs on either side of the fireplace. "I have to say something and I need you to listen." He pulled the chairs away from the wall and positioned them so that they were facing one another. "Please," he said, guiding her into one of them. He sat down in the other one and looked into her eyes.

"I'm listening," she said.

"I have every intention of helping you discover what Luke was thinking when he pulled the trigger that day," he said.

"And you have every intention of writing an article about it," she said, her words an accusation.

"Yes, I will write the article," he said. "but I won't submit it if you don't want me to. You may be the only person who ever reads it, if you decide that it isn't a fair analysis of what your boy may have been thinking when he walked into school on November 23rd," he said.

Gina was weighing his every word. She looked down at the journal in her hand and her boy's neat handwriting. She turned to the last two pages. "Lost brave," she read aloud. And then, "'I can see you all.'" She closed her eyes and shook her head. When she raised her eyes to once again face Adam Stoller, she was resolute. "Yes," she said.

"Yes?"

"Yes. You can write the article. But you have to help me to find the evil that my boy saw. You have to help me uncover it, so that I can see it too," Gina Clayton said.

Chapter Twenty-Two

WHERE DO WE GO FROM HERE?

Gina took a pen and the notebook out of her bag and began to copy from Adam's laptop a section of the notes they had made together. The list was brief and she had already committed it to memory, but somehow the act of writing it down was reassuring. It was proof that she and the author were moving toward something concrete in figuring out the mystery that was Luke.

They had designed a simple code of asterisks to distinguish the importance of each of the potential sources. They used question marks to signify the level of reluctance they might meet from each.

Travis **???**

Katie **

Ron Byers*?

Wendy???

Walker???**

Joe Gloss???

Monday Prayer Vigil**

AM Jamesburg**

"So where do we go from here?" Gina asked Adam Stoller as she finished writing. They studied the list on his laptop screen.

"I think the first thing we need to figure out is how Wendy Levy found out about the *Rolling Stone* assignment. If it's common knowledge, I need to know that and possibly use it to our advantage," he said.

"She made it pretty clear today that she wouldn't talk to me again," Gina said.

"That's okay," Adam said, picking his phone up from the desk. He pressed a contact number and put the device on speaker.

"Hello." She heard the man's voice answer on the third ring.

"Hello, Ron. It's Adam Stoller."

"Yes?" the teacher said. Gina could hear an infant wailing unhappily in the background.

"I wanted to thank you and your wife for what you did today," Adam said.

"I hope it's helpful, Adam." Gina could hear the resistance in his tone in spite of his words.

"It most definitely is, Ron."

Before he could say any more, Byers said, "But I can't talk to you."

"If this is a bad time…"

"No, I don't mean I can't talk to you right now. I can't talk to you ever again," the teacher said.

"I'm sorry to hear that, Ron. What's happened?" Adam asked, in spite of the fact that he already knew.

"My principal has told me in no uncertain terms that I shouldn't speak with you because of the *Rolling Stone* assignment. Apparently your publicist called his office and wanted to arrange for some photographs to be taken of you in various places on the school grounds. Mr. Walker was pretty upset with me for letting you into the building in the first place," Ron said.

Adam realized that Marie Lanphere must have done Jesse Olson's bidding. His idiot agent seemed to believe that no cost was too high for a wide-reaching market, even if it involved hurting innocent people. "Ron, I'm so sorry. I had no idea," he said.

"I figured," the teacher said, "but you need to lose my number, Adam. I can't afford to risk losing tenure over this," Byers said, "so I don't want you to use my name in the article."

"I understand, Ron. You've done so much already."

"Luke seemed like a good kid. I'd like to know what happened to him too, but the ball is totally in your court now," he said, and hung up without saying goodbye.

Adam turned to Gina. "Well, now we know who blew my cover," he said. "The enemy is in my own ranks. I'm positive that Walker will make sure that the whole staff knows, so the school is out as far as a further source for us."

"It's pretty amazing," Gina said.

"What is?"

"That both Ron Byers and Wendy Levy have helped us, in spite of the fact that they could lose their jobs for doing that."

Adam was taken aback by the smile on her face. "You look pretty pleased about the fact that two of sources of information have washed their hands of us," he said.

"I'm thankful that they each took a huge risk to show us that Luke was not some blood-thirsty monster. Wendy's impression of him, and his own journal, which Ron Byers copied and delivered to you *after* Walker warned him to stay away from you, show us something entirely different. According to Wendy, Luke and Travis went to the principal several times this fall, possibly looking for some kind of support from him and maybe from the school resource officer too. Maybe these "cowards" and "bullies" were making life miserable for him. If Walker knew this and did nothing...no wonder the bastard doesn't want to talk with me," she added disgustedly.

Her analysis trailed off and the two sat in silence. After a few moments, Gina stood and walked to the bank of windows that framed Lake Hinon. The haunting burden of guilt that she had carried for months, the sense that she was responsible for the massacre of innocent victims and her own son's death had seemed irrational up until now. It was merely an emotional phase in her journey with grief, she would tell herself. Now, she knew she was to blame. It seemed likely that Luke had been harassed and bullied, perhaps physically. Her son had suffered, but he had not come to her, nor did he say anything about it to his siblings or even his father when he made his secret trip to Auburn.

If only she could get to Walker. If she could confront him in a place where he couldn't wriggle away, like the worm he was. Suddenly, it came to her. The school board meeting. According to Wendy, it was on Monday. Walker would surely have to be there. As she gazed out at Lake Hinon, Gina took a silent vow—she would be there, too.

A blue heron was flying low. She watched as it pulled its long legs up and made a smooth landing close to the Inn's shoreline. "Beautiful," she said aloud. She turned away from the lake and saw Adam staring at his computer screen. "What are you thinking?" she asked. He began to type as she came closer to him. Over his shoulder she watched as he backspaced across Wendy Levy's, Mr. Walker's, and Ron Byer's names and added several asterisks next to Travis Worthing's.

"He knows. I'm sure this boy knows if Luke was being bullied," he said to her.

"Not according to the interviews Travis had with the police," she told him.

"He said next to nothing to the police," Adam said with certainty. "I've read the reports. And besides, the police already knew that Travis and Luke had been to see the principal. I'd be willing to bet that at least one cop knew what these meetings were about, even though it's not on record," he added.

"Joe Gloss?"

"Joe Gloss," Adam replied. "Wendy told you that he was with the boys in Walker's office that day, right?"

"Yes. He does seem to have been everywhere throughout this miserable experience," Gina said.

"What do you mean, everywhere?" he asked her.

"He was in the room where they took me to identify Luke's body. He was present, kind of lurking in the background at the station during some of the police interviews, and then he let me into the school building the other day *and* let me out."

Adam was staring at her. "Yeah, he was my official escort out of the building, too," he said, nodding his head.

"He would know if Luke was in Walker's office to talk about being bullied. But there's no way he'll talk to *me*," Gina assured him.

"Well, I guess that means I'll have to get him to talk to *me*," Adam said, still nodding.

"How?" she said, astonished by the certainty of his tone. "Where?" she asked when he didn't answer her first question.

He smiled broadly and said, "Where do you find most cops on Monday nights?" He didn't give her a chance to answer. "In church," he said.

CHAPTER TWENTY-THREE

KATIE AND THE THUNDERBIRD

Adam was starving. The more time that passed since inhaling his last cigarette, the keener his appetite became. Yesterday he had walked at least ten miles and eaten only one meal. He decided to treat himself this morning to the Sunday brunch in the Lakeside Inn Oak Room. He looked around the cozy space and hoped his fellow diners could not hear the rumbles of his digestive tract.

As he sat drinking a first cup of coffee the hostess had poured for him, he pulled out the pamphlets from yesterday's excursion to Ganondagan. Since his time at Syracuse University when he had driven there to do research for the writing of "*Seneca Optical*," he had been fascinated by the place. The three-hundred-year-old site marked the spot where thousands of Seneca people had once lived and thrived. The Peace Village, they had called it. Yesterday, just as he had done on his first trip there, Adam had walked the trails and climbed the mesa to view the huge palisaded granary where the early native people had stored thousands of bushels of harvested corn.

He leafed through the literature until he found the brochure on the latest feature of Ganondagan. This past October, the newly constructed Seneca Art and Culture Center had opened to the public. Yesterday he had watched, enthralled, as a dozen or so costumed dancers performed on a stage in front of a huge screen. The original animated feature created by a young Seneca film student was projected as a backdrop to the dance. The spectacle produced a three dimensional version of the Iroquois Creation Myth.

Adam was particularly engrossed in the interactive exhibit of the Thunder deities. The message on the large poster that had been set on a tripod in front of the display was also noted in the brochure that he read this morning. *"When you're a native person, your story is often told by other people. Here, we tell our own story."* Indeed. Adam had told their ancient story *his* way, and look how that had ended.

"Good morning, Mr. Stoller," Katie said as she reached for his cup to give him a warm- up. "Will you be having the brunch buffet or would you like to order off the menu today?"

"Katie," he said, more relieved than he wanted her to know. "I'm glad to see you. I wanted…"

The girl was staring at the cover of the brochure that lay on the table. "The Thunderbird," she said.

"Yes," he said. "I went to Ganondagan in Victor yesterday. Have you ever been there?"

"Yes," she answered. "When I was in elementary school. All the fifth graders go on a field trip there while they are studying the Iroquois. The longhouse was my favorite part." She picked up the brochure and stared at the cover a few seconds before setting it down. "But now everyone wants to get rid of the mascot," she said.

"That was you on *AM Jamesburg* yesterday, wasn't it? I thought I recognized your voice," he said.

She answered without hesitating. "I was driving into work when I heard the other callers. It's just not right what they want to do. They think by getting rid of the Thunderbird, they can get rid of Luke. In my opinion, neither of them deserves to be forgotten."

The hostess walked behind the girl, guiding a couple to the next table. Katie replaced her somber tone with a warm, "So what's it going to be, Mr. Stoller? The buffet or something from the menu?"

"The brunch looks great," he answered. The girl gave him the customary instructions for lining up at the omelet prep area and told him she would be back with more coffee. Adam had to figure out a way to talk with her outside of this dining room, ideally away from the Inn, if he wanted her to open up.

After he had finished his breakfast, she brought him his check. He could think of no subtle way of asking, so he just blurted it out. "Katie, did you know that I'm an author?"

"No." She was polite, but unimpressed.

"I write fiction, novels and short stories. I wrote "*Seneca Optical*," he added tentatively.

"Oh," she said.

"Have you read it?"

"Every kid at Hinon High has read it because of what happened on 11/23," she answered.

"I came here to try to figure out why Luke Clayton had my story with him that day. But I've come to realize that before I can solve that puzzle, I need to understand who Luke was. Would you be willing to talk with me?"

"Look, Mr. Stoller, I really wasn't tight with Luke."

"I understand that Luke didn't have many friends, but as I listened to your call to *AM Jamesburg*, I realized that you might know a lot about the dynamics, the interactions of the kids at your school." She began to clear his dishes and stack them on a tray, but he could tell she was listening. "I think it's important for me to understand that before I can try to understand Luke." She set the tray down and was looking at him now. "I was impressed with what you said on the radio about this." He pointed to the cover of the brochure. "That the Thunderbird is the symbol of courage in the face of evil. How the school district needs this mascot, especially now..." Before he could finish, the hostess appeared behind the girl.

"Excuse me. Katie, your table six is looking for a refill," she said.

"Sure. Thanks," Katie said to her. "Is there anything else I can get you, Mr. Stoller?"

"No," he answered. "Thanks for the great service this morning," he added for the benefit of the hostess. "And thanks for the information about the trails at Ganondagan."

Adam left the Oak Room and returned to his own, intent upon writing about the purity of adolescence. He had been inspired by Katie's uncomplicated convictions as she expressed them to Jim Andrews yesterday and to him this morning. He knew that most adults viewed teens as entitled slackers with nothing on their minds but posting banal crap and lewd pictures on one social media outlet or other. Maybe it was easier for Adam to see beyond those generalities to the essence of a young person because he had never had to raise one. But as a grad assistant he had witnessed in his own eighteen-year-old students, as he could see in Katie, an innocence, a nobility, an intention, if not always the fortitude, to do the right thing. He opened his journal to record his sentiments, but that's as far he got. For the first time in his stay in the Mahogany Room, the landline rang.

Katie did not bother to say hello. "I'm not sure if I know anything that will help you, Mr. Stoller, but if you want, I can meet you at the state park pavilion before I head home," she said.

"That would be great, Katie," he said.

A few minutes later, he pulled the Range Rover next to the red VW bug in the marina parking lot that the girl had described. Adam stepped out of his car into the mild March day. He noticed the sticker of the Thunders' mascot on the back of Katie's window as he passed it. Several yards away stood a large redwood pavilion. The girl was sitting at a long picnic table on the bench that faced the lake.

"I have to be home in a half-hour, Mr. Stoller," she said as he walked around the table so that he could face her. "And I'm really not sure that I can help you."

"Thank you for meeting me, Katie," he said, as he sat down on the bench across from her. The entire length of the table was filled with carved graffiti, most of it advertising the names and relationship status of dozens of strangers. "I guess what I want to know is what it's like to be a high school kid at Lake Hinon. From your point of view," he said, looking into her eyes.

She thought for a moment. "Well, before 11/23, whenever I would complain about school, my mother would tell me that she didn't want to hear it, that this was the best time of my life. And that someday, when I was out on my own, I would see that." She shook her head as she explained her mother's naiveté. "My mom graduated from the old Jamesburg High, when there was such a place," she said. "When I was in middle school, whenever she would talk to me about her experiences back in the day, I'd picture the school that Sandy and Danny went to. You know, from *Grease*?"

He smiled and said, "Yes. I'm aware of it."

"I guess that's kind of dumb. *Grease* was set in the 50's. My mom isn't that old, but still, the way she described it, it seemed so much simpler, more wholesome, if that's the right word, than my school experience."

"How so?" he asked her.

"Well, in the first place, there was no merger controversy in her day. No nasty merger politics."

"So the kids at Lake Hinon were aware of that conflict?"

"Were and *are*," she corrected him. "Oh, yeah. Definitely. At first, most kids heard about it at home before the vote was final. And when we merged, even though the teachers weren't shouting about it like the parents were, it was obvious that a lot of them were pretty unhappy about it, too. So it was no wonder our student body was split between the "White Trash" Langston kids…" She seemed to be waiting for some sign of disapproval from him, and even though she got none, she defended herself. "I can say that, even though it's not PC, because I went to elementary school there," she explained. "So it was "White Trash" versus the upper class Jamesburg students. "The Lakers," as they're called, even though not many of them live in mansions on the lake." Katie glanced over his shoulder at the body of water in question. Her eyes tracked a gull that shrieked as it flew over the pavilion.

"That must have made for a pretty tense environment," he said.

"Yeah. But it got worse in high school. Kids argued all the time, and there were some pretty bad fist fights, too. Jamesburg versus Langston kids, mostly. It got really scary to walk through the halls some days. Even off campus, at parties, or at the beach in the summer, you could be attacked. So much for school spirit," she said. "And the mean-girl thing—you know what that is, right?" she asked.

He nodded and said, "I think so."

"That got totally out of hand," Katie said. "Especially with social media as a weapon. It was a nightmare for some kids."

"Do you think the administration knew about this?" he asked her.

"Oh, sure. We had several assemblies about bullying and how bad it was. Mr. Walker told us that it wouldn't be tolerated at LHH. At least, that's what he said. But as far as I know, he never did much about it. There were lots of kids who were targets. I knew a girl—she transferred to the Catholic high school in Lincoln last month—who went to him to complain about being harassed in gym class, and he didn't do a thing to stop it," she said, obviously agitated at the thought of this ineffective jerk of a principal. "Unless you call having Joe Gloss do his dirty work…"

"The school resource officer?" he asked.

"Yes. The kids had him pegged from the beginning. He was Jamesburg all the way. He had been a big-time jock there. At least, that's what he told kids. If you lived in the old Langston district, he had no time for you," she said, "except to call you out and discipline you for something he couldn't prove you did."

"Katie," he said when she had grown silent for a few moments. "Do you think Luke had been bullied?"

"I really don't know, Mr. Stoller. Like I told you, Luke and I were more like acquaintances than friends. We had a health class together last year. He was shy, but then he was a freshman and I was a junior, so that would explain why he never talked to me unless I started the conversation."

"Can you remember anything you discussed when you did have a conversation?" he asked the girl.

"Nothing personal," she said. "He was kind of secretive. No, that's not the right word. That makes him sound suspicious. It's just that he didn't share much about himself, even when we were supposed to be doing that very thing in some class exercise. I was a little shocked when he told me about entering his Thunderbird design in the mascot competition. That was the longest talk we had ever had," she said.

"He must have thought he could trust you," Adam said.

"Maybe," Katie said. "The day they announced over the PA that he had won, we were in health class together. I stood up and walked over to him and gave him a hug. All the kids and our teacher started to applaud. Luke looked embarrassed, but I think he felt proud."

She paused and glanced over Adam's shoulder again, as if looking to the lake for confirmation before she spoke. "But everyone knew that his dad was in prison for dealing drugs and he lived in Langston, so he was definitely considered a loser…um, an outsider, as far as his social status at school." Adam nodded, but remained silent. "So I suppose he could have been a target because of those things. And he was on the football team." She stopped talking and he waited patiently for her to elaborate, but she seemed distracted again by something on the water. He turned and saw a rowboat near one of the marina docks with three Amish boys fishing from it.

When he looked back at her, she seemed to be miles away. "What about the football team, Katie?" he asked.

"Well, they were great," she said as if everyone, including Adam, already knew this. "They won the states, even without, even after…" she shook her head. "Everyone was so proud of them. Their bringing a trophy back to LHH, it seemed to make people forget about November 23rd. At least for a little while. But those guys had a lot of pressure on them, for sure," she said.

"Pressure?"

"Yeah. Football had to come before everything. The coaches made that very clear, and Scott, because he was the team captain, never let the guys forget that. On and off the field. They even did some weekend overnights. For team building. Even if you had a job or some other commitment, you had to go, or you'd be kicked off. Everyone knew that it was pretty intense to be on the team."

"So do you think Scott might have given Luke a rough time?" he asked her.

"I don't know. Scott was always nice to me. I'm just saying that the training and the practices were like extreme workouts, and supposedly they were like toughest on the second string and JV kids, in an emotional way, I mean." She stopped talking when the three Amish teens walked past them, fishing tackle in tow. They headed toward the horse and buggy that was tied to a lamppost at the far end of the lot.

Adam waited for the boys to be out of earshot. "Did Luke ever mention anything to you about the football team?"

Just then, Katie's cell phone buzzed. "Yes, Mom. I'll be home in a few. See you soon." Katie swung one leg over the long bench.

"I've got to get going, Mr. Stoller."

"Okay, sure," he said as he stood.

"I want you to know that I think Luke was a good person, and the mascot he designed proves that. I was never aware that he was being picked on by anybody. Something just went wrong with him somehow," Katie said with the same assurance in her tone that she had had on the radio yesterday. She stood up and took her bag off the bench next to her. Adam rose and the two walked toward their cars.

When they got to Katie's VW she turned to Adam and said, "Where do you live, Mr. Stoller?"

"New York City," he answered.

"Jamesburg and Langston must seem like horrible places to you, right?" She didn't wait for his answer. "In a lot of ways, I can't wait to get out of here myself, to go to college in the fall," she said, her eyes scanning the side road where the Amish buggy could be seen driving away. "But as weird as it seems, I know I'll miss it, too."

Katie opened her car door and slid into the driver's seat. "I wish I could have helped you understand Luke better," she said, looking up at Adam. "To tell you the truth, he was one of those people who I thought I could be friends with. Like in the future, you know, when real life started, not school life."

He watched as the VW drove away, the Thunderbird decal illuminated by the afternoon sun.

CHAPTER TWENTY-FOUR

THE WHITE STAR

Adam's conversation with Katie had been enlightening, yet troublesome. Political pressure, peer pressure, parental pressure, it seemed all were brought to bear on Katie and her Lake Hinon High schoolmates. As he drove out of the state park, the writer tried to imagine how those burdens might have contributed to the transformation of Luke Clayton from a mild-mannered sixteen-year-old into a murderer.

The thoughts were unsettling and Adam realized that he was not in the mood for the quiet pleasantries of the Inn, so he made a U-turn and headed away from the lake. Soon he was driving on Main Street through the downtown portion of Jamesburg, passing the stone church where he had attended the vigil the other night. He drove past the four blocks of Jamesburg businesses. Moments later, he saw the *Welcome to Langston* sign and pulled over and parked.

On Sunday the few downtown enterprises that were not for rent or boarded up were closed. In between vacated buildings, Adam passed a hardware store, an Agway, a 7-11, a dentist's office, and a coffee shop. A small pawn shop and an antique store shared the same storefront on the corner. Adam crossed First Street which delineated the end of Langston's commercial district.

Hands in his jacket pockets, he slowed down to a stroll as he approached a residential block of Main Street. The houses were shabbier than the tidy bungalows of Jamesburg, most of them begging for a paint job. Broken windows, torn screens in front doors, garbage cans whose contents had spilled over onto the curb, all lent this area a particular kind of small-town squalor.

Adam passed kids playing on scabby front lawns where a random daffodil or two bloomed. The unusually warm March day had lured them away from TV's and video games, he imagined. Most of them were engaged in pantomimes of battle; brooms and mop handles, tree branches, and other makeshift weapons were brandished, coming perilously close to the faces of their enemies. The kids shouted and screamed at one another and every group he passed seemed to be running in circles. Chained dogs pulled on their fetters and barked ferociously at the kids. Or at him. Adam wondered if the animals were vicious or just hungry.

Most city-dwellers would not have expected this version of small town America, he thought to himself. The ramshackle neighborhood reminded him of the one in Southside Chicago where his father's bar had been until a fire had destroyed it ten years ago. This was the "wrong side of the lake" that Adam had been told about since he arrived.

He crossed Main Street and headed toward an older wood-framed building on the corner. What had caught his eye from across the street was the eight foot wire outline of a star that was attached to the peak of the roof. Another storefront church he guessed, like the ones that seemed to be on the main street of every village in this part of the state.

When he reached the building, he tried to look inside, but the black shades on the windows prevented him. The gold-lettered sign painted on the window glass read *White Star Tavern*. Adam hesitated. It was only three o'clock in the afternoon. As he turned to walk away, his peripheral vision caught something that made him reconsider. In the corner below the establishment's name was a glossy decal. It looked like the one on Katie's car except that underneath the mascot were the words *Thunders Football Fan*.

As soon as he opened the door, he was assaulted by the odor of musty beer lines that had not been flushed in a while combined with the smell of old cooking grease. The place was packed and Adam had to push his way through the throng of mostly men to reach one of the few empty seats at the bar. ESPN was broadcasting a NASCAR event on the small screen over the bartender's head, but the level of noise made it impossible to hear what the announcer was saying. While Adam waited for the guy to come to his end of the bar, he surveyed the room: a jukebox with an *Out of Order* sign stood in the corner, a pool table took up most of the rest of the space, and the adjoining larger room had several tables and a big-screen television.

Adam turned back to the bar. He thought about ordering scotch, but a layer of thick dust atop the magnum of Johnnie Walker Red discouraged him. As he scanned the long row of bottles, he noticed that taped to the oak-framed mirror behind them was a panoramic picture of the 2015 Lake Hinon varsity football team. One kid's face had been X'd out with a black sharpie. Adam guessed it had to be Luke's.

"What can I get you?" the bartender asked as he approached him.

"I'll have a Labatt's Blue," he said. "Bottle, please." As the man set the beer in front of him Adam said, "Pretty busy in here for a Sunday afternoon, isn't it?"

"Always is," came the man's flat tone.

"Really?"

"Yup," he said. It was obvious that he had no time for small talk or Adam.

"My dad owned a bar for years. He always said Sundays were dead," Adam said before the guy could walk away. "My mom wanted him to shut the place for the day, but when you own a business, it's not that easy." The bartender gave Adam a second look. He grabbed a towel and started drying glasses in front of him.

"Tell me about it," he said. "My wife is always bitching at me too, but Sundays are my best days, even after the NFL season ends."

"Really? Why is that?" Adam asked.

"Hammermill factory starts and finishes early on Sunday. Most of my business happens when the shift is over. Thank God we still have that plant," he said.

"So all of these people work there," Adam commented as his eyes scanned the room.

"Not all. On weekends I get some farm workers who come in before evening chores, and seven days a week, morning, noon, and night I get some customers who don't have any work right now." He nodded his head toward a corner table where a man sat alone, his head propped in his hands, three empty shot glasses in front of him. "Like that sorry son-of-a-bitch."

Adam watched as the man put his head down on the table. The bartender picked up a rag and wiped the bar around him. "You're not from here, I take it."

"Nope. Just passing through," he answered.

"I'm Mike," the man said. "Let me know if I can get you anything else."

Two men sitting further down the bar held up their empty glasses to signal the bartender. Adam could read their body language as they spoke with Mike. They were asking about him, obviously suspicious about his presence in the White Star.

He rotated his stool a couple of inches to the left and concentrated on the conversation between two youngish guys who sat on stools next to him. A third man stood unsteadily in front of the pair with a beer in his hand. There was a pile of mud on the wooden floor where he was standing. No,

Adam realized as the distinctive smell hit his nostrils, it wasn't mud on the guy's boots.

"Fuckin' Jamesburg asshole," Shitty Boots said. "How does someone that stupid end up making the money that he makes?"

His companions didn't even venture an opinion. It was understood that their friend would answer his own question. "I'll tell you how." He raised his voice so that everyone at the bar and in the front room could hear. "Fuckin' corporate farmers! They pay us minimum wage and roll in the dough they make off our backs! Fuckin' government is in on it, too!"

His friends nodded, probably hoping to appease him. But he turned it up even louder. "Fuckin' illegals used to do the shitty jobs that white guys like us are stuck with now!" He punctuated his disgust with a huge beer belch.

When Shitty Boots' passionate discourse about the "dirty fuckin' one percenters, dirty fuckin' politicians, and dirty fuckin' Mexicans" dissolved into indiscernible mutters, Adam rotated on the stool and looked around the room. He watched as two young men, each clad head to foot in denim, began a game of eight ball. In his periphery, he could see Shitty Boots glaring at him now. He turned and waved at Mike and ordered another beer. When it came, he vacated his stool and offered it to the glowering man, and then he joined the small crowd gathered around the pool table.

Before he turned his back on them to watch the match, he noticed four women, two wearing Hammermill jackets, at the table behind him. "Her kid killed eight people! Her other kids should be taken away and she oughta be arrested!" Adam heard one say. A shiver ran through him—she was talking about Gina.

"Husband's already in prison. Drug dealer. Jesus," said a second disgusted voice. "But she always acted like she was better than everyone else anyway. Walked around in that lab with her nose in the air." Adam was confused by this last remark, and then he remembered that Gina had been employed by Hammermill for a brief time.

"Daughter's knocked up, you know," the first added.

"What kind of mother doesn't know her own kid is a psycho?" a third voice asked the group. The level of their vitriol was unsettling to Adam. How could Gina live in this place where this shaming Greek Chorus could pop up anywhere?

He moved away from them and walked toward the pool table. The two players, who looked to Adam like they couldn't have graduated from high school too long before, were involved in a conversation that immediately drew him in. "Coach Harrison replaced by a guy with half his experience? Goddamn shame on top of the whole stinking tragedy, if you ask me," one said as he backed up to watch his opponent's next move.

"Yeah. But Coach was a quality guy off the field, too." The young man took his shot and chalked his cue stick as he spoke to his opponent. "Took me to division games with him, took me to college visits when my old man wouldn't." As he stepped back from the table he said, "Not that I ended up going to college. But coach listened when I needed someone to talk to. He knew life at my house wasn't easy."

His friend nodded and said, "His kids came through for him and Coach Davis in that state title game. Hell, that team lost two, maybe three of their best players on 11/23," the other answered as he chalked his stick.

"You can't deny it took a lot of guts for high school kids to perform under those circumstances," his friend said. "Just to show up for that last game was something. Proves what good coaches they were to get that level of performance from the team without them being there."

"That team had talent *and* guts," said a spectator on the opposite side of the table from Adam.

"Coach Harrison and Coach Davis would have been proud of them," said the second player as he crouched over his next shot.

"Yup! They did it!" his rival said. "State champions!" Several of the on-lookers loudly agreed with this assessment.

"Faggots! Whole team full of queers and faggots!" The slurred shout shocked the room to near silence. It had come from the corner table where the sleeping drunk had been. He was awake now and perilously on his feet. All of the bar patrons including Adam turned toward the hollering man.

"Shut the fuck up, Turner, you low-life waste!" Shitty Boots said as he crossed the room and headed toward the shouter. His two buddies were right behind him. Adam watched as Mike rushed out from behind the bar. The proprietor was pushing people out of his way, taking long strides toward the drunk's table.

"I gotta right to talk just like anyone else! My kid was in that class-room!" Turner said as he swayed back and forth. "Said he would have saved that fairy Wallace if the teacher hadn't stopped him!"

Adam watched as the farm workers and the pool players grabbed the drunk. The cue stick lay in pieces on the floor next to Turner by the time Mike reached them. The tavern owner pulled the man up by his jacket collar and held on to it as he guided him through the parting crowd and out the door.

After the cops had arrived to escort Turner home, Adam ordered his third Labatt's. By the time he took his last swallow, the place had emptied out except for a few people talking quietly. He placed the bottle and his tip on the bar and got up. "Thanks, Mike," he said, and when there was no re-sponse, he walked out the door. It was dark as the writer crossed the street. A line from Leon Russell's "Stranger in a Strange Land" came to him, and he knew it would stick in his head for a long time. When he reached the sidewalk, he noticed that the tall white star was flashing on and off. Every so often, he would turn back and look for it as he walked the several blocks back to the Land Rover.

He could still see it as he started the car. Adam stared at the blinking star and thought about the characters he had come into contact with inside the tavern. He knew some of the flamboyant people he had observed in the White Star would show up sometime, somewhere in his fiction. That was a consoling thought; thinking about culling from real life and writing again. At the same time, the reality was that the White Star and its hostile patrons were a part of Gina's everyday life. She *was* the stranger in this strange land. The realization made him sad. His objectivity about Gina as a subject for his article was gone, he knew. He had known her only a short time, but he was grateful that she had come into his life.

As he stood on the curb and watched, the rooftop star blinked one more time. Adam waited for it to come back on, and when it did not, he took that as the signal that it was time to head to the Inn. There was no other traffic on Main Street as far as his eye could see, and so he pulled a U-turn and headed back toward the lake. Within seconds, he spotted in his rearview mirror a Jamesburg Police cruiser following close behind.

Trying to stay calm, he inventoried all the possible reasons he could be pulled over. He had left the brights on when he started the car; maybe the cop would give him a warning about that. The Land Rover was a pretty conspicuous luxury model of a rental car and that might make him somehow suspicious. Maybe the cop would simply check his ID and let him go. The most likely reason for the policeman following him was the overtly illegal U-turn. Adam preferred any one of these scenarios to the possibility that he would be pulled over and breathalyzed. Would three beers put him over the legal limit? He wasn't sure.

But the cop did not pull him over. Instead, he followed closely behind the Range Rover for the seven mile drive back to the Inn. Adam had broken into a sweat long before he approached the hotel and turned his signal on. He fully expected the cruiser to tail him into the parking lot. Instead, the cop sped by the Inn.

Adam watched as the cruiser's flasher came on. No siren, just the blue light emanating from the bubble. The writer got out of the car and stared as the light blinked on and off until it rounded a curve and disappeared.

CHAPTER TWENTY-FIVE

SKYPE

Gina had worked both Sunday breakfast and lunch. By the end of her shift, the free-floating anxiety she felt as she waited on people at the counter had intensified to a keen homesickness. She knew what was at the root of it. She was missing her kids.

As soon as she and Shelley finished eating their dinner, her daughter opened the laptop for the weekly Skype session with her siblings. Gina cleaned up the kitchen while Shelley chatted and laughed with her brothers and sister. "I've got the day off next Friday and I'm driving down to see you all before this baby makes it impossible for me to fit behind the wheel," Shelley told them before she vacated the chair and let Gina sit down.

She looked at the screen. There they all were crowded together on her parents' couch smiling at her. "Hey, babies," she said, and she felt the relief wash over her as she spoke.

"Mommy, check these out. Nana bought them for me," Lisa said, standing up and modeling the high leather boots. Her youngest seemed to have grown three or four inches since the last time Gina had gone to visit them in Buffalo.

"Those look great!" she said. "I see Nana is spoiling you, Lisa," she added.

"She's earned them," she heard her mother say from somewhere outside the scope of the camera.

"I've been teaching Nana how to use her computer better," Lisa said, as she sat down next to her brothers again. "And I've been helping her in the kitchen, too. She's going to teach me to make sauce next week." Her youngest child, who had always been so painfully shy, had a new tone of confidence in her voice.

"John and I have been helping Papa unload the delivery trucks at the stores," Tommy said.

"That's great, Tom!" she said, astonished. These were the boys who she could not get to take the garbage out or mow their tiny lawn. "How's school going, guys?" Her parents had assured her each time she asked them that everything was fine. All three of them seemed to have adjusted well to their new school. Their grandmother made sure to ask them each night at the dinner table, but Gina would never again take for granted that her kids were okay just because they said so.

"Good," the twins said in unison.

"I'm going out for the cross-country team next week and Johnny is trying out for baseball," Tom said. Gina was further amazed. Her younger boys had been such sources of worry for her from the time they were tweens. They had never been interested in any activities beyond video games. And before they had gone to live with their grandparents, Johnny seemed bound and determined to be thrown out of school and into jail.

"And Mom, you need to know that I'm never coming back there, to Langston," Tommy said.

"What do you mean, Tom?" she asked. "This is your home…"

Her son's face flushed with anger. He stood and shouted at her. "You don't get it, do you? Everybody hates us there! They hate all of us! Because of Luke! Because Luke killed people! I don't want anyone to know that he was my brother!" Gina sat in stunned silence as Tom clenched and unclenched his fists. He took a deep breath and said, "I have to go give Papa a hand now. He's working on getting the boat ready."

"Okay, hon," she said, watching her lanky teenager disappear from view. Although she had been taken aback by Tom's outburst, she understood his anger. There had been moments in the past weeks when her guilt for not being there for Luke was supplanted by flashes of raw rage toward him. Luke had taken eight lives and then killed himself! The selfishness of that act made her so furious that she had to do whatever she could to distract herself from those thoughts, or she knew they would poison her.

The sound of the doorbell made Lisa jump up from the sofa. "I think that's my friend Robin," she said. "We're going to watch a movie. Bye Mom, love you," she said as she blew her a kiss.

Gina's mother took Lisa's place on the couch. "Hi, honey," she said. "How are you doing?"

"Better," she answered. She fought the urge to tell her mother and her kids why the weight of grief seemed more bearable during this past week. She would have liked to tell them about Adam Stoller and their joint mission to find out what happened to their dead brother and grandson. But she couldn't. Not yet.

"I'm so glad to hear that, Gina!" her mother said. "I think these will make you feel good too," she said as she held up to the camera the report cards of each of her three kids.

"Wow!" Gina said as she read over the columns of mostly A's and B's. There was a time when her parents' efforts on her kids' behalf would have made her angry. Why couldn't they understand that she could handle this, that she could do this parent thing just fine all by herself? In the past, she might have been resentful of the fact that in the Lombardos' home, her kids were happier, more responsible than they were in hers. But all she felt now was gratitude. She understood that her parents were doing this for her, for their only child that they had always loved more than anything in the world. It had taken the worst possible tragedy to convince Gina she could permit them into her messy life, but they had proven over these past months that they were a positive force in her life and her kids' lives, especially. "Thank you, Mom," she said simply.

"Thank you, my darling, for these wonderful children," her mother said as she stood up. "Take care of yourself, Gina," she added as she left the room.

It was just John now. As she looked at him, she marveled at how much he resembled his father, the way Pete had looked when she had first met him. As he spoke, she recognized how much his voice had deepened in these past months. "Mom. You should move here, to Buffalo. With us." He leaned forward, closer to the camera.

"Johnny, I'm not sure that's…"

He interrupted her, "We miss you and you miss us." He hesitated a moment and then he said, "And we all miss Luke, even Tom. He's just pissed at him for what he did, but he misses him, too."

"I know that, honey," she said.

"Papa and Nana make sure that we talk about him every day," he said.

"That's wonderful, John." Gina felt tears forming. She had been wrong to keep her kids so far away from her parents all these years. Their love and wisdom were obviously helping her kids cope with this great loss.

"Sometimes we look through old pictures and talk about how funny he was, how he always acted like a little old man, even when he was a kid himself," he said. "When Tom and I started kindergarten, he would hold each of our hands everyday and make sure we got to our classroom. And he was only in first grade himself."

"I know," she said, smiling brightly at the memory of her three little boys walking together toward the school, Luke always in the middle, in case one of the twins tried to make a break for it. In the afternoon, with Lisa in her car seat, she would pick them up and they would be in the same formation, their sweet faces smiling at her, excited to see their mom again.

"Mom, Luke hated Langston," he said, the words and the change in his tone shocking her.

"What do you mean, Johnny? Did Luke tell you that?"

"Not exactly, but you know Luke. He always had to take care of us, no matter how old we were. He would never tell me anything that he thought I would worry about. But I could just tell. I would see him at school, and he was a totally different kid."

"Different? How?" she asked.

"I'm not sure I can explain it. But this year especially, he seemed to be like, on his guard kind of. In the halls, you know? He never smiled like Luke always did. Something was really bothering him. He didn't talk to me or Tom about it, though. He always thought of us as little kids," he said. "Anyway, one thing I know about Luke is, he would want us all to be together."

Gina felt the tears coming again and fought them. "You're right about that, John. And if you guys are happy in Buffalo, that's where we all should be. But it will have to be after Shelley has the baby. And there's one other thing I have to do before I can move. Can I tell you something that you won't share with the other kids and your grandparents, at least not at this point?"

"I can keep a secret, if that's what you need me to do, Mom," he said.

"I've been trying to figure out what was in Luke's head that day. There are people who know more than they've told the police, I'm positive of that, and I need to find them and what they know before I can leave." Gina didn't want to complicate her explanation to her son by telling him about Adam Stoller.

"Ask Travis," John said abruptly. "I think if anyone knows something, it's Travis."

Just then, Tommy came back into the room. "Sorry, Mom, for before," he said sheepishly.

"Tom, it's all right," she said. "It's okay to feel angry, honey. I'll call you soon. We'll talk more."

"Okay, thanks," he said turning to his twin. "John," Tom said, "Papa needs us both ..."

Gina said quick goodbyes to her sons. As soon as she closed the laptop, she picked her phone up and dialed the Worthings' number.

Chapter Twenty-Six

ARE YOU ON FACEBOOK?

The church doors were unlocked when Adam arrived twenty minutes early for Monday's prayer vigil. He wanted to be sure to get a seat in the last pew. From the vestibule he noticed several supplicants already seated with their heads bowed. Three of them, sitting in a row from shortest to tallest, wore Lake Hinon High varsity football jackets. As he slid into the back pew, he tried to determine if the boys were a faction from last Monday's larger group, but he couldn't tell. Clad in their identical jackets, they appeared to be a unit rather than individuals, so they may or may not have been at last week's gathering.

Dozens of people slowly walked past him as the organist played. Within several minutes the small church was filled almost to capacity, as it had been the week before. He searched for those who had spoken so emotionally that night. He recognized the nervous mother of the senior girl sitting in the pew across from him. But by the time the minister had walked to his pulpit, Adam had not seen Scott Wallace's uncle, nor could he find Ron Byers.

With a sweeping glance from one side of the church to the other, the young reverend signaled that the vigil was about to begin. Adam focused his eyes on the minister, but when he spotted the uniform of Joe Gloss passing by, the tiny hairs on his neck bristled. Two rows in front of him, the line of people shifted to give the cop the aisle seat.

The evening unfolded differently from the ritual of the week before with prayers followed by hymns and then more prayers. This time the reverend delivered a short homily based on the words of Isaiah 40:31. "'*Those who hope in the Lord will renew their strength. They will soar on wings like eagles. They will run and not grow weary. They will walk and not be faint.*'"

As the reverend expounded upon the Bible verse, Adam wondered if he was the only one in the church who was struck by its parallel to the Iroquois Thunderbird myth. The legend of Hinon lifting the lost warrior aloft had perhaps inspired Luke to do what he had done. Wasn't that why they were all here tonight? Had the minister chosen this particular chapter and verse for that reason? Adam looked to his left at the man sitting next to him. He looked across the aisle at the senior girl's mother. Each appeared to be unaware of any connection.

When Ray began his walk down the middle of the congregation with the microphone, this time no one raised a hand to express his or her personal testament of grief. Within the hour, the final hymn was being sung, the "*Our Father*" was chanted, and when it was over, the minister asked that everyone keep their places. He had an announcement to make.

"Friends, this will be the last of our Monday evening prayer vigils," he said. Adam listened to the murmurs of the congregation, and a few soft gasps signaled that the minister's pronouncement had taken them by surprise. "These gatherings have been important for us as a community, but the time has come to move on. Easter is two Sundays away. During this season we celebrate the resurrection of our lord Jesus and the renewal of hope in each of our hearts. We should look to His coming again as a sign that we, His children, have the power to recover and heal from the horrible tragedy that was visited upon us." He looked around at the congregation and in his most conciliatory tone he spoke again. "Of course, should any-one need me, I will be available at any hour to provide private guidance. May the Lord bless you all."

As the organist played, the processing congregants lifted their voices and sang a hymn whose lyrics Adam knew. "*And He will raise you up, on eagle's wings / Bear you on the breath of dawn / Make you to shine like the sun / And hold you in the palm of his hand.*" Again, he was struck by the correlation between the Iroquois myth and this Christian hymn. He was convinced now that the minister had intentionally chosen the verse and the hymn. Or was it just English majors and writers who thought this way, he wondered.

He walked through the vestibule and into the chilly March night. A light snow was falling only a day after the temperature had reached the 60's. He paused by the electric signpost where he had encountered Ron Byers the week before and watched as the people walked past him toward their cars. Some nodded, but most, including the three football players, ignored him.

Behind the group of boys walked the man Adam was waiting for. "Of-ficer Gloss?" he said before the policeman could pass by. Gloss turned and squinted into the light cast by the sign, trying to ascertain who Adam was.

"Yes?"

"I'm Adam Stoller. I saw you at the high school last Thursday."

"Yes," he said.

"I was wondering if I might have a word with you. About Luke Clay-ton."

"That's a police matter. The investigation is still open," he said as he turned to walk away.

"I know that," Adam said as he followed him down the sidewalk. "I'm wondering if you might share what you know about the boy from a more personal point of view. As the SRO at Lake Hinon High, you get to know the kids pretty well, I imagine." The cop was walking more briskly now. "Especially the troubled ones," Adam said from a few steps behind him. "I understand you were in a meeting with Luke and Travis Worthing in Mr. Walker's office several days before Luke opened fire on the school."

Adam had caught up to Gloss. The cop did not flinch. He was a cool bastard, Adam thought. "Can you tell me what Luke said in that meeting?"

"Have a good evening, Mr. Stoller," Gloss said as he walked to the Jamesburg Police car that was parked at the curb.

It suddenly dawned on Adam that more than likely it was Gloss behind the wheel of the cruiser that had tailed him last night. Now the writer followed close behind the cop, emboldened by the memory of the flashing blue light. "I think that meeting might be significant in the timeline of events leading up to the shooting. Don't you agree, Officer Gloss?" Gloss ignored his question. He opened the car door and got in. "Luke was troubled about something, troubled enough that he wanted to talk to Mr. Walker, and you were in the room when that happened."

"Mr. Stoller, I suggest you turn around, get into your car, and go back to New York as soon as you can. You're on a fool's errand. No one here knows anything more, and if they did, they would not talk to a journalist. You have a good evening," he said and slammed the vehicle's door. Adam was left staring at his disappearing taillights.

"Prick," he said aloud.

He had parked his rental in the lot behind the church. As he turned the corner he thought about how disappointed Gina would be when he told her that the Monday vigils had to be crossed off their list as a potential source of information. His confrontation with the cop had gained them nothing, and the odds were against him getting Bob Walker to agree even to meet with him, never mind relate what had happened in his office that day.

"Excuse me." Adam whirled around and turned toward the voice. It seemed to be coming from the hedgerow behind him that separated the church property from the sidewalk. The dark figure stepped into the light cast by the corner lamppost. Adam recognized the shortest of the Lake Hinon football players at whose backs he had stared during tonight's service. The kid's flaming red hair was another feature that had set him apart from the others. "You're the writer, right?" the boy asked.

"Yes, I'm a writer," Adam said.

"You're the one who wrote the story about Hinon, right?"

"Yes, I am," he answered.

"Can I talk to you a minute? About Luke Clayton?"

Adam felt the hairs on his neck stand up. "Sure," he said in a casual way, trying not to scare the kid off. "What's your name?" he asked the boy, who he saw now could not be more than fifteen.

"Um, I'm sorry, but if you write about this, I don't want my last name mentioned," the boy said, as if he had practiced these words.

"That's fine," Adam said. "What's your first name?" he asked him.

The kid hesitated. "Jeff," he said, and Adam doubted that this was true. "I didn't know Luke that well. I guess none of us really did, but what he did shocked everyone. No one on the team would have expected that from him. Look, Mr. Stoller, I don't have a lot of time. I'm supposed to be home by now."

"I understand, Jeff. Is there a better time and place we can talk?" Even on this dark street, Adam could see how nervous the kid was.

"No. This is the only time I can ever talk to you," he said gravely. "Are you on Facebook?" he asked.

Adam's publicist had insisted that he set up two accounts on Facebook—one personal, and the other his author's page. "Yes, I am," he answered the boy.

"I'm going to invite you to a Facebook group page. I think it will tell you a lot."

"What group is that, Jeff?"

"It doesn't matter. You won't be able to search it. I'll send you an invitation. S-T-O-L-L-E-R, right?" he said, already walking away from Adam.

"Yes, that's right," he answered.

"Just look for an invitation from Jeff," he called as he sprinted away and was soon swallowed up by the darkness.

CHAPTER TWENTY-SEVEN

THE CIRCLE

Gina followed the long corridor to the meeting room. In spite of the fact that she felt stronger than she had in months, by the time she reached it, she was on tip-toe. She wanted to be as unobtrusive as possible so that Bob Walker would not be forewarned and manage to dodge her again. After talking with Wendy and reading Luke's journal entries, she was almost certain that Walker knew more than he had told the authorities.

To her relief, the back door was open. Flashes of light flickered on the adjacent wall, as though a film was being projected on the theater-sized screen in the front of the room. Gina waited for the next interval of darkness, and when the moment came, she slipped into the room. A massive brick structure appeared on the screen. From her seat in the last row, she could see the outlines of several men and women sitting at a long conference table in the front. As her eyes adjusted to the dark, she recognized Wendy, and beside her sat the person Gina had come to see. Her plan was to approach Walker as soon as the meeting ended. He wouldn't be able to avoid her or have Wendy make excuses for him. She would be polite, but firm. She would make it clear that she wouldn't leave until he agreed to talk to her.

A middle-aged man in an expensive suit stood in front of the room, clicking a remote as he spoke. "In conclusion, let me say that this addition, ladies and gentlemen, will make the Lake Hinon School District the envy of all other agricultural programs across the state of New York and, in fact, the whole northeast. Our consultants and architects look forward to working with the fine people of your community to make this happen." With that, the screen went white, and with another click of the remote, the overhead lights came on.

"Thank you, Dr. Barnes. The board and I appreciate your enlightening presentation on this exciting new space, and we look forward to your return in a month when the public will vote on the proposal." Gina recognized the superintendent, Dr. Graves. "We'll return to our monthly agenda now," he said.

As he walked to his place at the head of the conference table, Gina glanced around the room. Fifty or so people sat in the tiered seats that faced the board members and the administration. She had not expected this many to show up to a school board meeting, but this was her first, so perhaps it was the norm. The woman in front of her suddenly turned around, startling Gina. "Did you get one of these?" she asked. Gina shook her head. A flash of recognition came over the stranger's face as she handed her the paper, and her cordial smile faded.

At the sound of the screen retracting, the woman turned to face the front. Where the screen had been, now an enormous silken banner was revealed. It bore the district's name in red and black, and below the letters was an outsized rendition of the Thunderbird. A shudder of surprise took hold of Gina as she stared at Luke's design.

"Before we wrap it up this evening, are there any comments from the floor?" the superintendent asked the audience. "Please raise your hand and state your name so that Mrs. Levy can put it in the board notes." As Wendy looked up from the papers in front of her, her eyes found Gina's. The secretary jotted something on a piece of paper and slid it to Walker. He glanced warily toward Gina, and she bowed her head to avoid his gaze.

"Yes!" A man wearing a Sabres jacket stood without being recognized and faced the people at the table. "I'm Bart Hawley and that...*thing*," he said, pointing at the banner, "is why I'm here. Why most of us are here," he said, glancing to the left and right for a consensus from the crowd. Nodding heads and a low group murmur gave him the reassurance he needed to continue. "Dr. Graves, Mr. Hall, board members, this mascot has got to be removed from every place on this campus! It's a cruel slap in the face to all of the kids and teachers who have to look at it every day when they come to school, and for the eight murder victims and their families and friends. It's a shameful disgrace!"

A woman on the other side of the room raised her hand, but stood before she was called on. "It honors the Clayton kid and mocks the people he killed!" she said. At the mention of her last name, a wave of dread gripped Gina. The resolve she brought into the room to confront Mr. Walker seemed to melt away at the woman's angry accusation.

The paper-passer in front of her spoke up. "It's on everything, from book covers to the school website!" Gina's anxiety grew. It was obvious to her that Dr. Graves could do nothing to restore this meeting to order.

A man wearing a Hinon High Sports Booster jacket chimed in. "It's painted on the gym walls, it's on all the team uniforms, for Christ's sake. What do you think it tells visiting teams about our school? About our community!"

"Mr. Walker," the superintendent spoke. "Would you like to address these concerns?" More a command than a question, Walker's boss gestured with his hand in a way that said "the floor is yours." Slowly, the principal got to his feet. He looked even paler and thinner than she remembered, shrunken inside his suit. She almost felt sorry for him. Almost.

"Folks, I understand your concerns about the mascot," he said, his voice strained.

"Bullshit!" someone across the room hissed.

"But we need to remember that it was voted on and chosen in a school-wide referendum of students, teachers, and staff. It represents a sacred image of the Iroquois people..."

"Here we go with the PC crap," the man in the Sabres jacket interrupted. "No, you're wrong! As of this past November, this thing represents the twisted kid who was sick enough to take innocent lives. And what did this school do to prevent it? To stop him? Absolutely nothing!!!"

"*You* are the same people that forced this merger on us! Who knows if the shooting would have ever happened if it weren't for that? The least you can do now is remove this constant reminder of your failure and this tragedy. At least do that!" another angry parent screamed from the crowd.

Gina had stopped breathing as this last woman spoke. She came here to find out what her son said to the principal in those meetings. Instead, she was witnessing first-hand the unmitigated hate that these people had for her dead child. A child she had carried for nine months and loved for the short sixteen years of his life. They didn't know and couldn't understand—Luke, her Luke, was so much more than his final legacy. Gina was on the verge of standing up and shouting at the room. "You don't' understand! For whatever reasons, he couldn't turn to me or anyone else with what must have been a terrible burden. To have been so alone, so sick, to do what he did. To do it and take his own life..."

But Gina did not stand up. She slid lower in her seat as Bob Walker walked shakily back to his chair, and the superintendent rose. "Folks, due to the late hour and the fact that the board needs to deal with some personnel matters in a closed executive session, we'll have to end this discussion for now. But rest assured ladies and gentlemen, we heard you."

As the board and the administrators followed Wendy out of the room, the disapproving rumbling of the crowd swelled to a near-roar and accompanied them as they headed into the superintendent's office. "Stooges!" "Cowards!" "Bastards!" The insults bounced off the walls of the large space.

Gina's fingertips were tingling, and as she stood up, she felt off balance. She had to get out of here, now. The woman who had handed her the agenda turned around before she could escape. "Excuse me. Aren't you Gina Clayton?" It was an indictment, not a question. Gina didn't respond. Instead, she turned, walking quickly to the back aisle.

Several men and women were clustered in the doorway talking, making it difficult for her to get past them. Gina put her head down and willed herself to push through the throng. The woman followed close behind her. "You're her, aren't you? You're Luke Clayton's mother!" Several people turned to look at the object of this woman's derision, and some of them began to follow the two into the corridor.

Cursing her decision to come here tonight, Gina hurried in the direction of the lobby. What had she been thinking? Why had she not enlisted Adam's help in getting Walker to talk? She was not strong enough to deal with any sort of questions about her son or herself. She should have stayed home and hidden like she had done for the past four months. She would race to her little house, and except for going to work, she would stay there.

She turned her head slightly to gauge her distance from the woman. What she saw in that peripheral glance caused her already racing heart to quicken. Following right behind her accuser was a crowd of fifteen or so people, and they were closing in on her. Gina had worn her woolen peacoat tonight. Wringing wet with a cold sweat, she sped up her pace to a walk-run.

A bank of double doors ran the length of the large lobby and the ones closest to the parking lot were within view. Positioned just beyond them she saw a policeman leaning against one of the glass panels. She said a silent prayer of thanks as she ran toward him, but suddenly, a pale man wearing a baseball cap stepped in front of her.

"Not so fast, Mrs. Clayton!" he said. He was smiling, but she saw raw hate in his eyes. He leaned in so close to her, she could smell cigarette smoke on his breath. "What's your hurry, lady? These people would like to talk with you. You owe them at least that, don't you think?"

Primal fear struck at her, from her toes to her scalp, and at the same time, something else. A simmering anger at her helplessness, at being out-numbered like this. A powerlessness that came from not being able to pro-tect her son from their blind loathing, from not being able to tell them the whole truth about Luke. They wouldn't want to hear that he had been someone else before November 23rd. Someone who was beloved by his family, just as his victims were by theirs. Someone who, like those victims, should have lived his life to its natural end.

Sweat rolled down from her hairline, stinging her eyes. She tried to push past the man, but he blocked her feeble attempts. The crowd formed a tight circle around the two. Their hatred for her and for Luke was palpable, like an electrical current. She felt its menacing power, its ability to burn everything and everyone in its path.

"Just what brought you here tonight, Gina? You've been pretty scarce these past months. Did you come to express your opinion about the mas-cot?" It was the man in the Sabres jacket.

She spun away from him. A short, middle-aged woman red-faced with fury stepped closer to Gina. "Maybe you came to apologize for what your son did! For what you *didn't* do!" Repulsed by the stranger's wrath, she turned away.

A younger woman wearing a Hammermill jacket faced her now. "You should be at home with your kids, lady! They need supervision, protection.

You of all people should know that!" Gina stood on her toes, looking for the cop, but he was turned away from the small mob. How could he be oblivious to what was going on a few feet away, she wondered. Gina opened her mouth to yell to him, but before she could, he turned and looked right at her. It was Joe Gloss.

In the aftermath of the shooting, Gina recognized that she was blamed and reviled for Luke's actions, but except for a few hate calls and some demeaning whispers in public places, the realization had been almost abstract. This circle of hate that confronted her now was real, almost intimate.

The man who had chased her down the hall blocked her again. "It would be a shame if your kids' mother couldn't make it home. If she were delayed somehow," he said. Every pulse point in her body throbbed. Instinct told her that this was not an empty threat. Her breath came in shallow pants and with each inhalation, she felt herself shrinking. She was the smallest of prey, a most vulnerable target, and Joe Gloss was not going to save her. Looming in front of Gina, the man obstructed her view of the doors and their promise of safety.

She had remained silent throughout the shaming and taunting, but at last, she whispered one word to the young man, "*Please*?" Slowly, he backed away from her and turned toward the doors. He gave her one last look of disgust and then pushed on the metal handle.

Dizzy with shock, Gina moved toward the open door. But the man in the baseball hat did not budge, and she could feel the heat radiating from his body as she squeezed through the small space between them. She heard the gagging sound from his throat before she understood what was happening. Her knees threatened to give way as she staggered out into the cool March night.

This, she realized, was her life now. Blame and guilt would follow her wherever she went. How could she possibly live this way? The target of scorn and hate. A mother who could not protect her children. She deserved their contempt. She would not hide from it. She prayed that one day, she would have the strength to face it and not run.

Gina stared straight ahead until she reached her car. She did not wipe the slimy glob off of her face until she was behind the steering wheel of the Pontiac.

CHAPTER TWENTY-EIGHT

BROTHERS OF THE LAKE

Adam resisted the urge to press the accelerator to the floor on his drive back to the Inn. Nerved up and jumpy, he thought over what had transpired outside of the church. After tonight, he and Gina could cross Joe Gloss off their list of potential sources. The cop's attitude made it pretty clear that the word was out about Adam's mission here. His demeanor had bordered on smug as he let it be known that from this point on, there would be no opportunity for Adam to move around in the shadows; if he tried to, he could expect a police cruiser to follow him. But then Joe Gloss had not seen his encounter with Jeff.

An electric buzz of anticipation, the same sensation he had while he was writing, ran through him. When he was "in the zone," a trance-like state of inspiration, his fingers would fly over the keyboard as he discovered a crucial piece of his plot or a key moment from a character's past. He was experiencing that same excitement as he thought about the possibility that Jeff might be leading him to a new clue in the mystery that was Luke Clayton. The more he thought about it, the more amazed he was that the kid had been so eager to speak to him. It could not have been easy to break away from his teammates tonight. Adam felt it in his gut--the kid must have some information that he was desperate to share. Why else would he want to send him an invitation to this Facebook group?

As soon as he got inside the room, Adam opened his laptop. How long would it take to hear from Jeff? The answer was there as soon as he logged onto his email. The subject line was ***BoyJeff has sent you an invitation to join a group on Facebook***. Adam clicked the link to the page, and instantly the group name appeared in bold, white letters. ***Brothers of the Lake*** spanned the banner photo, a black and white close-up of an outdoor scoreboard. *Jamesburg 54 - Langston 21,* it proclaimed. The archaic board captured a time before the sophisticated digital devices of today. It reminded Adam of his own high school days when metal panels with single numbers on them were inserted from a catwalk behind whenever the score changed.

The profile photo was a thumbnail of the 2015 Lake Hinon High School Varsity Football team. Adam squinted at the tiny image of each boy's face. A few smiled, but most, including Luke Clayton in the second row, imitated the bellicose expression worn by many collegiate and professional athletes. Beneath the team picture was something Adam had never seen on any other Facebook page. Next to an icon of a metal lockset bolted closed were the words ***Secret Group***. What the hell was a secret group, he wondered.

Anxious and jittery, he did a Google search and within seconds he was reading about the three kinds of groups on Facebook—public, closed, and secret. The secret group differed from the others in that the only way to join was to be added by a current or former member. Only members could see the list of those who belonged, as well as the tags and posts. If a non-member did a search on Facebook, according to Google, the secret group would not be disclosed. Could it be possible that the authorities had never discovered the *Brothers of the Lake* page?

Adam returned to the site and clicked on the **Members** list. His own name appeared along with thirty-one others, including Luke Clayton and Travis Worthing. But several on the list were obvious pseudonyms. Each of those was similar in its anonymity to that of *Jeffboy*, although some were much more menacing: *Monster, Nightmare, The Crippler, Rampage, The Beast,* and *War Machine* were the most intimidating. The profile picture for several members was identical: a cartoonish depiction of a wolverine. Under **Events**, the team's 2015 practice and game schedules appeared. The last date listed at the bottom of the page was ***December 1st – Lutheran Camp Team Retreat.***

Adam noted that the most recent post was the only reference to the shootings. Twenty members had made the same statement on November 25th, 2015—"*R.I.P. BROTHER AND COACHES.*" Some of the earlier declarations were what might be expected from the members of a winning team, boasts and hype meant to psych each other up. "*Birds reign SUPREME!*" "*INVINCIBLE,*" "*THUNDER DYNASTY.*" *There were links to several* newspaper articles about the team and its stellar record.

But there were other statements that struck Adam as oddly threatening. "*Kick the weak out of the NEST,*" "*Beware of the SHOWER little BOYS!*" "*December 1st! Motherfuckers,*"and again the sentiment that was reflected in the group's banner photo, "*Jamesburg will WHUP Langston Losers ASSES!*" Katie's understanding of the hostility still felt about the merger two years later seemed to be borne out here.

Interspersed among the threats were some obscenely morbid quotes, some of which Adam recognized from his brief infatuation with rap during his college years. The misogynistic stuff of those early days of the genre had turned him off, but as a young man, he had been attracted to the over-the-top aggression of those 90's rappers. His 17th Century British lit professor had published articles and then assigned them to his undergrad students. In them he posited that the raw and brutal street language of rap was comparable to the bawdy and violent vernacular of Shakespeare. As a nineteen-year-old English major, Adam had been convinced of the legitimacy of that assessment. But a couple of decades later as he read the posts made by the Brothers of the Lake, he was more disturbed than analytic.

> *"For all those who wanna profile and pose/Rock you in your face, stab your brain with your nose bone."*

> *"When the slugs penetrate you feel a burning sensation/ Getting closer to God in a tight situation."*

> *"Be like Richard Pryor set your balls on fire/Better yet, go hang yourself with a barbed wire"*

> *"I got blood on my hands and there's no remorse"*

> *"I be placin' snitches inside lakes and ditches"*

> *"Fuck around, I'll introduce you to your ancestors"*

Adam wondered how these mostly white, mostly Christian, nearly all middle-class boys from small town America could relate to the viciousness of the urban streets, and who were they intending to threaten by posting this savagery? Certainly not their opponents, who were not members of their secret group. He clicked on the **Photos** section, and by the time he finished looking at the hundreds of stills and the four videos posted there, he was sick to his stomach, but he had the answer to his question.

Among the pictures were typical shots of sweaty boys being boys, mugging for the camera in the locker room, shirts off showcasing flexed biceps and tightened abs. Some had been taken on the practice and playing field, some in the classrooms and hallways of the high school, and a few were shot off campus at parties, players with their arms around pretty girls. The only picture of Luke Clayton that he could find was a benign shot of him at the far end of a cafeteria table filled with boys wearing game day jerseys. In the center of the table sat Scott Wallace. JeffBoy, or whatever his real name was, sat next to Scott.

As he scrolled through the pictures, he came upon one of a tall boy, grinning from ear-to-ear as he applied a tube of Icy-Hot cream to the inside of a jock strap. Adam remembered that trick from his own high school wrestling days. Another showed a smallish kid, probably a JV team member, being shoved into an equipment locker by a boy who was twice his size. The photo of a kid kneeling in front of a toilet bowl as two teammates pushed his face into the water and a third boy stood poised to flush—the old swirly was something Adam was familiar with, too.

The first of the more disturbing pictures was a shot of a kid in the shower lying face down, t-shirt pulled over his head. Two boys were apparently holding him down while another stood over him and dumped white powder onto his wet and naked body. The next one showed a skinny boy being held down on a locker room bench by two of his teammates, while a third straddled him and rubbed his genitals on the captive's face. Adam couldn't be sure of the authenticity of the next one. A boy lay naked on the locker room floor, curled up in a fetal position, covering his head. A circle of six of his "brothers" appeared to be in the act of violently kicking him.

Adam stood up and poured a tall finger of Scotch. He had seen enough in the still photos to rattle him. But there were four videos yet to be viewed, and his gut was in a knot.

The first one was dated October 1st, 2015, midway through Lake Hinon's winning season. Adam reached out to turn the volume down as the deafening bass came through his small speaker, hip-hop blaring apparently from multiple sources. Several partially clad and sweating boys stood in a

265

circle. They were shouting something that sounded like, "Fresh flesh!" but the loud music clashed with their chant, so Adam wasn't sure. The camera zoomed in on the naked victim lying on the locker room floor. The tall boy's face was turned away from the camera and his hands and feet were bound with what looked like jump ropes. Suddenly from above, a stream of thick white cream, toothpaste perhaps, was squirted just below the prone boy's shoulder blade to his lower back. Adam could plainly read the number *12*.

The kid turned his head and now Adam got a partial view of his face as he tried to kick and twist his torso to escape his tormentors, but the circle closed tighter and two boys stepped forward to grab him so that the "artist"could continue his work. From the kid's lower vertebrate through the crack in his ass Adam watched as the anonymous painter drew another number - *1*. The video stopped and captured the message.

12-1, December 1st. Adam looked at the team picture again. He scanned the names under the photos until he found Travis Worthing's. He clicked on the picture to zoom it in. He couldn't be sure, but his gut told him, the kid on the floor might have been Luke's best friend.

The second video, was taken on October 15th, the same day that Luke and Travis had been in Walker's office, Adam remembered. This time the camera opened up on a benign scanning of a row of lockers. He turned his speakers up, but again the music exploded so loudly, he turned it down again. He watched as the camera focused on a short, muscular redhead lying on the floor, enfettered and encircled in the same way as the tall boy in the first video had been. Christ! That red hair! This had to be Jeff.

Suddenly, the camera panned up to a close shot of a face familiar to Adam, and since November, to most of the nation. The team's slain captain, Scott Wallace. In his hand, he held a shampoo bottle. The circle of boys closed in on their victim and held his hands and legs still. The camera tracked the container downward as it was inserted into the boy's body. In spite of the lowered volume, Adam could hear the victim's stifled screams. Just as he turned the speakers up again, the video stopped. "Jesus Christ!" Adam said to the empty room. He took another swallow of Scotch.

The third video, shot on October 22nd, started with the same cacophony; there were multiple phones and Ipod screens shining out of the darkness as country music blared this time. The first frame was a pan of the aisles taken from the back of a bus; a fleeting shot showed two adults, the coaches most likely, in the first two seats, their backs to the players. Then the camera sought the target. Sitting close to the middle of the bus, the boy was grabbed from behind by two of his teammates, one with his hand covering the kid's mouth. They dragged him to the back of the bus, and with the help of six or seven others, they pulled his pants down and knocked him to the floor. There was not enough light to make out exactly what was happening to him, but Adam watched the shadowy outlines for two more minutes as the blows and kicks kept coming.

The final video was not as graphic, but Adam found it the most disturbing. This time there was no music. For several seconds of the opening shot, all that could be seen was a glowering blue eye, and then two. When the photographer panned out once more, Adam recognized that the glaring eyes belonged to Scott Wallace. In the team locker room, the captain was flanked by two other boys. All of them naked from the waist up, to Adam, they seemed drunk with the power of their youthful virility. "To all you low-life pussies from Langston; beware." Scott warned. "The Brothers will make men out of you in a couple of weeks. At the Camp." Now there was a thwacking sound accompanying Scott's words. The camera pulled back farther to show a dozen or so boys, none of them Travis, or Jeff, or Luke, flanking their captain. In his hand he held a plastic bat, the kind little T-ballers used. Scott slapped his palm with it over and over again for what seemed to Adam like a full minute, then the screen went black.

"Goddamn it," Adam said aloud. He forced himself to look at the photos and replay the videos again. Except for the one picture in the cafeteria, he could not find Luke in any of them. Something wasn't adding up. If he had been victimized in some way like these other boys, there didn't seem to be any photographic evidence of it.

As he pushed away from the desk and stood up, an involuntary shiver crawled down his back. The room had grown colder. He picked up his phone and called Gina. As soon as she answered he said, "When can we get together? I think I've found something."

"I was just going to call you," she said. "Can you meet me tomorrow morning at the Worthing's place?"

"Has Travis agreed to talk to us?" he asked.

"No. But he's going to have to tell us that to our faces," she said.

CHAPTER TWENTY-NINE

TRAVIS

"Stay in the car," Adam told her. "I'll text you when the time is right."

Gina's eyes followed the gray suede jacket until it disappeared around the bend of the Worthings' tree-lined driveway. The warmth of the March sun coming through the windshield did nothing to assuage her nervousness. Moments before, she and Adam had watched from the road as Mrs. Worthing backed her Jeep out of the driveway and headed north toward Jamesburg.

After Johnny's final words to her on Sunday, Gina called Travis' grandmother. She hoped that she sounded determined rather than desperate as she asked once again for the woman's permission to talk with Travis. When silence on the other end of the line was the response, she added, "I've uncovered some disturbing facts since I saw you, Mrs. Worthing. Adam Stoller, the writer, has been helping me. We think that the school was aware of some things, issues that they should have dealt with. If they had, the tragedy might have been prevented." Travis' grandmother still did not respond, but she hadn't hung up. "Please, Mrs. Worthing. Travis might find some relief in talking about it."

At last, the woman spoke. "My grandson is hurting badly, that's for certain. If talking with you could help..." Gina held her breath. "Come tomorrow morning around ten. Travis will be doing his coursework on the computer. We've insisted that he get his high school diploma, and he is doing that online. I'll leave the house for an hour or so to do my grocery shopping. He won't know you're coming, and hopefully, his grandfather will never find out about it," the woman said.

Gina's heart filled with gratitude. She knew that this woman had suffered, too. This was the predicament of so many grandmothers today, she thought. You raised your kids, took care of them, and watched them destroy themselves, as Travis' father had done. You still loved your child in spite of his flaws and missteps. And then you proved your love by taking in a troubled grandchild at a time in your life when you should have been enjoying the freedom from maternal responsibilities.

"Thank you, Mrs. Worthing," she said and hung up.

Now she cast an anxious glance at her phone as she sat in the Land Rover. Adam had been gone for five minutes. When no text came ten minutes later, she couldn't wait any longer. She got out and walked cautiously up the winding driveway. Reaching the porch that surrounded the entire A-Frame, Gina walked from window to window, shielding her eyes from the sun's glare. The great room was vacant, as was the study, where she saw a laptop on the desk and a couple of textbooks lying open next to it. She reached the kitchen at the back of the house and peered into the bay window. No one was there, either. She took the three steps down onto the attached deck and stood looking out into the thick pine woods. Cardinals and finches and a couple of robins were pecking at whatever the Worthings had provided for them in the feeders.

Suddenly the birdsong coming from the tall trees was interrupted by three successive blasts of gunfire. Gina's heart froze. She clutched the rail of the deck and listened in terrified anticipation of more shots. Instead, she heard the low tone of a man's voice. Adam.

She took a running start off the deck to the dirt path and followed the sound through the woods. Within fifty yards or so, she came to a clearing. On the trunks of two felled pines sat Adam Stoller and Travis Worthing facing one another. Just beyond them, Gina saw a target stand. Tin cans, the apparent victims of the pistol that Travis had placed on the ground at his feet, were strewn all around it.

"What's she doing here?" the boy asked Adam as he stood up and faced Gina. He stared at her with huge gray eyes. She was amazed that the kid looked inches taller than he had just last week in the Worthings' kitchen. He had shaved off the scruff above his mouth, and she noticed that his lips were red and chapped. He wore a vintage Metallica t-shirt and ripped jeans. Folding his arms and glaring at her, she could see him shiver slightly in the shade cast by the huge pines.

"Luke's mom and I, we've been working on figuring this out together." Adam walked slowly toward him as he tried to reassure the skittish kid. Travis looked down at the ground and scuffed one boot and then the other in the dirt. His long hair fell over his eyes as he did. "Please sit down, Travis," Adam said. "We just want to have a conversation with you. You don't have to answer anything you don't want to. It's just that there doesn't seem to be anyone who can speak for Luke now, except maybe you."

Travis raised his head and looked at the stranger, trying to judge his authenticity. Gina watched as a thin layer of Travis' resistance seemed to thaw. The teen lowered his body slowly to the tree trunk and stretched his long legs out in front of him.

"What do you want to know?" he asked, ignoring Gina, who had sat down on the opposite end of the log where the boy was. He looked only at Adam as he spoke.

"How did you get along with Scott Wallace?" Adam asked.

"I didn't. He hated me," Travis said with obvious bitterness.

271

"How do you know he hated you?" Adam asked, keeping his voice even.

"From the time I first moved here, in middle school, he hassled me. Walked behind me in the halls with his buddies. Called me names like 'Crack Baby,' 'Meth Boy,' shit like that. Tripped me whenever the opportunity came. Shoved me into the lockers, and his friends would join in. Whatever Scott did or said, they did too," Travis explained with derision. "Scott was powerful that way."

"Why do you think they picked on you, Travis?"

"I'm not sure, exactly, but I wasn't the only one. Anybody they thought was weaker than them somehow. Smaller, poorer, bad parents, pretty much any kid from Langston got bullied by Scott and his followers," he said matter-of-factly.

"So that was during seventh and eighth grade, right?" Adam asked.

"Yeah, and then I met Luke. We hit it off from the very beginning. Luke was quiet, like me. We liked the same music and the same video games. I eventually talked to him about Scott. He knew how bothered I was by the harassment. He's the one who talked me into trying to deal with it instead of running from it."

"How did he think you should try to deal with it?" Adam asked.

"Through sports. 'If you can't beat 'em, join 'em' was what Luke said. Over the summer before ninth grade, whenever he wasn't babysitting Lisa and the twins, he and I would run or lift weights in my barn. We were both going to go out for football in the fall."

"So that was the plan. Did you do it?" Adam asked.

"Yeah. We both made the JV team. I played linebacker. By then I had gained ten pounds. Luke was a starter, a running back, but he was moved up to varsity before the end of the season. He was much better than me, smart and fast," he said.

"So, was it any better with Scott and his friends once you made the team?"

"At first. They seemed to pretty much ignore me in the halls, anyway. But after summer practice this past year, things got way worse, and not just for me. The locker room was hell for a lot of us kids from Langston because of Scott and his posse of assholes." Gina heard the frustration and anger in the boy's voice.

"Travis, you're a member of the Brothers of the Lake group on Facebook, right?" Adam asked. He had filled Gina in with the basics about the secret group on their drive to the Worthings, and although he knew the answer, he wanted to hear what Travis had to say about it.

"Yeah. If you were on the football team, you had no choice," he said. "It was supposed to be a secret group, but Scott and his friends made sure everyone in school knew about it. They used Snapchat and sent lots of pictures and video to kids who weren't on the team. It was disgusting," Travis said.

"I want you to know, Travis, that I've seen that page. There's a lot of disturbing stuff there," Adam said. "Can I ask you a few questions about that group?"

Travis stood up and began pacing back and forth between the clearing and the target and didn't answer. Adam decided to ask a question that seemed innocuous compared to inquiring about the sexual assaults that some of the photos and videos had captured. "Do you know why many of the profile pictures of the members were of a wolverine?"

"Yeah," the boy answered with a sarcastic snort. "The Wolverine was the old Jamesburg mascot. They could never get over the fact that there was no more Jamesburg High School. Assholes," he added under his breath as he continued pacing back and forth.

"Travis," Adam said gently. "Were you or Luke involved in any of those pictures or videos that I saw? There were several where the victims' faces were only partially visible." Travis stood still and glowered at him.

"No! They would never try to do that stuff to Luke!" The kid was shouting now.

"Why not?"

"Because, for one, he was a good football player. They had some kind of weird respect for him. They left him alone, mainly."

"Mainly?" Adam prodded.

"Yeah. They might say some rude things about his family once in a while, but that was about as far as it went." The boy met Gina's eyes in that moment and then he looked down at his boots. "Luke just shrugged that shit off. Then his design won the mascot contest, and Scott and his stupid friends kind of moved out of his way from that point on."

"What can you tell me about the acts I saw in the pictures and videos, Travis? How did those boys get away with those attacks?" Adam asked.

"Easy. They had all the power. It was impossible to stop them. They mainly targeted the younger, weaker kids, mostly from Langston, like I said before. It happened ninety percent of the time in the locker room after practice, but sometimes after a game. Most guys skipped the shower and tried to get away as quick as they could. They knew what was coming as soon as the music started," Travis explained.

"The music?" Adam wanted to hear Travis' explanation of the blaring sound he had heard on the videos.

"Yeah. One of them would flick the lights on and off three times and that would start it. Guys would pull out their phones or their iPods. Turn the speakers up to max and blast the music, so in case Coach H or one of the assistants walked by, they wouldn't hear the commotion. Lots of stuff happened--stuff that you didn't see on Facebook."

"And what about you, Travis? Did they hurt you?" Adam asked quietly.

The boy lowered his head and stared at the ground. "Only once. I'm sure you know what I'm talking about if you watched the videos. That was the only time they laid their filthy hands on me. Luke had to be at work right after practice that day, so he wasn't there." With a nervous energy, the boy began to pace back and forth again. He stopped and stood in front of Adam. "After that, Scott and his boys started with threats on a daily basis."

"How did they threaten you?"

"One of them would come up behind me in the locker room or in the halls, always when I was by myself, and kind of whisper in my ear," Travis said, his anxiety obvious as he spoke.

"Whisper what?" Adam asked.

"Typically it was about my parents being druggies. About being a Langston low-life. But in October, the threats about December 1st started."

"December 1st, that was the date that the overnight retreat was scheduled, right?" Adam said.

"Yeah. The *team building* retreat." Travis' derision was obvious. "Scott and his boys kept harping about how me and a couple of other guys from Langston were going to get '*reprogrammed*'--that's what they called it. They would say shit like, 'Just wait 'til we get you pussies at the Lutheran Camp. Wait 'til the lights go out. We wouldn't fall asleep if we were you'--that kind of crap," Travis explained.

"And then they assaulted you in the locker room," Adam said quietly. "That must have been a terrible time for you."

"Yeah. It made for some long school days and longer weekends. Just thinking about practice and Scott marching around the locker room with his little yellow bat." He looked up at Adam to see if he recognized what that meant. He nodded to let the boy know that he did.

As Gina listened to the harrowing details of Travis' account, a powerful realization washed over her. Last night in the school lobby, she had walked in Travis' shoes. Surrounded by a circle of strangers, they brazenly spewed their hatred for her. True, they had used only words to weaken and attack her, but they had effectively made her their victim. In those few moments, she was forced to reckon with the power of the bully, and the utter vulnerability of the target. No one interceded, no one came to her aid. Not even the cop who saw it all. She, an adult, had been shaken to her core last night, and now as she looked at Travis, she experienced clarity. No one had come forward to shield those kids either, some of whom, like Travis, had been tormented for years. Had Luke believed that he was the only one who could see this evil and stop it? Did he believe that his bloody solution was the only feasible means to end it?

A heavy sadness threatened to overwhelm her, but she pushed it off and stood up. "Travis," she said, "why didn't you tell your grandparents that you were being harassed that way?" He turned and looked at her as if she had lost her mind.

"My grandfather is seventy years old and he still has to go to work every day because he's stuck having to raise me! I didn't want to make trouble for my grandmother, either. I needed to deal with it on my own," he said. "Besides, it's embarrassing to have to admit that you're being picked on, especially when you're my age."

Travis' answer resonated with Gina. On the drive to the Worthing's home this morning, she had every intention of telling Adam about the board meeting and what had happened to her. But everytime she opened her mouth to explain it to him, she felt the shame drag her under, and she couldn't bring herself to share it with him. How difficult it would be for Travis, or any kid for that matter, to have to relive the degradation by telling someone else about it.

Adam asked, "What about Coach Harrison. Did you go to him?"

"No. But Luke did. He talked to him and Coach Davis. He tried to tell them that there was some bullying of younger players going on, and Coach Harrison lost his shit."

"What do you mean?"

"He told Luke that he was overreacting. That he was a whiny baby. That a little hazing was normal and even good for every team. He said he and Coach Davis had both been through it when they were kids. And besides, he said, Lake Hinon High School was counting on us. We were on our way to winning States."

"So is that when you two boys went to Principal Walker?" Adam asked.

Travis looked at the writer with a newfound respect. "I guess you *do* know a lot about it," he said. "No. Not then. Luke had already been to see him a couple of times before. He told him about how the younger kids, especially the Langston kids were being treated. And guess what Walker the Wacker said! He told Luke that he couldn't do anything about it if the boys who were being attacked did not come forward. So when Luke told me that, I said I would talk to Walker. I went with Luke to see him—twice. It was ridiculous!" Gina noticed that Travis' face had reddened with the emotion of telling his story.

"That was a couple of weeks before the shooting, right?"

"The second time, yes, I think so," Travis said.

"How did the meeting with your principal go?" Adam asked.

"Bad," Travis said. "We got nowhere."

"What do you mean?"

"After I told him about all the taunting and bullying that I had put up with for two years, he told me I should try to use my head to work things out with the Jamesburg guys. Use humor, use my intelligence," Travis said disgustedly. "I asked him what he thought the kid who had been attacked with the shampoo bottle should do to work things out with them, and he got really pissed off."

"Wait," Adam said. "You told Mr. Walker about that?"

"Yes," Travis said.

"And he got angry at you for saying that?" Adam was incredulous.

"For sure. He stood up and started shouting—spit was flying at me and Luke, he was so mad. He told us that he didn't want to hear these lies. That we were not to tell them to anyone else. He said that we would disgrace the new school—that the success of the football team showed everybody that the merger was working."

"Christ," Adam said, looking across the clearing to Gina.

"Then he said something to Luke, like, 'And you, Mr. Clayton, you designed our new school mascot. How could you get involved in something like this that would dishonor', yeah he said, 'dishonor' Lake Hinon High?'" Travis was becoming more and more incensed at the memory. "And then his buddy Joe Gloss walked in. I don't know if he'd been listening at the door or what, but he seemed to know everything we had said to Walker."

"What did your school resource officer have to say about it?" Adam asked.

Travis raised his voice to a shout. "He told us to stop whining!" The boy's yell had startled a hawk off a high branch of an oak overhead, and the three raised their eyes to it. They watched as it disappeared into the tall pines. "Yeah," Travis continued, "he told me to get over it; that it was no big deal to have a little toothpaste dumped on your ass. Then he said something like, 'Maybe your captain and the rest of the varsity need to hear about your disloyalty to the team.' And he told Luke to mind his own business and stop sticking his nose into things that didn't involve him. Then we were out of there. I was so pissed off that we had bothered," Travis concluded.

"How did Luke seem after that meeting?" Adam asked.

Travis appeared to be culling his memory. "Quieter. Calmer," the boy said. "That week, he came over to the house for target practice a few times.

He had never wanted to do that before." Travis paused again. "I didn't know it until I thought about it later, but I think that day as we walked down the hallway from that meeting, that's when he made up his mind."

"Made up his mind?"

He walked toward Adam and looked him in the eye. "Maybe Luke thought that he had been chosen, like the warrior had been, like the kid in 'Seneca Optical,'" he said. Adam was startled when Travis said the title of his story. It was as though he had come face to face on the street with a long-forgotten acquaintance.

"Travis," he said, "Is that why Luke carried my story with him on November 23rd?"

"I can't be sure, but maybe it all clicked for him after we saw Walker." Luke's friend stood in the clearing delivering the truth about Gina's son as he had come to understand it. "Maybe he carried the story to explain his actions. He knew that only people who understood the story would understand that he had no choice. That he had been chosen."

"You were with him before school that morning. Did he tell you what he was planning to do?" Adam asked the boy.

"No!" Travis was insistent. "I had no clue when he drove me to school that day. I did all the talking, as usual. I was freaking out about December 1st. Told him I was thinking of quitting the team and running away to my mother's in Indiana. He didn't say anything, just listened like he always did."

The boy looked at Adam and then at Gina. "He pulled up to the drop-off area. Told me he had to run to the pharmacy for his mom. That he would see me at lunch. And then he said, 'Travis, you're not going to have to go back to your mom's. You don't have to worry about those bastards hurting you.' He seemed like the same old Luke that morning. It wasn't unusual for him to be trying to calm me down. But when I got out of the car and slammed the door so it would shut, he was saying something I couldn't quite make out."

"What do you think he said?" Adam asked.

"I definitely heard him say, 'December 1st.' I've had all these months to think about it, and I'm pretty sure what he said was, 'There won't be a December 1st.'"

"Did the police ever ask you about your last conversation with Luke?" Adam asked.

"In a half-assed way, I guess they did. But I didn't tell them what I'm telling you. Cops have never done anything for me or my family," the boy said. "Joe Gloss did nothing to help Luke or me." Or me, Gina thought.

Travis' disgusted tone changed to one of earnest conviction. "Luke was a good person. But I think the evil finally got to him. As strong as he was, he knew he couldn't get rid of it all. He knew that. That's why I think he killed himself."

Gina's heart stopped at his pronouncement. She forced herself to breathe and then she asked the boy the question she had asked herself thousands of times since November. "Travis? Why do you think Luke didn't come to me? Why didn't he tell me what you were going through?"

"He didn't say," Travis said quietly. He seemed to have softened toward her. "But he always made it clear that he wanted to protect you and the kids." Gina felt the familiar bolt of guilt mixed with grief run through her. She could not deny it. Even Travis knew. Very early in his life she and her son had traded places. Without her realizing it, Luke had become *her* guardian.

"He loved his family. He was pissed at his dad for fucking up, but he loved him too." The boy let that sink in and then said to the mother of his dead friend, "He admired you, though. He told me you had a lot of shit in your life and that you were handling it better than most people could. He didn't want to be a problem in any way for you."

Problem One. Her oldest son's nickname. Gina stood up. She wanted to take this boy in her arms because she could never hug her own son again. Adam stood too. Travis put his hands up as if to stop either of them from coming any closer.

"You wanted to hear what I had to say about Luke, so let me finish." The adults stood still and listened.

CHAPTER THIRTY

DARK RIDDLE

"*I wrote a short story fifteen years ago. It was different from anything I'd written before or have written since. It was an assignment, an experiment. I chose to follow the elements of an Iroquois myth as the prototype. I liked the way the story turned out, but because of the circumstances of its inception, it always felt like a step-child, not a natural-born progeny. Still, it fit the bill for the graduate class assignment, and it was there when my editor demanded one more story for a collection years later. It was also an appropriate reading assignment for the Lake Hinon High School students enrolled in the Myths and Legends class as they studied the Seneca mythology of that region of New York State.*

On November 23rd, 2015, Luke Clayton, a sophomore student in that class, put a copy of "Seneca Optical" in his pocket and went to his high school and committed an atrocity. He shot and killed Edward Gatto, Jr., a sophomore, coaches and physical education teachers Rodney Harrison and Brian Davis, Ryan Johnston, Richard Varos and Tad Burke, all seniors, English teacher Janet Shelkowski, and Scott Wallace, also a member of the senior class and the captain of the Lake Hinon High School football team. Then he put the gun to his own head and ended the massacre. In those twenty minutes of horror, my story was transformed. It was no longer a creative work. It was *now and forever the manifesto of a mass murderer, and in its ultimate meta-morphosis, it became sixteen-year-old Luke Clayton's suicide note.*

The unsettling sense of responsibility I felt when I heard the news of the bloodbath intensified as each day passed. By the time I got the call from Rolling Stone, I was barely functioning on a personal level, to say nothing of my inability to write during this period. I agreed to undertake this assignment because I wanted to discover what role my fiction played in the horrible turn of events. I wish I could say that I accomplished that goal. Instead, I have to admit at the outset of this article that Luke Clayton is almost as much of an enigma to me today as he was when I first heard of the tragedy in upstate New York.

I spent three weeks in the Lake Hinon region, in Luke's hometown of Langston and in Jamesburg where he attended school. I approached some people who refused to talk with me, as did his mother at first, but there were others who did speak with me, in spite of the pressure that ensued from co-operating with a journalist. I talked to students and teachers and staff at Lake Hinon High School, most of whom didn't know Luke very well, but who described their impressions of him before the shooting as "quiet," "a good student," and "a good artist."

Conversely, I listened to local talk radio where the subject of the day almost always took a left turn back to Luke Clayton's violence. The commonly held consensus of the callers was that Luke was the evil spawn of a criminal father and a negligent mother from "the wrong side of the lake." I talked directly with community members who knew Luke, at least as well as anyone seemed to know Luke, and I met people whose lives had been ruined by him. I read Luke's own personal reaction to "Seneca Optical" from the journal that his English teacher had assigned. I spent most of my time in the company of his grief-stricken mother, Gina Clayton, who eventually decided that I might be able to help her discover how the boy she considered her good son became the perpetrator of those atrocities.

My time there and the information Mrs. Clayton and I uncovered served only to reveal single pieces of the puzzle that were this boy. When we tried to put them together in a precise way, we could not. Each piece would not exactly interlock with any other. In the end, Gina and I failed to create a complete picture of her son and his motivation to kill innocent people and himself."

Rog and Tess sat on the couch together. For the next forty-five minutes, Diane, leaning against the kitchen counter, continued to read aloud from her copy of this month's *Rolling Stone*. Adam noticed that at some point in Diane's monologue, Rog had taken his wife's hand. The writer got up and poured himself another Scotch. When his phone rang, she stopped reading. "Keep going," he told her as he put down the glass and headed to his study to answer it.

"Mr. Stoller?" He didn't recognize the voice on the other end.

"Yes. Who's this?"

"It's Kevin Laird from *The Times*," he said. "Do you have a comment about the firing of Officer Joe Gloss and the suspension of Bob Walker as principal of Lake Hinon High School?"

"No. No comment."

"Your article in *Rolling Stone* seems to have blown the lid off the hazing and the cover-up that was going on there," the reporter said. "The superintendent is working with the board and community members to bring in experts and counselors to help the students find the appropriate strategies to deal with, and end, the bullying."

Adam said nothing.

"Did you know that a public referendum to remove Luke Clayton's Thunderbird mascot will be voted on at the end of the school year? How do you feel about that?" Laird asked him.

"I have nothing to say about it," Adam said and hung up.

As soon as he returned home in late March, he had done almost nothing else but work on the "Dark Riddle" piece. When it was finished, he sent it to Gina, inviting her to make any changes or additions. Two days later, he read her email out loud to his empty kitchen. *"Wouldn't change a thing. It's perfect."*

The few weeks spent in Luke's world with Gina's approval of the article seemed to release Adam from the stranglehold of fear that had been blocking his writing. During his time in the Lake Hinon region, he had witnessed Gina's resolve, her determination to discover what had taken Luke down that dark path, in spite of the fact that she had to confront her own part in it. He marveled at her courage to do this in the midst of the brutal public shaming that she was subjected to, and that, as the mother of a mass murderer, might very likely follow her throughout her life.

Although he had not written about it in his article, on the morning that he was returning to New York, she admitted to him that last December she had thought seriously about ending her life. "I changed my mind when I realized that I was one of a handful of people on the planet that carries the 'good' Luke in my mind and heart. The rest of the world will always view him as a monster, but I knew another boy. The one who tried so hard to take care of his family, even though that shouldn't have been his responsibility. That's when I decided that for Luke's sake, I would live, that I would get up every day and be the best mother I could be to his brothers and sisters."

Adam had never witnessed such fortitude. Gina's brave search for the truth had inspired him to write once again, because what was writing if not the search for truth? It had not been easy, but when he struggled with his words and ideas, he didn't surrender to the self-doubt. Instead, he dug deeper. Last week, he sent his editor the first draft of *Valorous,* his third novel. On the dedication page were three words: *To Gina Clayton.*

Adam went out to the balcony and closed the door. Leaning on the rail, he scanned the tops of the trees that lined his street. The early June sun was sinking slowly and he watched the orange orb until it was out of sight. He listened to the evening birdsong and the conversations of people passing below. His phone rang again. He didn't recognize the number and he turned the phone off.

Adam did not need or want a cigarette, but he was on edge in spite of the beautiful evening. The reporter's call had rattled him, and he couldn't stop thinking about Gina, wondering how she was feeling since the publication of the article. He would call her later and ask.

He stepped back inside the darkened study, and stood still and listened to Diane as she read the last paragraphs of his article.

"I do believe that there are lessons to be garnered from the tragedy at Lake Hinon High School and I want to share them with you.

I don't believe that we can ever measure exactly the impact and the effect that we as mothers and fathers, friends or bullying enemies, teachers and administrators, police officers, creators of songs, films and stories, make on others with our good intentions or our mean-spirited actions, our love or our hate, our art.

I say this because there were other kids living in the Langston and James-burg communities who had tough home lives, many that were much more turbulent than Luke's. And yet those kids did not resort to violence as an expression of their feelings of frustration or neglect, as Luke did.

Mrs. Clayton and I discovered that there were many boys and girls who were bullied or hazed at Lake Hinon High, and many others who witnessed this harassemt, but because of the failures of the school system, most of them chose to remain silent. A few brave kids made futile attempts to seek help from the adults in charge of their safety at school, including the police, just as Luke had. When their fears or concerns were labeled as exaggeration or entirely dismissed, unlike Luke, those kids did not take justice into their own hands.

Throughout our nation, teens live in places that are rife with hypocrisy and class bias, just as Luke and his classmates did. The school merger in the Lake Hinon region brought that ugliness into the homes of most kids who were growing up there. They heard their parents revile their schoolmates from "the other side of the lake", and yet only one of those children reacted to that prejudice with violence.

I talked with other kids who had read my story "Seneca Optical." They did not see it as a call to arms, as it seems that Luke may have.

None of those young people, whose lives ran parallel to Luke's, committed these terrible acts that left their families and two communities in ruins.

But Luke Clayton did.

Why exactly he did remains the dark riddle.

Luke's best friend, Travis Worthing, and a target of hazing himself, told Gina Clayton and me, "What Luke did was not anyone else's fault. He didn't do it just because he thought he understood the message in your story. He didn't do it just because you were his mother and you and his siblings relied on him too much. And he didn't do it because I was his best friend and he wanted to protect me. But all of those things and other things that no one will ever know were all mixed up in his head that day. I think something inside him broke in the days before the shooting. None of us saw it, maybe because he was hiding it from us, or maybe because we weren't paying enough attention. But something broke. Luke made a crazy, horrible decision that day. One we'll never be able to completely understand. That's what I believe."

I agree with Travis. I believe that, too."

Diane looked up after she read the last sentence of the article. His friends were silent as Adam walked back into the room.

CHAPTER THIRTY-ONE

THE BURNING POINT

Gina gently pressed her lips to the temple of the sleeping infant in her arms and inhaled deeply. With the birth of each of her children, this first stage of motherhood had been the most satisfying. A baby's needs were so easily understood and met at this phase in life. Keep me fed, warm, dry, clean, and safe and I am a perfectly happy little person. This was the message these tiny beings exuded. And the serenity a mother received in kind was comparable to nothing else—no massage, no exercise, no spiritual practice of any kind could provide the same synergy and bring the peacefulness that holding a baby close to you could, Gina thought.

Miles Robert Clayton had been born on April 30th, Shelley's due date. His entry into the world was a smooth one and he was a healthy eight pound newborn. Her maternity leave was over, and his mother had gone back to work this week. Mrs. Simpson next door was thrilled when Shelley had asked her if she would watch Miles while she worked. But Gina was taking care of her grandson today. She stood up and carefully placed the sleeping infant on his back in the bassinet next to Shelley's bed.

She tiptoed out of the room and quietly closed the door behind her. Her father would be here by three o'clock driving one of his panel trucks from the store, and he and her two sons would be her moving crew. The spacious rental that Gina had found in Buffalo was two blocks away from her parents' place and three blocks from the kids' school. She had applied for a job and been hired at the large pharmaceutical company on Elmwood Avenue as a lab tech, and her hours would be nine to five. No more night shift work to keep her from her kids. John, Tom, and Lisa were thrilled that she was coming and that they could stay in Buffalo. There would likely be an opportunity for Shelley to transfer to a branch of the bank in the city this summer. In the meantime, she would come with the baby to visit them whenever she could.

Gina peered over the banister and looked at the dozen or so plastic bins she had already stacked in the foyer. The final room in the house that she needed to work on was her bedroom. The baby was still sleeping an hour later when she put the lid on the last bin. Before her father and the kids arrived she needed to do one more thing.

The door that had not been opened for months now was stuck, and she leaned on it and pushed with her shoulder. She went to his closet and then to his dresser and touched every article of clothing. She held a flannel shirt against her cheek and breathed in his smell that was still to be found there. Every object on his desk she touched or held for a moment. She had decided that nothing from his room would come to Buffalo with her, at least not for now.

Gina sat down on the bed and stared again at her son's original drawing of the Thunderbird. She had had a lengthy discussion with Adam about the words that appeared below. **Power – Transformation – Unquestionable Authority**. Had that been Luke's mantra as he took his school hostage and brought carnage and unspeakable grief to hundreds of people?

"How could he have been so selfish, so....arrogant to take those lives, to take his own? How could he think that that was the solution?? Why didn't he come to me? How could he have possibly believed that I wouldn't have done everything in my power to help him?" she cried out after they had left Travis Worthing on that March day. "I miss him so much! But I'm so incredibly furious with him, too!" she admitted for the first time. "And how could I have been so blind, so deluded, to not have seen that my son, my dependable, responsible son, was the child who needed my attention the most?"

Adam had pulled the car over on the side of the road near a stand of oak trees. He had not seen the woman cry until this moment. He sat and silently waited until she finished. When they reached her house he turned to her. He needed to ask the question. "Do you think you can forgive Luke, Gina?"

She lowered her head and stared at her hands for a moment before answering. "Someday. I think I will. But forgiving myself? I'm not sure that will ever be possible."

Gina stood and walked to her son's desk. Picking up the copy of Joseph Cambell's *The Power of Myth*, she opened it to the page she had bookmarked months before. Into the empty room, she read the highlighted passage aloud. "*Love is the burning point of life, and since all life is sorrowful, so is love. The stronger the love, the more the pain. Love itself is pain, you might say—the pain of being truly alive. But love bears all things.*"

From across the hall came the sounds of her waking grandson. Gina closed the book and carried it with her as she went to him.

EPILOGUE

"Four years ago, my son Luke Clayton, murdered five students and three teachers at his high school. Then he put the pistol to his head and ended his own life."

This opening sentence was the most difficult part of her speech. If she could get through it without breaking down, which she had done the first time she spoke publicly, she was pretty sure she could keep going. Looking up from her notes, she scanned the group in front of her. Most of the five hundred people at this statewide PTA conference in Albany were strangers, and the thirty or so who had shown up to this break-out session on effective parenting were more than likely hostile ones. There was a unity in their body language, arms crossed and pulled close to their bodies. Maybe they had shown up to give her a hard time, and Gina could not blame them for that.

She took a deep breath, attempting to rid her voice of its noticeable quaver. In the third row sat Jane Penn, the grief counselor who had encouraged her to speak out publically about her experience. "You're not going to gain total redemption this way, but little by little, you'll begin to accept and forgive yourself," she told Gina. "And you'll be helping other people at the same time."

Next to Jane sat Lisa. A junior in high school now, and the only child living at home these days, her daughter had insisted that she be able to miss school on this Friday to accompany her mother. And on the other side of Lisa sat Adam Stoller. They locked eyes, and he smiled at her. The slight nod of his head gave Gina the strength she needed to go on.

She adjusted the podium microphone, steeling herself to continue. "My son did so much damage that November day. He devastated the families and friends of his victims. Most of the survivors, who had to return to the same building where their classmates and teachers, their colleagues and friends were killed, were never the same. Luke robbed those kids of their youth, their optimism. He robbed the staff members of the pleasures of their profession, and he left his family in a state of shock and grief. And to this day, I am not completely sure why he did what he did." Gina paused and looked up. A woman in the front row slowly shook her head. Most of the people in the second row had cast their eyes down, gazing at the papers in their laps or at the floor, so they would not have to look at her. Lisa sat up straighter and stared at her mother. Her steady gaze calmed Gina enough so that she could continue.

"I know many of you are thinking, 'But you are his mother. There had to have been some signs. He was your kid, you lived with him. You should have seen it!' And you are absolutely right. I should have seen it long before November 23, 2015. I should have seen that his father's arrest and our move away from his grandparents left Luke lonely and vulnerable. I should have seen that his protectiveness of his siblings, and especially of me, was an extraordinary burden for a young teen, a reversal of natural roles. I should have seen that my own stubborn resistance to accept help during a very trying period set a horrible example for my children, especially for one as sensitive as my oldest son. I should have seen that Luke and other kids in his school were facing an epidemic of bullying and violent hazing, a kind of terror which I also have experienced.

But I didn't see it, because I wasn't looking. Now all I have is hindsight, my only qualification for being a member of this panel on parenting. *Now* I see, that in those days leading up to November 23rd, 2015, my face was often turned away from my kids, turned toward work, toward paying the rent, toward figuring out how much more I needed to work to pay the bills that were always due. I had plenty of reasons for it, but the truth is, I was not present in my kids' lives, which is where they needed me to be. Especially where Luke needed me to be.

Before November 23rd, I should have listened, too. I should have asked my son more questions and been more engaged in his answers. If I had listened more closely, more carefully, I might have understood that something was terribly wrong, not only in his school, but inside his own head. I confess that his quiet reserve was a relief from the chaos and noisiness of the rest of my life. I was satisfied to look at it as a sign of his maturity. I viewed my boy as responsible, self-reliant, and protective of his siblings and of me. I didn't see a need to probe, to ask questions about how he was doing, how he was feeling."

Gina paused and looked directly at Adam. "You may have read that Luke did not leave a suicide note; instead, he carried a short story with him that day. It told the tale of an abandoned boy who was given a special power to see evil and destroy it. A psychologist I met at another parenting event speculated that Luke may have had a Messiah complex, that he may have believed that his mission in life was to become a savior. Perhaps he felt it was his fate to do what he did, to protect others from harm. I don't know. But because I was not looking closely, listening closely, I did not see or hear any sign that he was carrying the weight of the world on his shoulders. That he believed so wrongly, perhaps psychotically, that he could be an arbiter of justice.

I stand at this podium today, not because I understand all the reasons my son chose to do what he did on November 23rd, 2015. I will search until the day I die to comprehend it. But in these first four years of introspection, of counseling, of reading and researching, I've come to one rock-solid belief, and that is: I failed as Luke's mother. That certainly doesn't make me an expert on effective parenting. But it qualifies me to deliver a message to all of you and it is this: Don't do what I did. Do not turn away from your teenagers, even if it looks like they don't need or want your help. Watch closely. Listen carefully. To your own kids, and to their friends, too. Talk to their teachers and their coaches, and even if you don't see or hear any signals that their lives are off balance, make sure their schools and communities have systems in place to offer help, guidance, interventions, in case, like Luke, your kids decide they can't turn to you."

There was not a sound in the room as Gina picked up her notes and turned off the microphone. The stillness of the audience was a relief. The last thing she wanted was applause. The silence continued as she walked back to her seat.

ACKNOWLEDGEMENTS

I am grateful to David George-Shongo, the director of the Seneca-Iroquois National Museum in Salamanca, New York, who referred me to Willie Ground. Mr. Ground is the museum's interpreter and collections assistant manager, and an enrolled member of the Deer Clan, Seneca Nation. Mr. Ground read *Dark Riddle* and approved of my representation of the Thunder Gods and the Hinon myth. I am also indebted to Andrew Solomon, whose essay, *The Reckoning*, in the March 17, 2014, *New Yorker,* was the only interview Peter Lanza, Adam Lanza's father, ever gave. The piece led me to Solomon's seminal work, *Far From the Tree: Parents, Children and The Search For Identity* (Scribner, 2012). Solomon's writing inspired the premise of my novel. His work uncovered what I have always sensed, that there is nothing more terrifying than a child who does not reveal his true self to a parent. For the purpose of the novel's depiction of the Myths and Legends class, I also had the pleasure of returning to Joseph Campbell's brilliant work, *The Power of Myth* (Doubleday, 1988). Thank you to my friend, Tara Reyda, English teacher extraordinaire, who invited me in to her 11th grade honors classroom at Chautauqua Lake Central School, for a reminder of what high school culture is like several years after I vacated the room across the hall. Thank you to my early readers, who delivered just the right amount of constructive criticism and praise to encourage the many edits that the book underwent: Kathy Holser, Jesse Stratton, Buddy Pace, Kimberly Brower, Gary Madar, my loving, but discerning, husband, and Susan Penn, who also aided me in the design concept of the cover. Finally, thank you to my Big Girls' Book Club, who have been together for twenty-five years, and whose voices I often hear in my head as I write.

About The Author

Safe behind her laptop on the shores of Chautauqua Lake in Western New York, Debbie Madar dares to explore the more mysterious facets of the human psyche. In both her 2014 debut novel, *Convergence* (NFB Publishing, 2014) and her second book, *Dark Riddle,* she invites her readers to delve into a catalogue of What If's? Madar's fiction makes great material for book club discussions, as the answers to the questions she poses often have more than two sides.

For many years before her first novel was published, Debbie was a high school and college English teacher. She and her husband Gary reside in Bemus Point. They have four children and six grandchildren.